ANAMIKA

ANAMIKA

ANAMIKA

*A Tale of Desire
in a Time of War*

MEGHNAD DESAI

RUPA

Published by
Rupa Publications India Pvt. Ltd 2020
7/16, Ansari Road, Daryaganj
New Delhi 110002

Sales Centres:
Allahabad Bengaluru Chennai
Hyderabad Jaipur Kathmandu
Kolkata Mumbai

Copyright © Meghnad Desai 2020

All rights reserved.
No part of this publication may be reproduced, transmitted,
or stored in a retrieval system, in any form or by any means,
electronic, mechanical, photocopying, recording or otherwise,
without the prior permission of the publisher.

This is a work of fiction. Names, characters,
places and incidents are either the product of the author's imagination or are used
fictitiously and any resemblance to any actual person, living or dead,
events or locales is entirely coincidental.
A small number of historical names have been used to
give an indication of the time period in which the story is set.

ISBN: 978-93-89967-30-2

First impression 2020

10 9 8 7 6 5 4 3 2 1

The moral right of the author has been asserted.

Printed at Parksons Graphics Pvt. Ltd., Mumbai.

This book is sold subject to the condition that it shall not,
by way of trade or otherwise, be lent, resold, hired out, or otherwise
circulated, without the publisher's prior consent, in any form
of binding or cover other than that in which it is published.

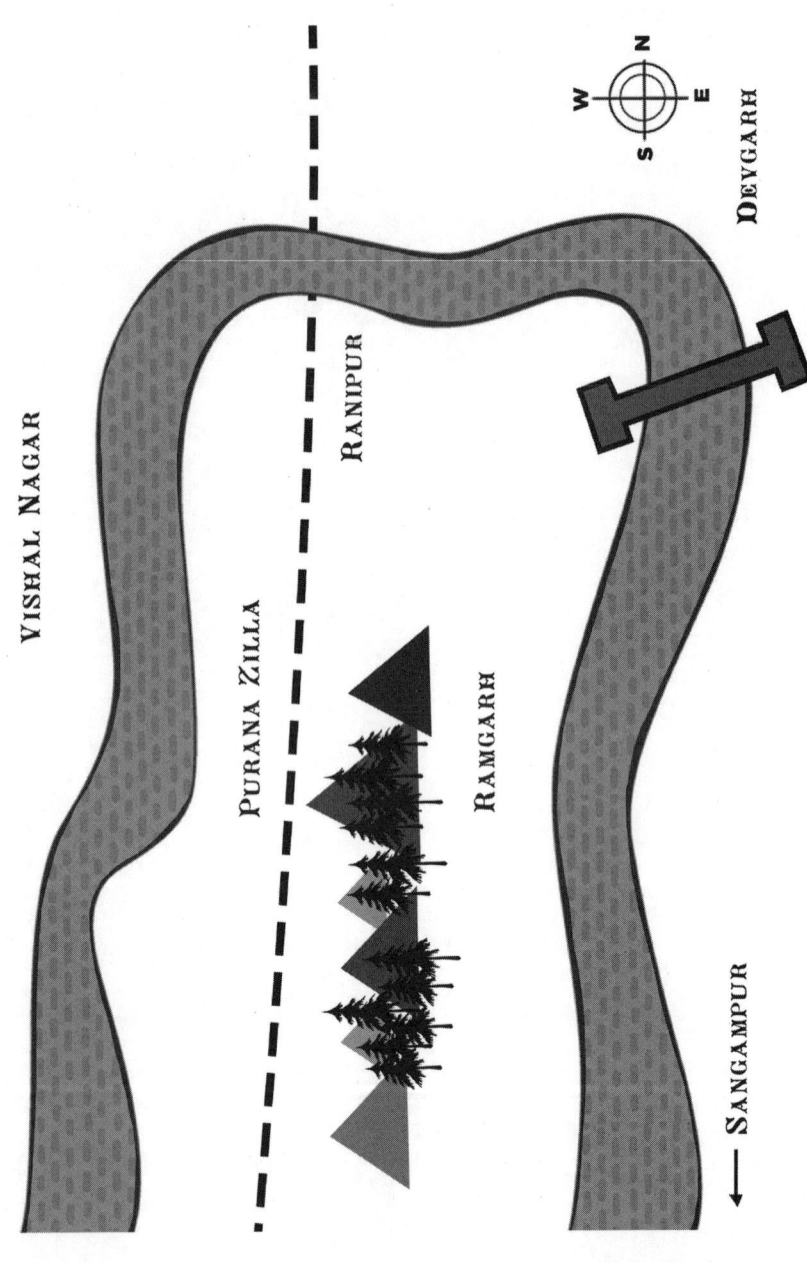

1. Anamika

*I*t was the light of that hour—long past midnight, yet still some time away from sunrise. The sky was just beginning to break out of its dark gloom and lighting up in preparatory glow before the coming of the dawn. This was the hour when the day started for her. She gently separated herself from him. He sensed that she was about to leave his side for the long day ahead; for the rest of the day, she would be able to get back to him only now and then, in between her many chores. She checked if he was still asleep, and he made as if to grab her. She hugged him and kissed him yet again. She wouldn't be keeping him warm anymore, so she covered him with a thick rajai.

It was time to fetch water. This might be a rich household, but the daily fetching of water was the responsibility of the daughter-in-law. She got up, wrapping her single garment around her. It was a coarse, long piece that had once been a white sari, but had since faded to grey. It suited her for sleeping in, and she could be sure it covered her well if she had to get up in the middle of the night to fetch help or go out in early daylight. Even as she hurried, she could not help looking at herself in the mirror. She had only her mangalsutra round her neck. She never took it off. It was her talisman, her good luck sign. Apart from that, no bangles, no rings, no other jewellery. She was a luscious beauty, younger-looking than even her mere twenty years, smooth and fair of skin with firm breasts, a small waist and hips that promised a woman who would bear many children to a lucky man.

He looked at her through sleepy eyes, and sighed. They had married only a year ago, but tragedy had already visited them—on the very day of their wedding. The wedding party had been large, as befitted the son of a great merchant, banker and leader of the community. Relatives had come from miles around and some would stay for weeks. Together, they went from his village to her town. Vishalnagar was the capital of Purana Zilla, a town that had a palace, a school and even an observatory, established by the enterprising young king, Raja Devi Singh. It was a slow journey of two days, through wooded country and across a river. Her father was no less important. Diwan Gulabchand was chief minister to the raja of Purana Zilla. He was a learned man, known throughout the land for his cunning and wisdom. His only daughter, Savitri, was his pride and joy. He had brought her up like a son—educating her and training her in the skills of horse riding, archery and all the martial arts, even sword fighting. His wife Meera complained that all this would make their daughter plain and ugly. No man would want to marry such an independent minded woman. But he persisted. She had to have the best and be the most accomplished daughter.

They had struck gold when they found Abhijit, the son of Ramdas Rathore, who was known in their community for his immense wealth. They lived over in Ranipur, in the territory of the shah. The astrologers had matched the horoscopes. The woman would bring fame to the house. She would bear a son and ensure a long life for Abhi and herself. Ramdas and his wife Revati could not have wished for anything more.

The wedding was a huge affair, lasting several days. Tents were set up in her home town for the groom's party as they arrived in scores. The bride's side was also present in considerable numbers. Several days were taken up by the henna smearing ceremony, music nights, and endless eating and celebrations for all—especially the young men and women on either side. This was, after all, also a time when parents could display their unmarried daughters to prospective partners. Each marriage had to be the cause of many more matches. Gifts had to be exchanged between the two parties, not forgetting the nephews, cousins and even distant relations who suddenly became close companions whenever weddings came around. But there was plenty of everything to go around, and the two fathers, Gulabchand and Ramdas, were not men to skimp in the slightest on such a happy occasion.

The climax came when the couple made seven rounds of the sacred fire, tied together with a knot, as the priests recited the holy mantras. The knot tied, the rounds done, the wedding party set off back to the groom's place. Gulabchand bade his lovely daughter goodbye. She was now another's. She would be given another name by her new family. Once gone, she would never return to her parents, come what may. It was a long tearful farewell. This was, for Meera and Gulabchand, the last glance of Savitri, whatever she may be called later on.

The wedding party left the bride's place, music blaring, women singing welcoming songs for the bride, firecrackers being lit, and everyone feeling happy and fulfilled. The groom and the bride rode together on a flower-bedecked horse.

Then tragedy struck. The horse, docile until now, suddenly panicked, broke into a canter, reared and threw the couple off. Savitri, riding side saddle, jumped off, as she knew about horses. But Abhi got caught under the horse's feet. There was mayhem and shrieks and cries all around. The wedding party broke up in confusion. The groom and the bride could not be taken back to her place—that would bring bad luck. They had to be taken all the way to the groom's place. It was clear that Abhi was badly hurt. Gulabchand sent his family healer. But the news was bad—very bad. Abhi had been mangled in the accident. He would never be able to walk on his own again.

There was no hope for him. He was to be bedridden for the rest of his life. He was not going to give her the children she was meant to bear. They tried many healers, went to many temples, and consulted astrologers and palmists to see if there was a cure. But there was none. She had no doubts; having made the seven rounds of the holy fire with one end of her sari tied to his kurta, she knew she was forever his. She wanted to be tied to him not just in this life, but in every life in the future.

His family had been very understanding, at first. They did not blame her for the accident. It was not her stars, but their own, that they cursed. The new name they gave her was Anamika—the nameless one. She thought that was the right way to start her new life. Her life was now tied to his; her name did not matter. What her fate would be was a question that never worried her. She wanted to live with him for as long as they could. She had loved him from the very first day; nursed him, cuddled him and kissed him when she liked, and made him as happy as she could.

He sighed again as he squinted at her fine form wrapped in her regular night garment, youth bursting out of her: that fine clear skin, those lovely eyes, and the way she moved, which excited him every time he saw her. She felt his eyes on him and smiled. Through all the troubles she had had since the fateful day of her wedding, she knew he loved her as much as he could. She loved him more than her own life. Ever since their first night back at his parents' house, she had coddled him, kept him warm at night and helped him to cope with his daily life. He could only sit up or lie down. But that was alright; she knew that was her life and her love. She was content.

She quickly took up the two brass pots she needed for fetching the water and moved to the door. She could see that her father-in-law was up and about. He always got up as soon as she did. It was a daily trial. Sometime after the wedding accident, Ramdas had begun to worry about the future of his family line. His only son would not bring him any grandchildren. He did not want to adopt. He could not wait till they found a cure for his damaged son.

They consulted the astrologers again. What had gone wrong? It was the planets. The wedding day had been carefully chosen but the leaving party had been delayed. The evil planet Rahu had entered the firmament and done his deed. But the rest of the prophecy was intact. She would bear a son and he would live a long life. They began searching for cures for him. They went as far as Kashi, and then Madurai, to find doctors who could cure. Everything was tried—Ayurveda and Unani medicines. They prayed and offered sacrifices; gave away cows and gold to Brahmins and sadhus. They would do everything to not let the family line vanish.

His wife had been the first to see the way out of their problem. Why let such blooming good looks go to waste? After all, the child would still be in the family; the family's patriarch would be its father. Ramdas had hesitated. He had to clear his conscience. But slowly his mind was made up. It was what he owed to his ancestors. It was the only way to keep the line alive. Anamika, on the other hand, had resisted from the start. She knew that once she had given them a son, her usefulness would be over. But even more, she could imagine Abhi's life shortened, since he required a lot of caring—which no one else would be willing to give him.

She faced constant pressure. Her mother-in-law was relentless. There was no harm, no sin. It was her duty for her husband's family. She had to say yes. They could wait but not forever. After all, her father-in-law was not getting any younger. It would be better if she agreed and gave her father-in-law the pleasure of doing what was his duty to his ancestors. He should not have to use force. Anamika had persisted with her resistance, but she knew she was trapped.

He was a light sleeper, and every morning, he knew immediately when she was awake. He had decided that early morning was his best time. If only she would agree. She could feel his excitement as he squinted from behind the door. She was a very attractive woman; no longer just his daughter–in–law, his son's wedded wife, but now the object of his desire. He had begun to look at her as his just dessert. He had to be fended off; his hunger for her was palpable. She meant to go on resisting. She just had to slip out before he could block her path. They would use force one of these days, she knew. Until then, she had to try her best to delay that hour.

Out of the door and into the narrow dark lane, she felt better. There were few people out so early in the morning, all women. She knew the women who would gather at the village well. Like her, they were young, hastily wrapped in some makeshift garment, all eager to draw the water from the well and rush back to attend to their men and their children. The well was in the village square. Ranipur was a prosperous village; it was cotton country, but there were also fruit orchards and farms that cultivated bajra and rice. There were weavers and tailors and carpenters; people from other villages often came to Ranipur for the services of its craftsmen.

On one side of the square was the imposing house, the haveli—two stories high and dominating the village. That was her house, or rather her father-in-law's. The house-front on the square was plain. The front door was never used, except for the royal guests who came to visit Ramdas. The door was not visible from outside as it was flush against the wall and was locked from the inside. A short plinth surrounded the front of the house. In summer evenings, Ramdas and Revati often sat outside while villagers passed by to speak to them. The only mark in the plain walls was a zarokha outside the first floor. The only way to get in was up the lane which ran by the house—the lane that she had just walked up. Across the way from the well was the road leading out of the village where there were only a few scattered huts. On the other side of the lane was a broader path down which there were many houses, each of them just one story tall, some small and a few large. There were about a hundred families in the village; theirs was the leading family.

Her two companions, Sushila and Rajat, were at the well as always. There would be more women soon but those two were always the first. They had to get the water and rush back to their children, who would be hungry when they woke up. She envied their troubles in feeding their children, fetching water, cooking and then ministering to their demanding husbands. Even so, they laughed as they helped each other. There was a wooden pail, which they had to lower with ropes down into the well and then pull up once it was filled with water. They would then empty the pail into their pots; any water that spilled over was collected in a trough and used to water the cattle. It was hard work, but they always helped each other. It was their time together, when they caught up on the day's news.

Sushila was the first to speak. 'I hear there is a lot of trouble around. People running around on horses, looting and killing.'

'Why does the king not control them?' Rajat asked.

'They are the king's men, looking for money to fight his brother, who wants the throne.'

'I hope they don't come here.'

Anamika said nothing. She had heard much more at home. Her father-in-law was worried about marauders coming for him and his treasures. As a leading trader in cotton and a banker, he had men who came to him from afar with news of trade and bags of money. He maintained a network of messengers, which was essential to his extensive trading business. He had heard a lot about the troubles brewing in the shah's territory now that there was a battle raging between princes disputing the succession. He had begun to wall up his gold and jewels so that no one would find them. He also had plans to send the women away to Kashi with a party of sadhus to keep them safe. But no one could say how soon trouble would come. For now, fetching water was the main task. What worried her most was how Abhi would be taken care of. Would they send him too with the women, or would they abandon him?

2. Abdul

*H*e had been riding all night with his small band of followers. He knew this was his last chance. He had received news that his step-brother, Hassan—his sworn enemy—was camped nearby in a field beside a large and deep river. The place was big enough to accommodate Hassan's many camps and followers. There were his officers and soldiers, his many mistresses and their hangers-on, cooks and food vendors, magicians and entertainers seeking a favourable review from the king, and supplicants for jobs. A royal camp was like a slowly moving town. For one fighting soldier, there were five useless appendages.

On the other side of the camp were steep hills. He had to amass his troops and strike hard. His idea was to trap his brother's army between the river and the hills. His brother had the larger army, of course, but he was also indulgent and over-confident. As the legitimate son and crown prince, Hassan had always had it easy. Abdul was not even legitimate. His mother was one of the many women in the zenana whom the king—indeed the shah—kept around; the litter born of these women had no rights and no claims. If they were lucky, they survived beyond the short life that the others had. Then they had to make their own fortune.

Abdul had been lucky. He had been present one day when the king was having a feast. The king loved his food and always had plenty to eat. It was a sumptuous meal as always, with kebabs and saddles of lamb, succulent pigeons, silken mounds of rice flavoured with cardamoms, cinnamon, saffron and cloves, yellow and black daal, and cheese with spinach and pakoras. He ate with relish and some speed, as if there was never enough time to have it all. Suddenly, the king choked and it looked like he was having a fit. The courtiers were aghast. No one knew what to do. The king was turning blue even as they looked on.

Abdul leapt to his feet, and before anyone could stop him, he quickly hugged the king from behind and squeezed him strongly. Something told him that was what he should do. Luckily for him, it worked. The king spat out the morsel of meat that was stuck in his throat, recovered his breath and felt better. Abdul was rewarded with a command of a hundred horses. This meant that he had the money to maintain his army, and himself, in the style necessary. He eventually advanced to a thousand, and then ten thousand horses. He held villages whose revenues gave him the means to finance his small army. Life was fine. He could see that he would one day be head of the army.

Then the king suddenly died and Abdul lost his sole support. Hassan, the crown prince, knew a rival when he saw one. He had never liked Abdul's advancement and had quarrelled with his father about the favours the king bestowed on Abdul. As soon as the king was out of the way, Hassan had stripped Abdul of his command, his salary and his palace. Abdul was rendered homeless and without his army. He had to avenge himself. The question was how.

The most likely way was the one that his father Ahmad Khan had taken. Ahmad Khan had arrived in Delhi as a young adventurer, with a horse and a gun, from Kandahar. Like many other Afghans, he had joined the services of one of the Afghan generals in the Mughal army. The powerful Mughal empire had flourished under the imperial rules of Akbar, Jahangir and Shahjahan. For over a hundred years, they had maintained peace and good order all across North India. Raja Todar Mull, Akbar's revenue minister, had carefully measured and assessed all the land under cultivation in the empire. The revenues assessed were collected regularly from the villages. The villagers were happy to pay, since they had certainty and regularity in their affairs. In famine years, the Emperor always waived the tax and provided relief works instead. Akbar had become king at a young age and had extended the empire his father Humayun had foolishly lost and barely regained before he died. Akbar conquered Hindustan and extended his empire up to Kabul and Kandahar. Across North India, he subdued many small and large kingdoms. The local kings had become his faithful vassals, and in the imperial territory, the officers appointed as nawabs and mansabdars carried out their tasks faithfully. People and caravans could travel in peace across the land and villagers could carry on their daily life knowing that they were safe from marauders.

Peace had led to prosperity and a happy populace. The Mughal emperors had built fine roads and magnificent buildings. The Taj Mahal, built by Akbar's grandson, Emperor Shah Jahan, was a lasting monument to the riches and the fine tastes of the Mughals. But the last king, Aurangzeb, tried to extend his territory south of the Vindhya mountains into the Dakkhan, as the country was called. Aurangzeb got entangled in a long battle that consumed the last 25 years of his life as an emperor. He was to be the last powerful Mughal emperor. While he was tied up in the south, the north began to get restless. The emperor's word was still law, but his faithful officers began to assert their own independence, as the power of the Mughal army was engaged in a war far away. Once he died, anarchy broke out over all of North India. The Deccan also slipped out of the grasp of the Mughals, as the Marathas fought them to a standstill and founded their own kingdom.

The emperor in Delhi steadily lost his power and influence over local kings and former appointee nawabs and subahdars. Aurangzeb's successors were feeble and lasted a very short while before usurpers threw them out. His son Muazzam took the title of Shah Alam—'King of the world'. But he only lived five years. Faithful officers became murderous agents who could change the Man on the Peacock Throne as and when they fancied. Thus Farukhshiyar, who succeeded his brother Shah Alam, was killed by his advisers. Then came Muhammad Shah. But his interest lay solely in his zenana, which had over ten thousand women. Ruling Hindustan was of no concern to him. The empire was left to run itself. Lacking Delhi's might as support, even the nawabs were not safe in their seats. Any brave soldier who could amass a small following could become a local king. Looting passing caravans and burning and pillaging villages under rival rule were sure ways of financing larger and larger armies. This, in turn, helped in winning territory and more loot. No woman's honour was safe, nor any man's life, when these new kings were about. These were the times of gardi—anarchy, in other words. The Marathas had added to the chaos by mounting raids from Poona, Nagpur and Gwalior. They were just as ruthless, if not more, as the Afghans and the Turkomans of the Mughal army. It was a game of dog-eat-dog, and to survive you had to be more of a wolf than even the vicious dog that your rival was.

Ahmad Khan had become an officer of a thousand horses in the dying days of Aurangzeb. He had been sent to bolster the subah of Ramgarh in the Chambal region. But as soon as the leash of Delhi slackened, he murdered his master and declared himself the subah. The emperor in Delhi did not mind as long as he got his tribute in revenue and women. But Ahmad Khan had higher ambitions. A dervish had forecast that he would be a king one day. Ahmad never forgot the dervish. Muzaffarshah Jalalabadi was a holy man, and people credited him with miracles. Muzaffarshah had seen Ahmad waiting outside the Diwan-e-Khas in the Red Fort at Delhi, where the emperor was granting audience. He said to the young man, 'I see it in your eyes that you were born to be a king one day.' Ahmad Khan hoped that the miracle-working dervish would prove right in his case, having heard of his prowess.

Emperors were changing frequently in Delhi, being murdered by their trusted advisers or by their own siblings. As one weakling followed another, Ahmad saw his chance. He stopped paying the tribute he owed and declared himself a sovereign king. He invited the dervish to crown him king. Muzaffarshah told him that he should be a shah not just a raja. So Ahmad Khan became a shah and named his capital Muzaffarabad. The shah then declared even higher aspirations by moving about in a camp with purple tents—the colour of the Mughal emperor's tent itself.

Abdul had to follow his father's example, build up his troops and strike to remove his half-brother, the crown prince, who was now the king. He had secured the loyalty of a few of his old troops, but that was not enough. He had to get some money so he could retain them and entice back the rest of his troops. He had friends among them who kept him informed of the low morale in Hassan's army and their hankering for Abdul's return. Ten days ago, he learned that Hassan had begun his march south to capture the kingdom of Purana Zilla. But given his lazy ways, he would take his time. He was camped by the river Sreni. Hassan had just acquired his father's zenana and he had much to enjoy. He had to have his pleasure with his new acquisitions before he could proceed further.

Abdul saw his chance and sped to a place he knew he could find a large treasure. He took twenty of his best men and started for a village where he knew there was a lot of gold and silver to be looted. It had once been one of the villages that paid him revenue. As they approached it, he told his men to hold back. He would scout ahead and figure out how to take the village.

Having ridden all night, he was now hungry as well as thirsty. He slowed his horse down to a walk so that it would make as little noise as possible. He entered the village square almost silently. There were three—maybe four—women at the well. His eye caught the beautiful one. They were busy pulling up pails of water from the well, helping each other. They were all young, but she was the most fetching one. Her bare arms were fair and her face was perfection. She was wrapped in a single coarse garment, a sort of sari that the Hindu women wore. She had a simple necklace as her sole piece of jewelry.

Suddenly, the horse neighed. The women saw him and panicked. They fled down a little lane on one side of the well. All except her. She just stood there and looked at him. He spoke up.

'I am a thirsty traveler. Will you give me some water?'

She replied by lifting her brass pot, summoning him closer to the well, where she was. He got off his horse and stepped closer. He held out his cupped hands, and she calmly poured water from her pot with a steady hand, all the time looking at him intensely. Then, suddenly, she was gone, walking away from him in the same direction as the others. He was about to thank her, but she did not give him a chance. She had given him only what he had asked for—a drink of water—and then had picked up her other brass pot and simply walked away. He was totally bewitched. She was a vision like he had never seen before. He had also never met a woman who could be so calm in the presence of a stranger, and that too a soldier.

As he began to turn away, he had a careful look at the big house in the square. This had to be the haveli of Seth Ramdas. It was a two-story house with a plain, high façade. Halfway up, there was a small zarokha jutting out. The house was a simple one, but it exuded wealth for those who could discern such things. He had heard about Ramdas and his wealth. He had to return for the loot, if not for the beauty.

3. Anamika

She put down the two brass pots. One would go in the kitchen, and one would be there for washing. But she had to first get dressed, before everyone began to demand their morning dues. Later in the morning her cook and her maid would come to help her, but in the early morning it was her turn to look after everyone. She went back into the bedroom and checked how he was doing. He would sleep a bit longer. Then she would wake him up after she had fed the others. She made sure he was warm, and again he drew her close to himself. This always pleased her. She liked it when he kissed her. She lingered just a moment longer today. She was thinking of the roving, admiring eyes of the stranger who had asked for water.

There was a commotion in the village. The women had run back to their houses and described what had happened. Soon men from the neighbouring houses came to their door. Seth Ramdas was, after all, the head of the village in some sense. It was unusual for people to come this early, but as he was awake, Ramdas let them in. They related the story of a horseman walking into the village square. The women had seen nothing else. They had just run away.

Ramdas was worried. He asked his wife to call their daughter-in-law. With the men of the village in the front room, the women stood behind the door. Ramdas asked his daughter-in-law, 'Bahu, did you see a man on a horse?'

'Yes, father.'

'What did he do? Did he say anything?'

'No, father. He asked for water.'

'Did you talk to him?'

'No, father. I just gave him water to drink.'

'You gave him water? Did he touch you?'

'No, father. I would not let a strange man touch me. He bent down in front of me and I poured water in his hands.'

'What did he look like?'

'I did not look at him. I hid my face.'

'Well that was at least a good thing', her mother-in-law said. 'But you should not have given him water.'

'He said he was thirsty.'

Ramdas gestured to his wife that the interview was over. He now had to take stock of the situation with the other men.

'So what do you think?'

'He was alone. We don't know who he was. He could have been some officer of the shah.'

'The Shah has embarked on a march on Purana Zilla. That much my messengers have told me. So it cannot be one of his men,' Ramdas said. He had his sources of information.

'Maybe he was from Abdul's army,' piped up another.

'Do you think they would raid the village?' Ramdas asked.

'I doubt it. Why would he come alone if he had an army with him?'

'Maybe he just got lost.'

'Maybe. But we must be careful. Let us meet at noon again.'

Her mother-in-law was not happy.

'Our women don't talk to strangers.'

'But mother, I did not speak to him.'

'You should have run back home without looking at him.'

'I did not look at him. I hid my face. I did not talk to him.'

'But you gave him water.'

'He asked for it. I had the water. So I gave it to him. I did not touch him.'

'We will have to get the pot purified. We must call the pujari later today to purify it.'

'Yes, mother.'

She went back to her routine. She had to warm up the milk and cook breakfast for the family. She had put on her makeshift clothes—a blouse, a petticoat, and the garment she had worn. Normally she would change that as well. But somehow, today, she wanted to hang on to it. There was something that had pleased her. She did not know what it was. Her parents-in-law were clearly furious, but she had held her own. She had lied a bit, but now she knew that she was on her own. Her little lie protected her. Perhaps that was it. Or perhaps it was the piercing almond-shaped eyes of the stranger as he asked her for water. Of course she had looked at him while he was bending beneath her with cupped hands. He had a stern but handsome face. He wore a turban and some rings on his fingers. His horse was a strong Arab horse as would be useful in battle. He was a powerful man, as she could see from his hands and his stature. And again, those penetrating eyes. Something had happened in Anamika's dull daily life. What did it portend?

4. Abdul

As he rode back to his companions, Abdul could not get the woman out of his mind. He conjured up that vision again and again. There she was by the well. She had on nothing but a thin necklace and a single garment that barely hid her lovely form. Abdul had seen beautiful women. In a life spent hanging around a palace with a large zenana, there had been no shortage of quick furtive liaisons. He considered himself well versed in recognizing female beauty. But this was something else. And not just her form—her attitude struck him as very forward. She did not run away in panic as the others did. She stood there, calm and in control. She looked at him with bold eyes. As she gave him water, she did not flinch from his eyes staring at her. She walked away with as much ease as she had displayed in confronting him.

Who was she? Obviously a married woman—her necklace was the Hindu woman's mangalsutra. But what was her name, her family? Where did she live in the village? Perhaps in the big house? He would have to find out.

When he reported back to his companions, he did not say anything about the woman. It was clear to him that the village could be raided with much profit and little resistance. Ranipur fell within Hassan's territory now and he should be offering protection, but he was far too engaged with expanding his territory to care about what he already had.

They had to attack the village and do it quick. But the rest of his troops had not yet had anything to eat or drink. The first step was to forage around the scattered huts where farmers lived. Abdul asked two of his men to gather whatever they could quickly and began planning his attack. Before they could set off, Quli Murshid, his best officer, was quick to react.

'We better hurry. The village women have seen you. They will begin to run away soon.'

'But the men are hungry and thirsty.'

'There will be plenty of food in the village.'

'Fine, Let us go.'

5. The Bargain

Once the men of the village had left, Ramdas began to make his preparations. He called Revati to the living room. Anamika pricked up her ears and eavesdropped from the adjoining room, where she had been talking to her mother-in-law earlier.

'You begin packing what we need for the journey. I better hide some more of our things before they arrive.'

'When do we go?'

'As soon as possible. Get ready and ask our bahu to do so as well.'

'Where do we go?'

'I have thought it all out. We can move quickly if we go now, taking the horse and the cart. We will hide somewhere while the storm passes. Then, if the trouble persists, we must reach the river before they catch up with us. We can get a boat that will take us to the Kali temple at Sangampur where the Sreni meets the Yamuna. Once we are there, we can go to Kashi. We may need to be away for a while.'

Anamika's worst fears were being realized. She could hide no longer.

'Father, how will we get him ready so quickly?' she interjected, entering the room. Like a good Hindu wife, she would not name Abhi in front of her elders.

'We will have to leave him behind for a while. I will ask Shivnarayan. He can send Sushila every day to check on Abhi.'

Shivnarayan worked for Ramdas as a muneem in his trading and banking business. Sushila was his wife.

'I will stay behind. I cannot leave him.'

'This is no time for such thoughts, bahu.' Revati was stern. 'We have to get out of here quickly. You have to be kept alive, as does he.' She was speaking of her husband. 'And I have to be with him in case he needs help.'

'No mother. I cannot leave him behind. I am willing to die alongside him if that is my fate.'

'Your fate is to come with us and give us a son who will continue the line. That is our command for you. Now go and prepare for departure.'

Anamika was stunned. She ran back to Abhi, who was now awake and sitting up. He had heard the commotion but did not know what had been said.

'Mika, what has happened?'

'There was a soldier in the village this morning when I had gone to fetch water. Father thinks he is from Abdul's side and they will attack the village. He wants us to run away.'

'When?'

'Soon. But they don't want to take you. They think we can return in a day or two so they will leave you behind and ask Sushila to come and look after you. But they may not come back for a long time if the looters are roaming around. I refused to go with them.'

'What did you say? Are you sure it is proper to defy father?'

'My place is beside you at all times. I will not go away without you. I stay here till the end, come what may.'

'Mika, father may have the better idea. He has lived through times of trouble and knows how to survive. Do as he says.'

'I will obey you in everything else but I will not leave your side even if you tell me to. I have gone round the fire seven times with you, and I will stay here even if you ask me to go away.'

Abhi clasped her hands and looked at her with a frown.

'You are incorrigible. But then, I chose you.'

'Or maybe I chose you. Now you are stuck with me in this life and in every future life, for ever and ever.'

6. Anamika

Anamika went about her daily domestic routine as if nothing untoward had happened. She lit the fire and put some water on for heating. Wheat flour had to be taken out of its large box and kneaded for the morning meal. She knew the routine, and today she went about it with greater care, as if to make sure that she was going to stay on.

Revati came in. She saw what Anamika was up to.

'Douse the fire immediately and get ready bahu. There is no time to lose.'

'But I want to be sure he has something to eat today, at least.'

'No time for that. Sushila will feed him.'

As Revati was about to throw water on the fire, there was a bang.

'What is that?'

'The soldiers must have arrived. They are firing their bandooks.'

Revati rushed back to where her husband was. In the main room, there was panic. A bullet had made a hole in the door that was kept shut. They heard a shout.

'Seth Ramdas, open the doors. We want to talk to you.'

Ramdas looked through the newly formed hole in the door, and saw some gun-wielding men on horses. He saw no choice.

'I am opening the doors. Don't fire. There are women in this house.'

As Ramdas opened the front doors, the men who had just left his house rushed back in through the side door. Everyone was shivering. Revati realized that she had to withdraw indoors. She ran inside. She could not see Anamika, and assumed that she would be with Abhi. She had no time to think of her wrong-headed daughter-in-law.

Abdul was on his horse, leading twenty other men. They were all armed and looked ferocious. Afghans, all of them. Ruthless booty seekers, ready to shoot and kill on the slightest pretext. Neither men nor women were safe from them.

'Ramdas, open your treasures. Let us see how many lakhs you can give us.'

'But Huzoor, you know I don't have money like that. The times are hard and trade has been affected by all the troubles since the old king, your father died. We have already paid the revenue to your brother.'

'He has no right to the revenue. This is my village. I will collect the revenue. Not just from you but the whole village. Where are the villagers? Bring them here.'

Ramdas came out trembling, along with a few of the men who had rushed to him. Shivnarayan was ready to help his master. He came forward and said, 'Huzoor, we are poor people. You are our protector. Please let us live in peace. Next harvest we will pay the revenue to you. This year we have no money.'

'I want ten lakhs from the village. How you give it to me is your concern.'

'But Huzoor, ten lakhs is not possible. You can come into my house and search if you like. I am not as rich as you think.'

Abdul was not that easy to fool. He knew what would work.

'If there is no money in this village then I will set it alight. My men will take the women, and then we will shoot all the men.'

Ramdas was perplexed. Was he to take the threat seriously and surrender, or could he fend the angry man off? After all, if ten lakhs was what he wanted, it was going to come almost entirely from his own coffers. The village might be saved, but what about him?

'Huzoor, please think of us poor people. We can get you as much as we have, but that would be not more than one lakh at most. You are our protector, please have pity on us.'

'I will count up to ten. Then my men will begin firing. One. Two. Three…'

'Stop this.'

Abdul looked up. At the top of the house, in the zarokha, she stood, looking as beautiful as before, but now angry as well.

'Call off the firing. You can have the money, but don't kill the people.'

Ramdas was aghast. Why had his daughter-in-law exposed her face to these marauders? What was she up to?

Before anyone could say anything, Anamika was at the bottom of the stairs and walking into the square where Abdul and his men were. She had on the coarse garment she was wearing in the morning, but she had wrapped a shawl around her shoulders for greater modesty.

'You can have what you want, but don't kill anyone. Father, you know you have the money. You owe it to the villagers to give it all to this man. While we live, we can always get more money.'

Ramdas was speechless. Abdul got off his horse. He came close to the woman and said softly, 'You quenched my thirst for water this morning—but can you now quench a bigger thirst?'

'You can have the money.'

'I want more than money, as you must see by now.'

'I do not know. But I cannot talk here with you. Come inside.'

The men standing around Ramdas froze. They were astonished. What would this woman do to the village? How could she talk so openly to this marauder? Had she no shame, no sense of propriety?

Before anyone could say anything, Anamika led Abdul inside the house and shut the doors behind her, leaving all the men outside. Revati had escaped by the side door.

Anamika led Abdul to a room where Abhi could not hear anything. It was the room where Ramdas would sit, doing his business. There were thick ledgers bound in coloured cardboard, pens and inkstands in various places. In the middle of the room was a perch on which Ramdas would usually sit, his feet touching the floor. In front of the perch was a sloping desk, on top of which there were pens and ink. If you opened the desk, you would find coins, bundles of chits and hand written notes, and inventories of items. This was a trading man's working desk, his galla.

Abdul sat down sideways, facing Anamika.

'How much to spare the men of my village?'

'You heard me. At least ten lakhs. More if I can get more.'

'Will you promise to spare the women of my village if you get the money?'

'All except you.'

Anamika smiled.

'I know that. I knew you would come back.'

'I would even give up the money if I got you.'

'Why? You can have the money and you can have me.'

'Is this a trap?'

'How would there be a trap?'

'Are Hassan's men coming to save you?'

'Who wants to be saved? Come.'

Abdul followed, astonished, as Anamika led him upstairs. There was a large four poster bed in the room they eneterd. It was meant for Abhi and Anamika's first night in the house—a night that never happened. The room had been left untouched, with its colourful decorations in place.

Before he could say anything, she removed her shawl. All she had on was the coarse garment.

'This is how you saw me this morning. This is what you want, isn't it?'

Abdul was speechless for once.

'You can have me and you can have all the money in the house. But on one condition.'

'I knew there would be a trick.'

'There is no trick. I want you to promise me, on your holiest book, that you will protect my husband with all your might. As long as he is alive, I am yours to do with as you please. The day he dies, I will die with him.'

Abdul was completely flabbergasted. He had never seen a woman talk so boldly, nor with such cunning.

'You are married? Where is your husband? Why is he not here to protect you?'

'He is in the house, but he cannot walk. He fell off a horse on the day of our wedding. I have nursed him since then. He is very precious to me.'

'Why would I need to protect him?'

'Because I know and I can see that you want me. I am here for you to have, as long as he is alive with me. Just promise me what I ask for.'

'How? I do not carry the Quran-e-Sharif with me.'

Anamika came close to him, put her arms around his neck, looked him in the eyes and said, 'Sign a promise in your blood.'

Abdul took out his dagger and made a small cut on his smallest finger. Blood rushed out.

'Here is my promise.'

'Smear my forehead with your blood.'

Abdul knew the rituals of Hindu women well.

'I will put sindoor in your hair. Then you know I will protect your suhag.'

Anamika took his finger and smeared the blood in her hair. She then sucked his finger while dropping her garment. She took the bloody finger and ran it all over her front making a red circle over her breasts. She invited him to lick it off. Abdul knew he was being invited openly by the most beautiful woman to do what pleased him. He was quick with his mouth against hers. She let him kiss her deeply. Then she took his hands and let him roam all over her breasts and hips and wherever he wanted, all the while kissing him. He held her tight. He licked his blood off her breasts. She had the feeling that he was very excited. She then took him to the bed and lifted up her breasts to welcome his mouth. She lay down on the bed, her feet still reaching down to the ground. She spread herself, inviting him to take her.

Abdul was in seventh heaven. His impatience with the woman who had led him on was palpable. There was no time for play. He dropped his belt and thrust himself inside her. She breathed heavily and soon started laughing and moaning. Abdul was astonished.

'You are a virgin?'

'Yes. I saved myself for you. Don't stop.'

Abdul did not, nor did he take long to thrust his way deep into her. He prolonged his pleasure as long as he could, but he was too excited. He burst inside her. She laughed and moaned the entire time. The bedsheets were smeared with Anamika's blood. She hugged him, pushed him gently away and then she quickly wiped herself. He sat down on the bed, still excited but happy.

Anamika calmly reached under the pillows on the bed and retrieved her blouse and petticoat. She had undressed and left them there before appearing in the zarokha, which was just at the end of this room. She put them on and wrapped the garment that had excited him so much in the morning around herself, so it would hide any tell-tale signs of her state.

'Let us go down and tell them what to do.'

'What do we tell them?'

'Let my parents-in-law go off to Kashi. This house is then my husband's by right. You can always come and have me here. You know I will never leave—we have now sealed our pact in your blood and mine. I can show you where all the gold and jewellery is hidden. There is more than ten lakhs.'

Abdul was again surprised by the coolness and determination of this woman. He had not expected any of what had happened in the previous five minutes. He had anticipated dragging her away and raping her by some wayside tree. He had expected to burn and loot the village and let his men carry away the women. He had not thought that the woman would willingly give herself to him, in her house, on her bed.

'You go out and tell them. I will stay behind, as I am only a woman.'

Abdul had no time to appreciate small ironies. He had to calculate quickly how he would benefit from this situation. He opened the doors. Ramdas and the men of the village looked at him, trembling.

'I have been pleased that the lady of the house is an honest woman. Seth Ramdas, you lied to me. I should kill you, but she has asked me to spare your life. You can go away to Kashi with your wife. I will send someone to escort you to the river. But don't try and come back. Don't seek Hassan's help, I am holding your son and your daughter-in-law hostage, so don't get up to your cunning tricks. One false step, and they will be dead and I will set fire to the house and the whole village.'

Anamika realized that Abdul had what it takes to be a leader. He had changed her bargain into his own victory. He was also not lying—she was hostage to him. Maybe Abdul was not like the others. Maybe he was someone she could trust. She certainly hoped so. She had now hitched her life and Abhi's to Abdul's trust.

'As for the villagers...' Abdul paused and waited for the trembling to resume. 'The lady of the house has asked me to spare all your lives. Your women are also safe.'

The villagers fell at his feet, crying and thanking him.

'Now feed my men. They are hungry and thirsty.'

The village was transformed in an instant. Ramdas was the only glum person, but no one paid him any attention. Abdul took him in his hand and directed one of his men to make sure he did not escape. He would be taken away after the soldiers had eaten. Ramdas had to ask someone to get his horse. Revati had also emerged from hiding. She had heard what had been said, and cursed her daughter-in-law. Her woman's mind had grasped that the young bahu had tricked them and thrown them out, taking advantage of the Afghan's lust for money. That was her revenge for Revati's insistence that she give them a son. Now there probably would never be a son to feed the ancestors in heaven when they got hungry.

7. Ranipur

The village was now in a festive mood. The relief was incredible. Never before had they heard of an Afghan coming to raid a village and sparing everyone except the rich man. Men rushed back to their houses and asked the women to fetch water and whatever food they had ready, for the soldiers. Normally the women would not step out of their doors when soldiers were about. But now they knew they had been reprieved. As the women rushed out, they heard how it had all happened and cheered Anamika with gratitude. The village began to prepare to feed the soldiers, as if they were a wedding party come from the groom's side.

The soldiers knew that no Hindu household would let them in the kitchen. But the village square was large enough to lay down mats for them. There were large plates made of leaves sewn together, which were always used in wedding dinners. You could eat off them and then throw them away. There were small clay pots for drinks, which would be smashed after the meal. This way, the Muslim soldiers could have their food without causing any ritual pollution for the Hindu villagers. No effort would be spared to feed them and give them water and milk to drink. This was something the village excelled at.

Anamika heard Abhi call her from inside.

'Mika, what has happened? Why all the noise?'

'The villagers know that they will be spared by Abdul Khan and his men. So they are now preparing to feed them.'

'Is this your doing?'

'I will tell you about it later when they are all gone. There is only one more thing you should know.'

'What is it?'

'Father and mother are going to Kashi now.'

'But they were going to go with you.'

'I have to stay here on the order of Abdul Khan. That is a condition for their being saved. Abdul Khan was angry that father lied to him about the money.'

'Have you been your father's daughter and done some shrewd

bargaining?' Diwan Gulabchand was known for his cunning ways in securing agreements.

'I said I will tell you all when we are alone. Now I have to see what there is for you to eat.'

Abdul was beginning to calm down after the morning's exertions. He stayed outside, as he did not want anyone to suspect what had transpired between him and Anamika. Even his soldiers had been astonished by the deal he seemed to have made. The village was saved; the women were to be left alone. How much money had he got? What had that beautiful woman done to Abdul? Quli Murshid saw that the waters were running deep, but he kept his counsel.

Anamika came to the door and gestured to Abdul that she wanted to see him. Surprised at her openness, he went in with some hesitation.

'What do you want?'

'I want you to meet my husband.'

'Why?'

'You have to see who it is that you owe your good fortune to. After all, you are saving him and I am the prize for that.'

Abhi had heard none of that, as they were still in the front room. Abdul followed Anamika in.

Abhi was sitting up. Abdul saw a handsome, strong, young face on what seemed like a tall person. This must have been the man she really loved. He could now understand why she was so keen on saving him. He smiled as Abdul came and stood at the door of their bedroom.

'This is Abdul Khan, our saviour and future shah. Huzoor, this is my husband.'

'Salaam Alequm, Khan saheb.'

'Walekum as-Salam, Sethji.'

'I am not the Seth. It is my father.'

'But your father is going to Kashi. You are now the Seth of this house.'

Anamika was overjoyed at Abdul's tact and graciousness. She had not thought he would treat Abhi with such dignity and honour.

Abdul turned to Anamika.

'Perhaps we should take Sethji to his galla. Let me ask a soldier to carry him.'

Anamika was speechless. How had Abdul guessed that as a Seth,

Abhi would sit in the room that they were in a while ago? Now that his father was gone, Abhi was indeed the rightful occupant of that room. He used to sit in that room every day, since before the wedding, below where his father sat. It was only in the last year that he had become unable to do so. Everyone had resigned to him being in bed all the time. But here was an Afghan, used to an active life, riding a horse and carrying a gun regardless of Abhi's missing limbs, who could see that Abhi would be happier doing what he was brought up to do.

Abdul went to the door and summoned a soldier. Again, everyone was curious. Abdul ordered the soldier to lift Abhi up and take him to the room with the ledger books. Abhi was astonished. He had not moved from this bed for a long time, except once or twice a day. Now there was someone lifting him up from behind and taking him ever so gently next door.

Abhi was put in the seat where Abdul had sat briefly earlier in the day. He knew the room well, and also knew what the various ledger books contained. There were cupboards built into the wall, some with heavy locks, that had the gold and the jewellery. Suddenly, Abhi brightened up.

'Shukriya, Khan sahib.'

'I am only doing what I believe will benefit us all.'

Abdul ordered the soldier to bring Ramdas in. Ramdas stepped in, still fearful, not sure what was about to happen to him. He was amazed to see his son sitting where he used to.

'Give your bunch of keys to your son, Sethji.' Abdul's voice was peremptory.

Anamika could not believe that Abdul had such an amazing sense for practical detail. Ramdas reluctantly dug into his inside pockets and took out a large bunch of keys. Before he could say anything, Abdul snatched the bunch and gave it to Abhi. He then instructed the soldier to take Ramdas out. He had sensed that Anamika did not want to be in the same room as her father-in-law. She had given away his money and got him sent off. This told him that there was little love lost between the two. He was also wary of any potential emotional scenes between father and son that may ensue. Ramdas had to be treated like the liar that he was.

Abdul also asked the soldier to send Quli Murshid in. Anamika could not figure out why.

Quli Murshid came and stood at the door, taking in the strange scene. He could see that Abdul wanted him to be a witness to some important decision.

'Sethji,' said Abdul, addressing Abhi, 'you know I have come to take money from the village and from your father.'

'I thought you had taken the money.'

'Not yet. I now have trust in your wife and in you. I know that you will not betray me. I will protect you. That much I have promised your wife, who was quite honest about the money. If I take all the money I need now, chances are someone might attack our party and loot us. We would rather loot than be looted. So I say let us agree that we keep the money in your safe hands. We will leave a guard outside, day and night. When I need the money, I will send a request and you will give it to us. Meanwhile, you carry on the trade of your father, and what you earn will be your's.'

'That is very noble of you.'

'I am not a nobleman. My mother was a simple but beautiful woman who happened to catch Ahmad Shah's eyes. I am the result. If I have got anywhere in life, it is by the strength of my arms and my guns, the swiftness of my horse, and the good blessings of the dervish Saheb Muzaffarshah Jalalabadi. If by his grace I become the shah like my father did, I promise you I will return the money.'

Quli Murshid understood what Abdul was up to. He had no palace and nowhere to store the money. This way, he could store the money while also earning the goodwill of the young Seth and the village. This left them free to pay the soldiers as and when they wanted and mount their campaign against Hassan.

Abhi asked Anamika to fetch a ledger. She gave it to him and placed the pen and ink pot on the edge of the desk, close to him. Abhi opened the ledger on a clean page.

'Let me start your account. How much should I record in your account?'

Before Abdul could speak, Anamika said, 'Khan sahib had demanded ten lakhs.'

'Done.' Abhi wrote it out with a flourish.

Abdul made a salaam to him and said, 'Let me take your leave. I have far to go. Quli Murshid will tell you how much we need. He has a head for figures, which I don't. Whatever he asks for, give it to him and make an entry in your ledger.'

Quli Murshid was ready with his request. 'Each horseman gets a rupee per day. We have a thousand horsemen to pay, but they have not been paid for the last five months. All of that has to be covered.'

'That would come to one and a half lakhs. But you have to allow for baggage and the train, plus the water carriers and the food suppliers.'

Abhi could see that he had to get down to business now.

'Anamika, could you see to it that Khan sahib is well looked after?'

Anamika knew even so that her first concern had to be Abhi.

'Will you be alright here? Shall I send Shivnarayan to assist you with the ledgers?'

Anamika wanted time for herself, but also for Abhi so he could be back to an active life. She went out and saw that Shivnarayan was still there, supervising the arrangements for feeding the soldiers. She asked him to come in and help Abhi. Shivnarayan was also surprised to see Abhi was up and about. He was quick to involve himself with the task. Anamika was now the villagers' favourite person; anything she wanted, they were happy to do.

Anamika went out of the room with a quiet glance at Abdul.

Abdul knew what was coming and followed Anamika back to the bedroom upstairs.

'Khan sahib, what can I say?'

'When we are alone, don't call me Khan sahib.'

Anamika came close to him. She held up her mouth for him to kiss. Nothing would now stop him from exploring her fully.

'So what do I call you?'

'My mother called me Lalla.'

'You are now my Lalla. You were amazing with him and...'

'You are amazing with me. Don't waste time talking.'

This time, they were less hurried. She was as eager as before and pleased that he could not hold himself back either. Soon they were inside each other's mouths and bodies, biting and kissing and rubbing thighs together. She luxuriated in his attentions. He lay back and lifted her on top of himself. She laughed and did whatever he wanted. He held her back, grasping her breasts with his strong hands as she rocked herself on top of him. It felt like an eternity before she collapsed on his chest, savouring her exultation and his release.

But it was only a moment or two before Abdul knew he had other things to do and his soldiers to worry about. He detached himself gently from Anamika. She knew he had to go. He was aware that his soldiers had eaten. He would pick something up from the square. But he had to move on before his men became impatient. Quli Murshid had been satisfied about the money, but knowing him, Abdul wanted to make sure that no one would think he had slackened in his campaigning just because he had seen a beautiful woman.

'I have many many more kisses to bestow on you than I can today.'

'You are a soldier and you want to be a king. I know that. When you are a king, you can have a large zenana. I am here for you when you have a brief break from your battles. I am yours, Lalla. Be sure of that.'

'What is your name? What do I call you then?'

'My name is Anamika.' She took his little finger in her mouth and said, 'This is your Anamika. But call me Saki. I can be your intoxication.'

He held her tight again, and kissed her. This time they lingered, making sure each felt the eagerness of the other. Their bodies were talking to each other.

He had to go. He had just one last question to ask her.

'What about him?'

'You have given him a new lease of life. I will tell him what I need to. I do not tell lies, not to him, not to you. Come again and come with more time.'

Abdul had to have his farewell kisses, his restless roaming, and then suddenly, as easily as he had taken her, he got up and left her. She lingered behind, as she did not want to be seen with him right now. Her life had changed. Abhi's life had changed. Could this be a portent for a happy future?

Abdul went to where his soldiers were now getting ready to march away. Villagers came to salute and thank him. They asked him if he wanted to eat something. Everything was available, and if not, the women were ready to make it for him. For Ranipur, Abdul was now their second-most favourite person. He could feel their love. He knew he could now treat Ranipur as a safe home.

He mounted his horse and said, 'Ranipur has been good to my soldiers and me. I want to come back to you and enjoy your hospitality very soon. I will rename Ranipur Raunakabad when I am the shah. Until then, farewell.'

Anamika thought it best to hear all this from inside the house. Once the soldiers were gone, the village women poured into her house to thank her. She suddenly remembered that in all the hectic happenings, she had not given any breakfast to Abhi. But the women were more than ready to help. From now on, Anamika was their queen as far as they cared.

She went in to the galla to see how Abhi was doing. He was busy like never before. He had given the money to Quli Murshid. Indeed, he had set up a sensible system for them to estimate their needs. Entries were made in the ledger; moneys counted out and put into bags and given to Quli Murshid. Now Abhi was busy catching up with the accounts with Shivnarayan's help.

'How are you? I forgot to feed you, but Sushila is bringing something for you soon.'

'I am busy, as you see. It is a pleasure to be busy again. It is also a great feeling to touch the ground below me with my feet.'

Anamika was also impressed. All these days, they had taken his disability as something they could do nothing about. He had not been allowed to leave his bed and go anywhere. Now, suddenly being carried into his place of work had done wonders for Abhi. She decided to leave him there. She had a lot to do and much to reflect on. She also needed a bath.

8. Niloufer

Niloufer had much to do as well. She was always taken along whenever the shah went on a campaign. This was as true of the older shah as of his son. Niloufer had been part of the zenana all her life. She was just seven when the marauders came to her village in Badakshan and snatched her away. The older women were killed and the younger ones raped. But the children were taken, as they would fetch good money in the slave market where young virgins were always in demand. She had been looked after and fed adequately till she was eleven. Then, as she began ripening into a young woman, her captors took her to Kabul and there the slave traders took her on. Hardly a day had passed when she was bought by an Afghan general who was going to Delhi. He did not want her for himself. He gave her away as a gift to the emperor in Delhi.

She lived in the zenana with ten thousand other women, all competing for the attention of the dissolute man. Mohammad Shah—the Mughal emperor in name alone, unlike his great forbearers—had no time for his kingdom, as he spent all of it in the zenana. She changed hands again when she was passed on as a gift to the subahdar of Ramgarh. The poor old man was flattered to get a luscious young woman from the emperor's zenana, but had no time to savour his prize. So it was Ahmad Khan who was her first man. By then, she was sixteen. For months, he could not have enough of her. He had many more, but Niloufer was his favourite. She knew how to please him; a different trick every night, a different perfume, a different dress, a different gesture to titillate his appetite. Niloufer was the connoisseur of sexual preferences.

But then she got pregnant. She cursed her fortune. It was a king's child, but not a royal one, as she was not the queen. Far from it. The queen had come from a noble family in Kandahar, as Ahmad knew he had to marry someone fit for a shah. So Niloufer went off to have her child alone. She had wanted a daughter, who could then be trained in the same arts she had learned. She could be introduced into the zenana when the time came. There were little meena bazaars held in the zenana from time to time. Here, older women of the zenana would display their nubile daughters to the king, who would come on a shopping spree. The lucky ones got bought, and they and their mothers had an assured lifestyle in the zenana. The less lucky ones had to catch the eyes of a general or a nawab. If that failed, there were slave traders in Delhi and Lahore and Kabul.

Niloufer was lucky. Her son grew up among the children of the zenana, but she did not see much of him after he was weaned. She had heard that he had made his fortune. She was happy, but unconcerned. The important thing was that she was kept on. As Ahmad got older and his energy began to fade, he liked Niloufer to be around. She knew how to revive his flagging spirits. She had learned about ointments and smears that she could apply to perk him up. She knew of aphrodisiacs and potent solutions that the shah could imbibe to charge himself up just before his mistresses crowded in upon him. She kept on asking unani hakims and ayurvedic vaids for new medicines and miracle cures for his diminishing libido. He kept her by his side even when he was sporting with younger ones, as she always came ready with what he needed.

Thus it was that Niloufer was there when Ahmad suddenly died. She knew what had killed him, but did not tell anyone. She earned the thanks of the women complicit in the act that had killed Ahmad. The queen was grateful for her discretion. When Hassan succeeded his father, her son Abdul quarrelled with him and was deprived of his rank and all his perks. But Hassan kept Niloufer on in his zenana. She was entertaining, and she could choose for him the kind of woman who would please him most. Hassan's problem was that he had just inherited a large zenana, but none of the women in it were of his choosing. They had to be kept around because of the unexpected death of Ahmad. Hassan needed to make his own selection and keep the rest under control. Niloufer was the selector for the shah and he was happy to have her around to ensure that if he did not like one, she would get another quickly.

Her tent was vast as she had 20 girls with her to look after and groom. Hassan had begun his first campaign since becoming shah, and this was his style. He had his ten thousand men, dozen elephants and scores of horses. There were large guns, and camels to pull them. The soldiers had to be fed and the horses and elephants had to have their food and water. All of this meant a big site with hundreds of hangers-on. But Niloufer was used to all this. She had been on many such expeditions before. She just needed to have ten women ready every night, and ten more waiting in case Ahmad's mood changed. What the rest did and how they would fight was none of her concern. But Hassan was different. She had to learn about his likes and dislikes.

Kings had to be watched before a battle, as they were full of bravado. The pent-up anger and energy meant that the women had to watch them, lest they got violent and the worst happened. Niloufer had to choose women who could be in control while simpering for the shah. But it was after the battle, when the kings were splattered with blood and gore but with their anger not fully spent, that the women knew the orgy would be endless. The battle would last a day or several, depending on how rough the enemy was. But after days of violence and abstinence from all comforts, the shah would have a gargantuan appetite for his women, and that required some special ones. Niloufer knew that the campaign was about to begin in earnest soon, and she had to groom her charges the best way she knew.

Her particular concern this time was a new girl. She had white skin, blonde hair and green eyes. She was taller than the rest, and bigger, too. Yet she had an exquisite figure: firm, large breasts, a slim waist and a large bottom. Her presence was a sign that this time, the slave traders had penetrated into the country beyond the Sea of Marmara. Nadya knew no Indian language when she arrived. She could speak fragments of Persian and Arabic or Turkic when she came to the zenana. You could see that she had been through a hectic life even at a young age. How she had been taken from her home in the land beyond the Sea of Marmara, how many hands had exchanged her, was not Niloufer's concern. But there was no doubt in Niloufer's mind that Nadya would end up as a favourite. Language was hardly required for what she had to offer, and the shah would convey very well what he wanted. But then, seductive words added to the thrill of the act, as Niloufer well knew. Turkic was a common language in which they could talk. Niloufer had to do with what she had.

Niloufer liked grooming the young women under her charge. With Nadya, she also started teaching her rudiments of the language she had to understand, if only to know what the shah was demanding. As she cleaned and combed her hair, Niloufer also told Nadya how to make a salaam and bow low, how to display her charms, how to move, and how to leave if the going got rough. Nadya's blonde hair was Niloufer's special delight. She had not come across such hair before, though they had told her that the Emperor Aurangzeb had had a woman from Abkhazia he was infatuated with. Abkhazian women were blonde, just like Nadya. Nadya's hair was short, and Niloufer thought that by keeping it short Nadya may yet retain her style amidst a bunch of dark-haired women with long tresses. She brushed and washed the hair, and then as Nadya lay down to let it dry, Niloufer began telling her what to say when she was confronted by the king.

As Nadya listened, she fingered the cross that she wore around her neck. She recalled how her mother used to take her to the church. It was vast and gloomy. There were old men with beards and tall hats. They looked severe and intoned in a language none understood. There was a smell of incense and a lot of music. Her mother had told her that what was said in the church did not matter. The cross around her neck would protect her forever. Now, more than ever, Nadya hoped she was right.

Niloufer was now demonstrating how Nadya should bow and show herself off at the same time. How she should be shy, but reveal herself so the king could appreciate her assets. How she should never say what her real name was. If asked, she should say that she would take whatever name the king gave her. How she should refuse any alcohol at first, and only take some if the king was likely to lose his temper if she resisted. But that happened only when he was already drunk beyond repair. Then she could pretend to drink and being drunk. The king would notice little. Nadya had to learn all this if she was to succeed as Niloufer wanted her to. She was the daughter Niloufer never had, and Niloufer wanted to make sure Nadya would be the favourite, like she was.

Nadya knew she had to become a favourite if she was to survive. There were too many other women the new king had inherited from his father. She was new, but she alone knew that she was no longer in the prime of her youth. She had been through many zenanas and had seen a lot. She had been captured in a faraway land that she had heard being called Abkhazia by everyone. She had seen young princes and old kings. One of them liked having women around him all the time—so much so that his guards were all armed women. Nadya had learned how to wield weapons and protect the man who owned her. Of course, she had to turn into an object of pleasure when the prince fancied. An armed woman in a soldier's dress was thrilling for the prince.

But he died because of his brother's intrigues. Nadya had learned how the conspiracy was carried out. One of her own troop had conspired with the brother and poisoned the Prince while he was playing with her. In return, she became the favourite of the brother who was now King. Nadya and the rest were thrown out of the zenana. Nadya knew then that her looks, or even her skill with the knife, were not enough. She had to learn to listen and guard against intrigue. Pick up gossip, make allies but not friends, and look after herself. Now, four more princes later, she was keen to learn how she could make it to the top. It would be that, or an early death.

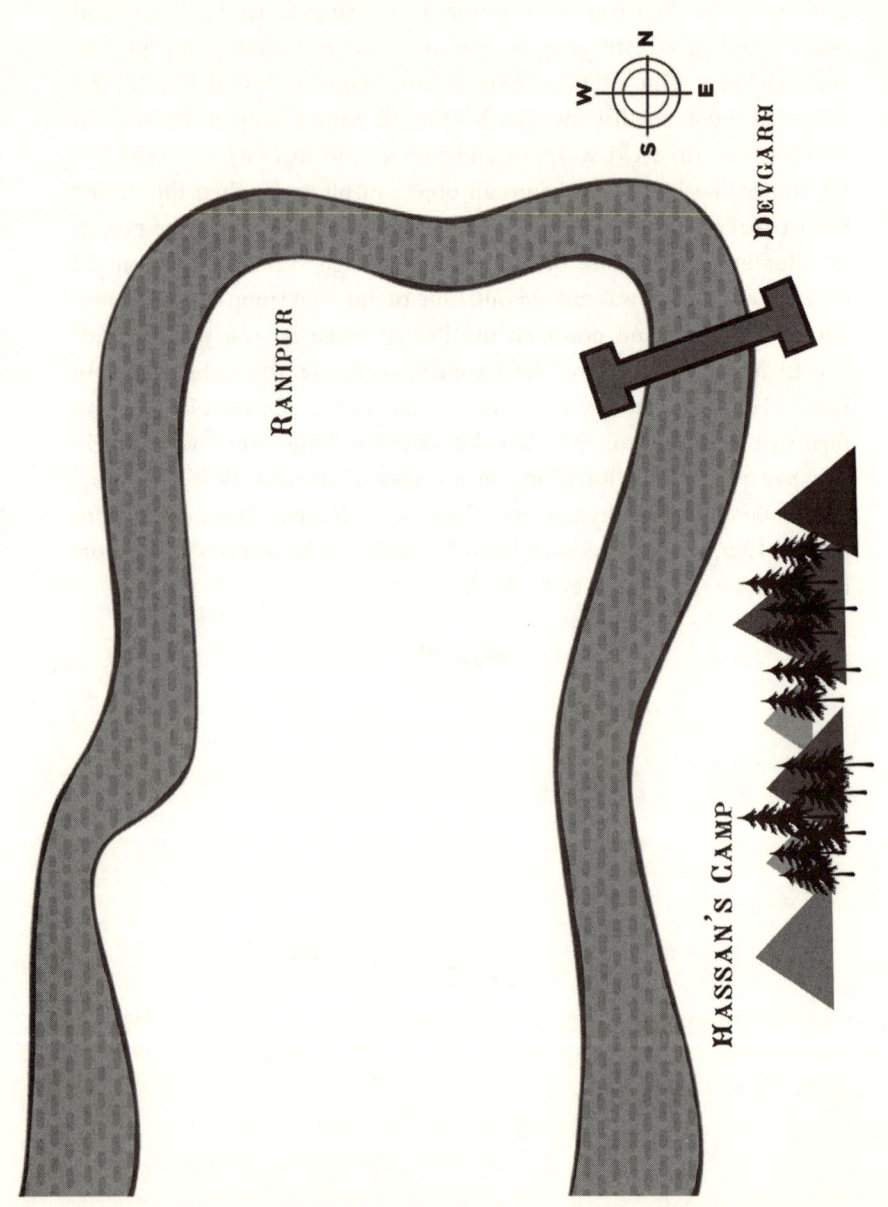

9. Hassan

The object of Niloufer's concern was holding court. His tent was large, with silken curtains and lush carpets. There were soft cushions and mattresses all around. His throne, while on campaign, was arranged on top of a pile of mattresses so he could perch higher than all around him. The throne was more like a divan than a chair. He could sit up or recline, as his mood dictated. At present, he was sitting up.

Hassan was a handsome youth, having inherited his Saiyad mother's fair skin and his father's stern good looks. He was tall and alert as he sat consulting his officers. His sword was at his side in its silver scabbard with encrusted pearls. There were his army generals, his revenue clerks, his wazir, and many hangers-on who were waiting upon his command to run errands. The officers were seated under him and the hangers-on were standing around. There were two men fanning him with elaborate chowries and a person sprinkling attar on him from an elaborate silver shaker. A gold covered hookah with a long silver extension was burbling for his attention.

This was a new world for Hassan. He had been busy studying the serious subjects as a student prince. He had had to learn philosophy, calligraphy, archery and sword fighting. He had been fond of reading about the great kings of history and their campaigns. His father had not yet taken him on a campaign. There was plenty of time, years before he would need to. But then his father suddenly died. Hassan had had to grow up quickly. He was just getting used to being a king and being saluted by the old generals. He had to show them that he knew his role.

'How many troops does Devi Singh have?'

'Huzoor, we think he has ten thousand foot soldiers, five thousand horses and a five hundred strong elephant force.'

'Does he have big guns or only jizails?'

'Huzoor, he has one big gun that is slow to move and fifty field guns, which are very effective. He has camels mounted with swivel guns. The big gun has been brought to him by the Frenchman Pierre. The big gun is called Padmini and can be very effective when fired, but is very heavy and requires camels to move it around. His horsemen have matchlock bandooks.'

'Has he any friends among his fellow Rajputs who may come to his aid?'

'Huzoor, Rajputs are always quarrelling about who has precedence over whom. As of now, no one is speaking to Devi Singh because he says his father was the senior Rajput king and so he is now senior to all the rajas. There is a dispute about that and few may come to his aid.'

'Have we troops ready for marching?'

'At your command, Huzoor.'

'How many days will it take us to reach the outskirts of Vishalnagar?'

'Two and a half for the horses and four for the foot soldiers. Huzoor, once we cross the river on this side, we have to find good places to ford the river. It will take time to take the camels and elephants across.'

'Tell them we begin our march tomorrow morning. Zail Singh!'

At Hassan's command a general rose up and saluted.

'Huzoor.'

'Get the boat bridge ready for us to cross the river. Get another boat bridge ready for the soldiers and the horses.'

'Yes Huzoor.'

'Tell the soldiers this is the last night they have to enjoy themselves until we finish our conquest of Purana Zilla.'

'As you wish, Huzoor.'

A man came in, panting with urgent news. He bowed low before Hassan thrice and waited for his permission to speak.

'What news of Abdul?'

'We hear that he was in Ranipur, but he failed to loot anything. All he got was some food and water for his men.'

Hassan laughed aloud, and as if on cue, so did the court present in the tent.

'Abdul is always a big talker, but when he tries to pretend he is a prince he fails. That is what you get when you are born of a low woman and not a noble queen. I am not worrying about Abdul. Once we have taken Purana Zilla, we will deal with him. Let them know that anyone who brings me Abdul alive will get five lakhs; his head carries a reward of two lakhs.'

Hassan clapped his hands. That was the signal that the meeting was over. The officers could go. Now the shah would get down to enjoying himself.

10. Anamika

All day Anamika had gone about the house cheerful and happy. It was a new feeling. She was now the mistress of the house, and Abhi was busy taking over as head of the family business. She luxuriated in her bath. Now there was plenty of hot water. Rajat had brought in two extra brass pots just for them. Anamika cleaned herself with care and then spent a lot of time pampering herself. She put on her sindoor and smiled at the memory of the last time sindoor was smeared into her hair. She took out a brightly coloured sari and matching blouse and petticoat. She dressed herself to show Abhi that she was happy.

Abdul had left two soldiers, Jibril and Wahid, behind to guard the house. One of them was ready to lift Abhi up whenever he wanted to go. Abhi was taken for his bath and Anamika stood beside him to help him as he wished. Until today, the only way he could be washed was by bringing a bucket and a wet cloth to his bedside. He would shift to a bench beside the bed and then Anamika would scrub him with the cloth and then dry him. It was not much, but that was a part of her daily routine. Now he could move and there was no one to check what they got up to. There was much splashing of water, as Abhi was now happy and relaxed.

That night, as they snuggled close, Abhi asked.

'Are you going to tell me what you did to save the village? And why did father and mother go away to Kashi so suddenly?'

'When Abdul Khan came to the village, he demanded ten lakhs and father said he did not have so much. At most he could give one lakh, but no more. Abdul Khan saw that he was lying and wanted to kill all the men in the village and abduct all the women. So I cut a deal that he could have all the money, but he must spare everyone's lives.'

'But why did he send father away?'

'Abdul Khan is a hot tempered Afghan. He could not abide being lied to. I requested that he should spare father's life but if he wanted he could see to it that father and mother could get to Kashi, which they wanted to in any case.'

'Is there more to it than that?'

'Can I tell you a story in answer to that'?

'Go ahead.'

'Remember, Yayati was a very powerful king. When he got old he regretted that he did not have any more strength to enjoy his pleasures. So he asked his son Puru to exchange his youth for his father's old age. The son agreed.'

'So?'

'Had he asked his daughter-in-law, she may not have agreed.'

Abhi knew what was being hinted at and did not probe further.

'Are there any more stories you wish to tell me?'

'You know the story of Satyavan and Savitri. Soon after their marriage, she found out that the God of Death was about to take her husband away. She had to trick Yamaraja when he came to snatch Satyavan away in his deathly embrace, by some device. She succeeded and he let Satyavan live '

'You were Savitri before you became Anamika. Maybe I should have changed my name to Satyavan.'

'You do not have to change your name or anything about you. You are mine and I shall be at your side for ever and ever. No Yamaraja will get near you while I am by your side.'

Abhi knew that Anamika had done some deal with Abdul. He chose not to probe any further. He had faith in her, and even more, in her love for him. In any case, he was enjoying his new life, and in some way Abdul Khan had been responsible for giving him this new lease on life. Maybe Anamika had also received a new lease on life. He wrapped himself closer around her tonight, so she would know he knew and did not mind.

11. Abdul

Abdul had left two of his soldiers with Abhi and Anamika. He sent one off with Ramdas and Revati to escort them till the river, where they would be put on a boat that would eventually take them to Kashi. With his remaining troops, he hastened back to his camp, where his loyal troops were waiting for him. There was much joy as Quli Murshid told them that they were going to be paid on the spot. But there was no time to lose. They had to set out by late afternoon to gain the element of surprise in their campaign.

The troops left behind had been foraging in the villages for their daily sustenance. Abdul sent someone to tell each village that they would be paid for what had been taken. He had been impressed by the willingness of the Ranipur villagers to help them. He now had an inkling that treating the villagers well rather than just robbing them might be the best way to win their support and loyalty. It was going to be a hard, long campaign to remove Hassan, and they would need much goodwill in the days ahead.

As they set off, Abdul addressed them.

'You have been my faithful followers in the days of exile I have suffered. I value your loyalty and will never forget it. Now we begin our fight to regain what is mine. Hassan is camped by the river. We will march further up the river and cross it. This requires us to be very quiet, fire no guns and keep the horses in check when we get close to the river. I know a place where the river is fordable and we will go across there. May Allah be with us.'

There was a loud cheer and some guns were fired. Then they set off in a disciplined manner, ten abreast, and hastened to the Sreni where it had an unusually high ground to flow over. The broad and deep Sreni was in full flow after the monsoon, but when it came to Devgarh, the ground was high enough to slow the river down. Abdul had marked the place long ago when he had ridden for Ahmad to try and gain Purana Zilla. The campaign had been at a stalemate then. After six months of fighting, a truce had been signed. Hassan was about to break that treaty.

Abdul's plan was to get to Devgarh, which was some twenty miles upriver from where Hassan was camped, and cross over to the other side. He wanted to surprise Hassan by coming in from the hilly side. Normally that would be the most well-protected side, as Muzaffarbad, the capital of Hassan's territory, was just beyond the hills. But Abdul knew that Hassan, being overconfident, would leave the back unguarded. Hassan had superiority in the number of horsemen and he had big guns. Abdul had to use his ingenuity to gain advantage.

Quli Murshid had sent an advance party to contact the boatmen at Devgarh to get a boat bridge ready. This way, some would ford and others would use the bridge. Now they had the cash to pay on the spot and the boatmen were happy to oblige. It had to be a strong boat bridge, as horses had to go across. The river was only about ten feet deep there. The danger of drowning was little, but speed was of the essence—so they had to get across in an organized fashion.

As they marched, Abdul went to Quli Murshid and began explaining his plan.

'We attack after dark. I expect the soldiers will be resting or just drinking. They do not expect an attack from the hills. On our left will be the foot soldiers' tents, and on the right the guns and the horsemen. You go on the side with the guns and try and capture as many as you can. Take about three hundred with you. Let the rest attack the whole camp from the front. I will head for Hassan's tent. It is easy to spot, as he uses his father's purple colours. I hope to capture him if I can't kill him. If we surprise them, they will scatter and leave us a lot of their baggage.'

Quli Murshid had his ideas as well. 'We must warn our men about the elephants. If they go berserk, we have to keep out of their way and let them crush their own side. If we could capture some elephants, that would be helpful in the future, but they are also expensive to feed.'

'If we succeed, we should get a lot of loot from tonight. We can then afford elephants and guns for our side.'

As they rode, they avoided villages and kept to the wooded countryside. These paths were well worn, as armies had marched back and forth in the age-old dispute between Ramgarh and Purana Zilla. But the urgency lent the march a lot of tension. Abdul knew that an army on the eve of a battle thrives on tension. His bounty had convinced his soldiers that they were on the winning side. Once they struck Hassan, then the rest of their comrades would join them as well. Armies grew on the promise of success.

12. Nadya

The news that the march would start the next morning had released a lot of tension in the camp. Soldiers now had a clear signal: *Enjoy yourselves tonight and be ready for the hard slog from tomorrow morning.* Suddenly, the noise level in the camp was higher and firecrackers, or even real guns, were being fired in the air. Music could be heard from several tents, and some soldiers had taken out their pet instruments that they fancied playing. There were drums and flutes and tambourines. All the hangers-on—sellers of delicacies and clothes and jewellery, women followers who were there to entice any soldier who would pay them well, astrologers and quacks and magicians and snake charmers. They had to get the best out of their last evening with the idle soldiers. Everywhere there was a festive atmosphere.

In his purple tent, Hassan was also enjoying himself. Again, he had not expected to have all the luxuries that his father had enjoyed thrust upon him so suddenly. Chefs had brought in his evening delicacies including several kinds of kebabs, roast lamb, pigeons and rice. He was being entertained by the women Niloufer had brought for him. She knew that, to begin with, they had to be charming in the way they waited upon him as he ate. He liked his food, but there was always too much of everything. The women were also a luxury he had yet to get used to… They were there to serve him, to coax him to have another mouthful of some delicacy. Niloufer moved the women about, as she knew he would get bored with them before long. New ones had to be brought in to keep him amused.

Niloufer was waiting for the dinner to end. Ahmad had had his routine. He would wait till he had sated his appetite for food. Then he wanted his other appetites to be catered to. With Hassan, no one was sure what he fancied. All that Niloufer knew was it would be better to have another set of women for that phase of the evening. He was eating with some relish and soon he had done what he could with the food.

He clapped his hands. Servants came in and took the trays away. Snacks would be brought in fresh throughout the evening in case he felt like eating again. The wines were already decanted in fine silver surahis and there were silver cups ready to be filled. Musicians arrived promptly and began to play soothing music from behind a curtain on the far side of the tent. They would play for the dancers but not see their faces, as only the king could see the faces of his women. Others would face death for casting an eye on the king's possessions.

Hassan drew Niloufer close to him. He had known her forever, as she had been in his father's zenana and was trusted by his mother. Now, suddenly, she had become the gateway to his sexual pleasures. This was something Hassan was familiar with, but again, the number of women around often bewildered him. He had not yet formed an idea about what he really liked in women. Most of them had been in his father's zenana. Until he acquired his own favourites, they had to be kept around. Hassan had to cope with being king in this way as well. He had to do the things that kings did. He hoped he would begin to have his own favourites soon. But Niloufer was a great help. He always indulged her vanity by playing with her as well. At 40 years, she was still an attractive proposition, but she knew her place and was flattered. Hassan had his hand on Niloufer's thighs as he caressed her. He drew her even closer and bit her ear. She laughed and reciprocated by moving her hands over his sensitive parts. She could feel that he was in an excitable mood.

'Who have you got for me tonight? Laila was mostly good last night, but she got tiresome when she wanted me to admire her singing. I need someone tonight who can fire me up for the battle tomorrow.'

'I have a gem of a beauty for you. Do you want her now or will you try your Salma first?'

'Who is this new one you have got for me?'

'She has a beautiful body you will devour the minute you see her. She is from beyond Istanbul, very white-skinned and frisky.'

'What do you say?'

'Huzoor, I would say let Salma do her usual stuff. You can begin with her and then get all fired up for my little pigeon.'

'Bring on Salma.'

Salma was waiting impatiently just behind the curtains at the back of the tent. Normally, she would be there the instant the food had been cleared away. Tonight, she did not know what the matter was. She had to be better than before. She had got a new choli made for tonight. It was held together by a thin string at the back that left the rest exposed for his eyes. She had a low-slung lehenga on, but with a split in the sides so her legs could be seen. She knew that if she played her cards right, soon she could be the number one woman in Hassan's zenana. She had heard how Laila was thrown out the previous night by Hassan as he got bored with her. She had to do her stuff. Tonight may be her big chance, as he was about to go off to fight. She wanted the whole night with him for herself.

Salma came and bowed deep. Hassan gestured for her to come close.

'Huzoor, what would your pleasure be tonight?'

'Come and fill my cup.'

Salma picked up the silver surahi and poured wine into Hassan's cup. Hassan took one sip and then threw the wine at her. Salma knew this was coming, but she played the distressed damsel and pouted with mock anger.

'Look what you have done to my beautiful choli. How can you be so cruel?'

'Well take it off, then, so I can pour another cup of wine on you and then begin the mehfil.'

Salma saw that he was doing what she wanted him to. Her mock anger might work again and wrap him around her little finger. She frowned and took off her choli and turned away from Hassan, hoping he would fancy her bare back. He grabbed her and turned her around.

'Where is my wine?'

Salma frowned again and filled another cup. Hassan threw it at her, this time splashing her breasts.

'Now look what you have done. How will I dance for you?'

Hassan suddenly got the feeling that Salma had done this act many times before for his father.

'Don't you want see my dance tonight, Huzoor?'

'Later. Now I want more wine.'

Salma tried mock anger yet again.

'You only care for the wine, not for me, tonight. Don't you find me intoxicating?'

Hassan lost his patience.

'Go away. You are tiresome. I don't like you tonight.'

Salma broke out in tears.

'Forgive me. I will do whatever you command. I will pour another cup of wine for you. Don't send me away.'

Hassan was not in the mood for reconciliation. He wanted something different. He called Niloufer, who was waiting just behind the curtain.

'Take this tiresome woman away. She does not please me tonight. Bring on your little one.'

Niloufer took the tearful Salma out and soon came back with Nadya. Nadya had just a simple single piece of silk wrapped around her that stopped much short of her knees and did not go above her nipples. Her tall form, white skin and blonde hair charmed Hassan. He immediately gestured Niloufer to leave. Niloufer bowed deeply, cast a glance at Nadya, wishing her courage, and slipped behind the curtains.

Hassan asked Nadya to come closer. She came coyly, not sure what would be expected of her. Hassan drew her close. She was now kneeling in front of his couch so he could admire her. Hassan was amazed to see this tall white woman. He could not take his eyes off the cross she was wearing, as it drew his attention straight to her chest.

'What a beautiful vision. What is your name?'

Nadya had practiced the response many times. She clutched her cross so he could see more of her. Haltingly, she spoke the lines she had been taught.

'Huzoor, creatures like me are too insignificant to have names. Call me tonight whatever pleases your noble self and I will be happy. Another night, you can choose another name for me.'

Hassan was pleased at this response, as he was meant to be.

'If you say you are an insignificant one, I will call you Nacheez. Now show me that you are what I crave for tonight.'

'Shall I fill your cup, shall I dance, shall I press your feet?'

'Come fill my cup and please me.'

Nadya came close and filled another silver cup. As she presented it to Hassan, she let her garment fall off. She had nothing on except her cross. Hassan could hardly believe his eyes. There, before him, stood the most beautiful woman he had seen in many years. Nadya took the cup from him and poured the wine over her breasts. Drawing his mouth to them, she said, 'Please yourself, Huzoor. Nacheez is all yours.'

Hassan was thrilled. He had not expected such a quick and bold response from Nadya. All the coyness and pretend anger of Salma were nothing compared to this woman, who boldly took initiative. Nadya kept it up, laughing and leading. Soon she was beside him, taking his arms and letting him explore her beautiful body. Hassan was happy to be led. She let him roam all over, opening up her legs. But she saw his excitement and suddenly moved away. She picked up her garment, covering herself seductively and said, 'Let me dance for my Lord.'

Hassan had no patience. He wanted to grab Nadya and have her right there and then. But before he could move, he heard screams and shouts. And amidst the commotion, out from behind the curtains where the musicians were sitting, came Abdul. He had been watching Hassan with Salma and then with Nadya. He could only see Nadya's back. But he did not want to strike at Hassan while she was close to him. As soon as she moved away, he burst in.

'Hassan, come and fight me.'

Nadya screamed. Niloufer did not think much of it, as screams were part of the fun. Hassan was shocked. He finally became aware of the noise outside. There were guns being fired, the shrieks of women and the cries of soldiers. Abdul's men had surprised them all and begun the attack. Coming down from the hillside, the descent gave their horses extra speed and their guns were effective. Abdul had made straight for the purple tent. He was sure Hassan would be in his cups by now and would not offer much resistance. Before Hassan could move, Nadya rushed at Abdul and clung to him. Abdul was thrown by the tall blonde woman. He brushed her off as gently as he could.

Hassan, in the meantime, had regained his composure and taken his sword out of its scabbard. He was ready to fight. Hassan was no mean fighter, but he was unprepared for this event. As Abdul rushed towards him, he parried him off. But Abdul was soon near him, slashing at him left and right. Hassan kept on dodging and hoping that he would find some weak spot in Abdul. But soon enough, Abdul had him cornered. Hassan crouched, sword in hand, but Abdul was above him and about to stab him.

Suddenly Nadya sprung into action. She came up from behind Abdul, grabbed the dagger he had in his belt, and plunged it into his right shoulder blade. Abdul cried out in anger. He was bleeding profusely. Hassan stood up. But Abdul had just enough strength to slash at Hassan's right arm, making Hassan drop his sword.

Niloufer came into the tent. Seeing Abdul and Hassan locked in battle, she shouted, 'Lalla, leave your brother alone. Let Hassan live.'

Abdul, bleeding even more now, was taken aback by Niloufer's arrival. Hassan saw his chance and ran out of the tent, into the melee. Abdul tried to chase him, but Nadya and Niloufer stopped him. Abdul was furious but helpless. His quarry had escaped.

'Why do you ruin my life, mother? This was my chance to get him and claim the throne. Why did you stop me?'

Nadya saw how Abdul was bleeding. She also realized that Niloufer was Abdul's mother. Her sympathies changed. She tore a long piece out of her garment and began to bandage him. Abdul was now feeling the aftershock of the wound. He did not know what to make of this beautiful woman who had stabbed him and was now dressing him. But he had little time to think about her. He rushed out, found his horse and rode away.

Outside, the fighting still raged. Abdul's men were on a rampage and Hassan's army, surprised in the midst of their revelry, was running away. Some were jumping into the river to escape. Elsewhere, some men were trying to regroup. It was a chaotic scene.

Quli Murshid was coming towards him.

'We have routed them. They are running away in confusion. We have the elephants and the guns. Did you get Hassan?'

Abdul gestured and showed his wound: deep, profusely bleeding. Quli Murshid said, 'Get on my horse I will take you away before they fight back.'

'Where shall we go?'

'Away from here. They may attack back and we have to save you. Can you bear to ride for a few hours?'

'Of course. I will be fine soon.'

'No, you won't. Not with that deep a wound. The safest place for us is Ranipur. If I ride fast, I can get you there by the morning. Stay alive and stay awake.'

They had known each other for years. Quli knew Abdul was strong, but he was also sure that Hassan's men would chase them. They had no safe haven of their own. The only place Quli could think of was the village that had been so nice to them just the previous day. He was sure Hassan's men would not get there any time soon.

As he rode away, he raised the standard. The soldiers soon saw what was being signalled and joined him. He gave them quick instructions.

'Leave the elephants and the big guns behind. We do not have the time. We must clear out of here. Just grab what you can carry with yourself. We will meet again at the old camp from where we started. I need twenty men to follow me to Ranipur. I will meet you in the village. I must be quick.'

Abdul knew he had some explaining to do for Quli.

'I had Hassan cornered and was about to stab him. But then this woman, a tall white woman who was with him, suddenly came from behind and put my own dagger through me. Then my mother sprang up from heaven knows where. I lost my concentration and Hassan ran away like the coward that he is.'

'Your mother has always been loyal to the shah's family. She runs Hassan's zenana, as she did with your father, as you well know. Hassan takes her everywhere with him. But don't talk much now. You must conserve your strength.'

Abdul could see that Quli Murshid was also annoyed that he had missed his quarry. He was trying to reconstruct in his mind the sequence of events, but it was difficult. He remembered the woman dancing, but had only seen her back. Then as he burst in, he only saw Hassan. He never thought of her staying back or doing anything. He was so close to killing Hassan. Then, of course, this woman had clung to him. Abdul recalled that it was a pleasant sensation even in the heat of the combat. She was stunning. What had embraced him was a hot, beautiful body. Who she was and what her name was, he would never find out. He did not hold it against her that she had defended Hassan and had stabbed him. He admired that, as it showed loyalty and courage. Why he had to meet two beautiful and courageous women in as many days was beyond his ability to fathom.

He was starting to feel drowsy. He knew what to do. He wrapped his arms around Quli's back, then, knowing he would be taken care of by his friend.

13. Abhi

It was again that hour of the night when Anamika could sense that she would have to start her day's routine. Perhaps not yet, as she did not have the lurking presence of her father-in-law to worry about anymore. She pressed herself closer to Abhi. They had their intimacies, even though Abhi could only do so much. She grabbed his arm and put it around her waist. He did what he knew she wanted. He squeezed her breasts and, drawing her closer, kissed her. She giggled.

Abhi opened his eyes and said, 'Mika, something very unusual is happening to me.'

Anamika was worried. She sat up.

'What, Abhi?'

'It is not something to worry about. But I can feel some movement in my toes and tingling in the soles of my feet.'

'Really? Let me see.'

Anamika threw off the rajai and bent down to look at Abhi's feet. There, she could see his toes moving ever so slightly. It was a sensation he had not felt in a long time.

'O Abhi, how amazing!'

Anamika had tears of joy in her eyes. She bent down and kissed his toes, then came up and kissed him full in the mouth, before bending again to kiss his toes. He drew her back to him and this time, took the initiative like he had seldom done before, kissing her deeply. They were happy, like it was their first night of illicit love. Anamika was crying and laughing. Abhi choked with emotion.

'It is thanks to sitting up all day yesterday, I think. Also the hot bath.'

'I do hope so. I must go to the Kali temple and make offerings of sweets and coconuts.'

'We must also thank Abdul Khan when we see him next. It is his doing.'

Anamika was glad that it was Abhi who remembered Abdul's gesture. She was going to offer prayers to Kali to tell her why she had done what she had. But now she felt that maybe there was some divine hand behind her bargain.

Suddenly, they heard the sound of horse's hooves and a loud shout. 'Open the door!'

Anamika got up and wrapped her garment around her. She went into the main room and asked, 'Who is it?'

'Open the door. I am Quli Murshid. Abdul is badly hurt.'

Earlier, Anamika would not have had to open the door, as Ramdas or Revati would be there. But now there was no time to think about her modesty. She wrapped her garment around her a bit more tightly and opened the front door. There, in the hazy half light, was Quli Murshid on his horse, with Abdul behind him. Quli got off first and then gently brought Abdul down. Anamika asked them to come in. Jibril and Wahid, whom Abdul had left behind, were sleeping just outside the house. They stood up and helped Quli take Abdul inside. Abdul seemed to be semi-conscious. He had a cloth bandage around his shoulder. He looked awful. Anamika took him straight to their own bedroom as Quli held him. Abdul could barely walk.

Abhi saw what had happened. He lumbered up and moved to the bench beside the bed, as he would do for his daily wash until yesterday, making room for Abdul on their bed.

Abhi had moved faster than Anamika or Quli could think. Abdul was now placed on Abhi and Anamika's bed. Anamika saw the wound in his shoulder blade. She said to the soldiers who had brought Abdul in, 'At the well, there will be two women. They will recognize you. Ask the one called Sushila to bring me some water now, as I cannot come to the well myself.'

Anamika went into the kitchen and lit a fire with the kindling and dry wood they stored there. She put a pan of water on. She recalled how her mother-in-law had wanted to douse the fire just as Abdul had fired his gun, only yesterday. Back then, she had been concerned about Abhi. Now, Abdul was her worry. She needed Abdul to recover and be her strong support, for Abhi.

Sushila came straight into the kitchen, avoiding the men in the other room. She had brought in a brass pot full of water she had just drawn from the well.

'What is it, behen? What has happened?'

'Abdul Khan has arrived with an injury. Can you tell Shivnarayanji to bring the vaid as soon as he can. But don't tell anyone about Abdul, and tell your husband also not to tell the vaid what he is being asked to come for. Just say I need him. They will think it is about my husband. They are used to that.'

Sushila left immediately. Her husband was up, and would be surprised to see her back so soon. But nothing mattered now except for what she had been asked to do.

The water in the pan was boiling. Anamika took it off the fire. She fetched a new piece of cloth from the cupboard in the kitchen and took it into the bedroom along with the pan. She knew how to wash a body, as she had done it everyday for Abhi. She did not hesitate for a minute to do the same for Abdul.

As she came in, Quli withdrew to the door and Anamika sat down opposite to where Abhi was sitting on the bench. She asked for Quli's help to make Abdul sit up and take off his clothes. Abdul's thin armour had been pierced by the dagger, and his shirt underneath was also torn. Quli raised him up and loosened his belt. He then took off the two layers of clothes from his upper parts. The torso was that of a strong man with a hairy chest. But the right shoulder was caked in blood at the back.

Slowly waking up, Abdul found himself in a strange environment. He saw Quli and then Abhi. He heard Anamika asking him to bend forward. Instinctively, he did so. She began to swab him with hot water. It felt good after a long night of pain.

Anamika was not thinking of Abdul's body now, as she had the last time they had been together. Her mind was fully focused on his injury and the urgency of saving him. She was patient but swift in cleaning the wound. Abhi looked on. He had firsthand experience of Anamika's deftness in washing someone's body. She was just doing the same for their benefactor.

The wound was now clean. Anamika asked Quli if he could open the cupboard near the door. Quli was not used to taking orders from a woman, but Anamika was different. He did as he was told. She asked him to take out a piece of cloth from the bottom shelf. It was one of her soft cotton saris, useful for daily wear. He handed it to her. Anamika tore out a long piece. She folded it up and put it on the wound. Then she tore out another long piece and made a bandage for the shoulder. Abdul was docile and cooperative, bending forward when asked and muttering his gratitude for Anamika's actions.

'You better rest a bit now. The vaid will come soon and we will give you some medicine.'

Quli Murshid did not like the sound of this at all.

'We do not want anyone else to see Abdul like this. People talk and then we lose face. We will go soon. He will be alright now.'

'If that is your wish, I will send the vaid away.'

Abhi saw the problem.

'Why not let the vaid see me? I will go to the galla as I did yesterday. He can see me there and Khan saheb can stay here out of sight of other people. I will make up some complaint for him to deal with.'

Anamika was impressed by his presence of mind. She had noticed how quietly he had moved out of his bed and made room for Abdul. Quli called Wahid, who was waiting outside, and asked him to take Abhi to his galla. As he left, Anamika said, 'Abhi, I will bring you your milk. Huzoor, if you can wait just a short while I will bring you the milk too. It will give you sustenance till you reach your destination.'

As Anamika went out, Quli could hear soldiers gathering outside.

'I will ask them to put up a tent just outside the village, so you can rest. We can then move somewhere before Hassan's army comes after us.'

'Let twenty stay in the square like yesterday, and I will rest in the tent. The rest should stay not far away. Remember we have to sort out what we have won; how much to carry with us and what to leave behind. You will need time to talk with Sethji about all that.'

'Even so, I want you in a safe place away from here. We will make a camp that can house all our men. Ranipur is not big enough.'

'As you say.'

Quli Murshid went out. Horses were clattering into the square. Now, of course, they no longer worried the villagers. Some women at the well offered the soldiers water and helped their horses drink as well, by pouring water into the large stone trough at the front of the well. Quli began to talk to the soldiers. Some had arrived with baggage that they had looted. Some showed him bags of coins and caches of guns. Ammunition had been captured as well.

Quli told them that everyone with bags of coins had to deposit them with Jibril and Wahid, who would then hand them over to Abhi. But the vital point was to begin moving out as soon as possible and find a place not far from here, but closer the river, so they could get away if attacked. Their old camp was fine, but the villages there may have exhausted their stocks of grain. They had to strike a new camp. He was still worried about Hassan's troops recovering and regrouping for attack.

As the soldiers began to leave the village square, Quli went back inside the house. He had to talk to Abhi first.

'Sethji, my soldiers will hand over to you the bags of coins they have got. Just keep an account for us. We will need much more soon.'

'Do not worry, Khan sahib. I will enter it all in my ledger. You will have it when you wish.'

'Shukriya.'

'Ranipur will be happy if you bring all your soldiers and put up your camp just outside. You know we will help you as you have helped us. We have blacksmiths and carpenters and tailors. Your people may need some help in these matters. We also have the vaid to look after their injuries. So please, stay close to Ranipur so we can be of help to you. This is now your territory.'

Quli was struck by Abhi's thoughtfulness. He had not expected a merchant—and one so badly crippled at that—to be aware of the problems an army had. But Abhi's advice was sound. They were safe near Ranipur, and there was plenty of water and many families ready to help them. There was open land nearby and smaller villages where they could forage for food.

Quli went in to see Abdul. He was alone. Soon Anamika came in with a bowl of hot milk for Abdul. Seeing Quli, she quickly went back into the kitchen and came out with a bowl for him as well—something he wasn't expecting.

'What about Sethji?'

'Don't worry. I am going to give it to him now.'

Anamika went back into the kitchen. She knew she had to be totally focused on the injured man and assure Quli that there was nothing else between them. The joy of being with Abdul would only come if it was their own secret. Hurrying it would diminish the pleasure.

'Here is your milk, Abhi.'

Anamika found the freedom of addressing her husband openly by his name one of the many gains from the departure of her in-laws. Now they were alone and able to do and say what they wanted. Her parents had always been close and loving, and had addressed each other by their names in front of their only child. Anamika had been warned by her mother that the world was not like her family. Now she could live freely, as she had grown up to do.

'Are you alright? You had to get out of bed suddenly. How did you do it without my help?'

'Things seem to be getting easier. I am really liking this desk and this perch. If only we can keep to this daily routine, I am sure things will get easier.'

'I will pray specially for that.'

Abdul and Quli Murshid appeared at the door of the galla.

'Sethji, give us leave to go. We have far to travel.'

'I wish you could stay and rest, but I know how your life is. Come back soon.'

'Yes, please,' said Anamika. 'Come back whenever you want.'

The warmth in her voice was not lost on Abdul. But like her, he too was walking a straight and narrow path today.

14. Gulabchand

Gulabchand was getting ready for his morning visit to the palace. His day started with visiting the raja alone for a while, where he could get him acquainted with the latest news and hear what was on the raja's mind. After that, there was an open darbar where other officers and petitioners came in. Gulabchand had worked for the kings of Purana Zilla all his life, as his father had done before him. Had his only child been a son, the succession to the Diwan's post would have been assured.

He had on his flowing kurta and his immaculate white dhoti, along with his leather shoes. He was waiting for Meera to come through with his long coat and turban.

'Here you are. Hope today is an easy day. What did the messengers say?'

'There was a pigeon that brought strange news of Ranipur.'

'What strange news? Is our daughter...'

'She is alright, as far as we know. But the news is that Ramdasbhai and Revatiben have departed for Kashi.'

'That is surprising. Who will look after the business? How will Savitri cope all alone in that big house?'

'There's more to the news, and none of it makes sense. Abdul and his men came to the village but left without looting or killing anyone. The villagers gave them food and water.'

'I do hope our Savitri is alright.'

'She is no longer ours, and she is not Savitri, remember?'

'Whatever the conventions, she is still my daughter and she will be Savitri for me as long as I live.'

Gulabchand kissed Meera as he always did, even after 25 years of marriage. He believed in showing affection to his wife when they were at home and she reciprocated. And now, even the two innocent eyes of their only child were not there to see what they got up to.

Raja Devi Singh was waiting for him as he got off his palki and entered the small private room. Of course, it was only a small room compared to the large public darbar room. Walking across its twenty feet, he found the raja seated on his jhoola as usual. It was an exquisite piece of furniture, hand-painted in gold and fitted with small mirrors. The arms that held the swing up were silver and the seats were of red silk. The raja loved his jhoola, which his father had got made for him.

He was a handsome young man, just twenty-five, and had only been on the throne for the last four years. He had a lot to learn, but he was also a shrewd and brave man. He liked his Diwan, who was like another father to him.

'What news, Diwanji?'

'Some good news. Hassan's army tents on the other bank of the Sreni were attacked last night by Abdul and his men. It seems Hassan's army was totally unprepared and lost a lot of men and much baggage.'

'How about Hassan himself? Did Abdul kill him as he has vowed?'

'We do not know as yet. The news is incomplete, as this is just the first pigeon our spies have sent us. Perhaps, by the evening, we may learn more.'

'So what do we make of the news?'

'At the very least, Hassan will be delayed in his plans to attack us. We have to find out if Abdul took his guns away or not. If he did, then we have more room to manoeuvre. Even if they haven't lost their guns, we still have a demoralized army facing us.'

'Are we in contact with Abdul?'

'Yes, Sir. I have maintained contact with his right hand man, Quli Murshid, for a long time now. He used to work for your father as a young soldier. But then he wanted to seek a fortune on his own. He did not succeed, but Abdul picked him up and he has served Abdul very well.'

'You should find out from him if Abdul can join forces with us against Hassan.'

'With your command, consider it done. I will send out my messenger now. If you give me permission, I will join you at the durbar later.'

'Permission given. But do not be late.'

'No, My Rajasaheb.'

Gulabchand retreated from the presence of his young master. He found Devi Singh very easy to deal with. The young raja insisted on asserting his authority, but only in minor matters. In big things, Gulabchand had his way.

15. Hassan

The meeting in Hassan's tent was gloomy this morning, after the debacle of the previous night. Hassan had found his way back into his tent soon after he had to flee. He had realized Abdul had fled on his horse. When he re-entered, neither Niloufer nor Nacheez were there. He was relieved. They had seen his humiliation. He was not quite sure what Nacheez had done to Abdul. At one point, she was in his arms, but then she may have struck him. He needed to find out from Niloufer what the new woman in his zenana had done. She was more than just a toy to play with.

Hassan hid his injured hand beneath a silk cloak. The pain had now subsided. The royal hakim had been effective and, as always, discrete about what he had seen.

His officers were gathered around him, dumbfounded.

'Who was responsible for this attack? Why were there no guards posted? How did they come and attack us when we have the big guns and the elephants and the horses? Wazir-e-Alam, what is the explanation?'

Qaramat Ali, the wazir, was in his seventies. He could hardly remind his king that the king himself had declared a holiday before the march the next morning. He had himself announced that the soldiers had one last night of pleasure before the battle began, and he himself had been, after all, deep in his cups. The wazir, being the shrewd man that he was, had found out the sequence of events in the king's own tent, but he was not going to say anything about it.

'Huzoor, let us thank Allah that you are unharmed. I hear that you saw off the villain Abdul.'

Hassan thought this was an excellent suggestion.

'The miserable wretch ran away just as I was about to drive my sword through him. Some women from the zenana came between us and he escaped.'

'Huzoor, we will punish those women if you tell us who they were.'

'We are now embarking on the battle. We shall deal with the women when we return, after we have killed Abdul with our own hands.'

The whole court cheered the king's declaration.

'What are your orders now, Huzoor?'

'Send the entire zenana back to Muzaffarabad. All the hangers-on have to be sent off. From today, we become an army on the march. Prepare to march this afternoon. Wazir-e-Alam should escort the zenana back safely with his troops. We shall conquer Purana Zilla within the week.'

Again, a cheer went up in the assembly. Qaramat Ali was impressed by Hassan's resolve. Last night's humiliation, though a well kept secret, had stung Hassan into action. Maybe he could become a warrior like his father, after all. Wazir hoped so for his own sake. He was not happy to be going back and taking charge of a bunch of frustrated women, leading them away from their pleasure-loving king. But that, he knew, was the least of his problems. He did not know how the young king would cope without him at his side. He would have to find a way around this command.

Zail Singh was happy he had not been held responsible for their losses. He piped up, 'We have all the big guns and all the elephants still with us. We can regroup quickly and march this afternoon, as you command. The boat bridges that you ordered last night will be ready by then, Huzoor.'

'Let us then meet for the march.' Hassan clapped his hands and dismissed the gathering. Qaramat lingered. As he expected, Hassan gestured at him to stay back. Qaramat knew from what he had learned about the previous night that Hassan would need some advice.

Hassan liked the old wazir. He had sat on his lap and heard many good stories when he was a boy. Qaramat had also been a good guide for the growing Hassan. Hassan had not expected to succeed so soon—he had still been studying and training himself. He had expected to have ten more years at least before responsibility called. Now, he suddenly had to grow up, and quickly.

'Wazir-e-Alam, you must know what happened. I was caught unguarded. Were it not for that young woman, Abdul would be king now.'

Qaramat was impressed that in private, Hassan was ready to face the truth. Qaramat had found out what had happened. He had spoken to the musicians, whom everyone else had forgotten.

'Huzoor, the young woman saved your life. She stabbed Abdul with his own knife. Not many people could do that. Even soldiers would be too slow. As a woman, she is brave.'

'So what do we do with her?'

'Huzoor, my advice to you is that you keep her at your side. She can be your guard, night and day.'

'But you know, Wazir-e-Alam, that I have taken a vow to never have a woman near me while I am fighting. No pleasure till the end of the battle. Now I must eliminate Abdul, or he will kill me. This is why I am sending the zenana back.'

'Huzoor, this young woman will not be for your pleasure. She will be your guard.'

'Even one woman in the camp will distract the soldiers.'

'Huzoor, she will be dressed as a man. No one need know. But she has to be at your side to protect you.'

'You are always one step ahead of all of us. Let it be done. How will you keep it a secret?'

'Huzoor, leave that to me. You begin marching now.'

'Well said. I will start now.'

Qaramat bowed thrice and took his leave.

Niloufer came in. She had heard what was said, but she kept her counsel.

'Huzoor, I am here to beg forgiveness for what happened last night. You know how a mother's heart is. Please forgive me. Allah be thanked that you are safe and sound.'

'You have to go back with all of them. We shall deal with you when we return victorious. In the meantime, pray to Allah for mercy.'

'Huzoor, please remember that I have always been faithful to the family. You have been my life.'

'We are well aware. Now just go,' Hassan commanded. Turning to an attendant, he said, 'Get my armour and tell them to get my horse ready.'

'As Huzoor orders.'

16. Quli Murshid

They had finally worked out a compromise. The army struck camp just a mile outside Ranipur. Even as the first batch put up a tent in the village square, the men found the vaid visiting Abhi. Abhi asked Jibril to take the vaid to the soldiers in the square. Soon the vaid was busy dressing minor wounds, applying balms and advising the tough, rough soldiers on how to take care of themselves.

They came back to find the other soldiers catching up with Quli and awaiting orders as to where to strike their tents. Quli told them to go first to the Ranipur square, water their horses and see if the vaid could help. He had sent some gold coins to the vaid, so he was ready to help anyone who needed it. The village blacksmith was out helping with horseshoes and repairing guns that had been damaged. Villagers had offered to help them strike tents and food was being arranged for them. Women were ready to mend their clothes, which had been torn during the battle. The soldiers were not used to such kindness.

Abdul needed rest, but not too far from Ranipur, as he would need his wound washed again. The large open land near Ranipur was adjacent to a small pond. The men kept busy building up the tents, cleaning their guns and washing in the pond. They had a single change of clothes each, and the other sets needed mending and washing, which their new 'sisters' were happy to do.

Abdul was feeling better. He began to plan the next stage of his campaign.

'I hope we hauled back enough ammunition from last night. If we need more, we have to send someone across to Purana Zilla, where there are dealers. Also send a message to the other groups of my soldiers and tell them to defect from Hassan and join us. Tell them we can pay better than he can.'

'Let them stay with him and turn to our side only when we are attacking them next. That way, they will have more information for us. They still have the big guns. Our next effort must be to capture them.'

'Do you think Hassan would have headed back to Muzaffarabad?'

'No. I think he will take a day or two to recover, and then march to Purana Zilla. We have insulted him in the eyes of his soldiers. He has to regain their loyalty. This is his first campaign and he can't withdraw now. That would be to admit that you have won.'

'So we can make another raid on his marching army as soon as he begins marching. Or should we wait till he has been exhausted by the raja?'

'The raja has a strong army, as you will remember. Your father could not defeat him, and that campaign took a whole year before the truce was signed. Hassan does not have the patience your father had, nor does he have the fighting experience that you do. I would say that you rest here for a week, at least. Our soldiers can also repair their guns, replace their horses and get some rest. Once we start our attack, we will be in the field for a long time. This will be your final battle with Hassan.'

Abdul knew that Quli had a fine strategic mind. Indeed, if he ever became king, he wanted to make Quli his wazir and the chief of the army. Quli had joined him just four years ago, but he had become indispensable. Abdul knew that it is clever people like Quli who someday lose patience with their masters and take over. He had to prove to Quli constantly that he was capable of decisive action. He had to do something soon that would wipe out the disgrace of the previous night.

'How long I rest would depend on what information our spies bring us about Hassan's movements. If the chance comes for a quick strike, I am ready to lead us.'

'Of course. Let us wait for some news about Hassan.'

17. Afghani Begum

Timur Langda was waiting for the call from the begum. Ever since her husband had died, Fatima Begum had been very lonely. She was used to power and constant attention. She was, after all, a daughter of a Saiyad family that was used to lording it over their clan. Ahmad had been good to her. He was overwhelmed by her beauty and her refined manners. He was secretly proud that she had agreed to be his queen. He had given her the title of Mallika-e-Alam and called her Sayyida Begum. While he was around, she had her court, which carried out all her commands. The women in the zenana were in awe of her, and she had the last word on who stayed and who went.

Timur Langda was the man in charge of the zenana. Or rather, the half-man—an eunuch. Early in his childhood, he had impressed people with his fine voice. He could sing the dirges of the Sufi mystics and move people to ecstasy. He was then taught to dance and trained in some classical Hindustani and Persian music as well. He was the favourite of the court. But as he grew older, his benefactors decided that Timur could not be allowed to just grow up normally. The risk was too great, if his voice was to break and turn out harsh. So it was that the due damage was inflicted on him. Timur kept his fine childlike voice, and went on regaling audiences with his singing and dancing.

But even that had its limits. His singing was no longer the best, and the sight of a thirty-year-old prancing like a ten-year-old was off-putting for some. But his impairment proved to be his redemption. He could go in and out of the zenana. His uncle Nadeem, who had also been a fine singer in his childhood, had traversed the same path as Timur. Nadeem had been rewarded by being made the Keeper of the zenana. He guarded the access to the women, and no man but the king was allowed in, unless Nadeem could be sure that the visitor was another like him. Timur knew that when the time came, he would succeed his uncle and get the coveted post.

Being a Keeper was not an ordinary job. Nadeem had his own staff of fierce soldiers, who could not enter the zenana but could be asked to stop anyone trying to get in. If anyone resisted, swift death would be their reward. He also had to go and attend to the needs of the women in the zenana. See to it that they had all the tailors and perfumiers and masseurs to serve them as and when they wanted. Timur was their guard and the supervisor, making sure that nothing untoward happened.

Slowly, he realized that he had other uses. The women in the zenana were all beautiful, or at least seductive. But there was only one king, and even he, try hard though he may, could not cater to them all. The languishing ones, if long neglected, would get frustrated and restless. No man could console them, as none would be allowed in. So it was that Timur became the sole source of solace for many of them. Of course, he had to keep his meetings with each of them secret from the rest. It was an intensely bitchy world, where women were perennial rivals and each wanted to bring down the others and get nearer to the king if she could. Gossip and innuendo would be rife, to malign someone who was getting ahead. Ailments and diseases would be alleged against some just to get them eliminated.

Women knew that while the king was with them at night, he often ended up in the begum's quarters at other times, where he found peace in her embrace. So they never saw themselves as her rival. They worshipped her instead, and saw her as an ideal that they aspired to. What the begum said was the law for the women. If they could get her ear about the latest gossip or scandal, she would reward them with a piece of jewelry or some special food. Timur was, of course, the go-between in these intrigues. He was in and out of the quarters all the time. He knew his advantages. He was safe as far as they were concerned. Thus it was that while confiding their troubles to him, he often ended up offering such physical solace as he could. There are, after all, many organs of the body that please and demand pleasure. For a lonely, languishing woman, what Timur could do with his hands and his lips and his mouth was welcome. He was an expert in these arts and, of course, discrete. Timur was a favourite of many, and his was a charmed life.

But dangerous too. If a woman felt wronged or exposed, she would turn on him, and if the king believed the woman, that would be the end of the road for this instrument of her pleasure. Timur knew that he had to be good but not boastful, effective but humble, and never

ever let anyone know what he was up to with the others. The most dangerous person to be with was the begum, of course. The young king was not yet married, and the only queen was his mother. She was, naturally, also the person who would decide who he should marry. Begum Afghani had already sent messages back to Kandahar to seek a suitable highborn and beautiful woman for her son.

Najma came and, as expected, informed Timur that Begum sahiba was demanding his attendance in her presence. Timur told her to report that he was on his way. He checked his dress and dabbed some attar on his wrists and neck. When he entered, the begum was reclining on a sumptuous divan with silk cushions and damask curtains. These were thick, rich curtains. Two women were fanning her, and Begum sahiba was playing with the ornate end of a hookah behind a thin silk screen. She was a beautiful woman in her early forties. She was wearing a richly embroidered caftan with pearl buttons and frilly lace sleeves, which showed off her fine form well. The high brows, the clear fair skin, the exquisite face with the perfect nose and grey-green eyes, the rosy cheeks—all were as they had been ten or even twenty years ago.

Timur stood outside and made a deep salaam, bowing low. She dismissed her attendants with a gesture and asked him to step behind the screen. This was a rare privilege that Timur had begun to enjoy only lately.

'How is the Begum sahiba? Are things as she wishes? Can your humble slave do anything to make you happier?'

'Come and sit beside me. I have an oppressive pain in my temples and my back is hurting.'

Timur knew that this was the signal for him to get close to her. Very hesitantly, he sat next to her and began gently massaging her arms. She lifted up his hand and put it behind her neck.

'This is where the pain is the worst.'

Timur sidled a bit closer and moved his hands so he could gently massage his queen's neck and back. She sighed with relief, and took a puff on her hookah. She sensed that he had dabbed his wrists with her favourite attar. Timur may be a half-man, but he had his uses. She let him move his hands down her back slowly. She sighed and lay down sideways so that he would have easier access. Sitting behind her, massaging her back, Timur judged the moment when he could move in and caress her from behind. Begum Fatima sighed, 'What news have you of my son's campaign? I hear that there was a raid by Abdul and some fight. Did Hassan get hurt?'

Messengers had galloped in advance of the returning zenana and the rest of the non-combatants. Timur had picked up the message from the wazir. The zenana was on its way back, and there was much bitching by Salma and Laila about what had happened. He had heard something about Niloufer but that was from the messengers sent by these women, whom he knew were now out of favour. So he had to be careful, but he also knew that the begum would have her own spies.

'Begum sahiba, what I hear is confusing. Some say that Abdul and the Huzoor had a fight and Abdul got injured. Others say that while Huzoor was about to strike Abdul down, some women from the zenana stopped him and Abdul ran away. But then some say that Huzoor was hurt in the fight.'

'Who would those women be? Have you found out?'

'Again, there are rumours. Some say that it was Salma or Laila. Others say it was Niloufer. There are some new ones in Huzoor's zenana whom I do not know yet.'

'You mean you have not been keeping them warm at night.'

'How can Begum sahiba say that? I am your faithful slave and only do your bidding.'

'Then do what you have to or my pain will get worse.'

Timur moved closer and began to caress her. She sighed and opened up her dress. Timur knew his limits. He did not do anything immediately. She took his hand and brought it inside her dress.

'Comfort me and tell me the truth. Was it Niloufer who let her son escape my Hassan's fiery sword?'

Timur was engaged in a delicate operation. He leaned forward and put his mouth first to the throat, just above the necklace she was wearing, and then worked his way down to where her breasts were. She drew him forward, and he did what she liked him for. He was gentle at first, and then as she told him to kiss harder, he did as he was meant to. It was a few moments of pleasure for Fatima, but she also knew she had to keep him in check.

'You are avoiding my question. Are you also Niloufer's solace?'

'How can Begum sahiba say such a thing? I am your slave and yours alone. I hear that Huzoor said in his court that he had Abdul in his sight, but two women stopped him. Niloufer is always there when the zenana is travelling with Huzoor. But I hear that Huzoor announced to his court that he will not punish anyone. He was gracious and pardoned them.'

Fatima took another puff from her hookah. The opium was now beginning to get to her. She drew him closer and let him open up more of her dress. He got busy and she led him on. They had their silent routines. Even if the servants were eavesdropping nearby, they would never hear a word that would make them wonder what their queen was up to.

'Let Wazir-e-Alam know that I want the names of the two women. I want them arrested before they do any more harm to my son. That Niloufer is bent on making her son the king and I will not let her. My son need not know. Let this be done without his knowledge.'

Timur realized that this was an order, and now the conversation would not proceed beyond this point. He had to get on with easing the pain of the begum. He looked up and said, 'Begum sahiba, it will be done as you wish. What else can I do?'

Fatima slid down and lay flat on her back, giving Timur full scope to perform the many delicate arts he could practice to please his mistress. At the end, he would be richer by some more jewelry, and later maybe even a grant of a village or two if she liked what he did for her.

18. The Message

*A*bdul came every day with Quli to get his wound cleaned and dressed. This became a routine. They would arrive after Anamika had given Abhi his breakfast and bath, and he was already at his galla. Abdul would come and be taken straight to their bed, and then Anamika would deftly do the dressing. She always wanted Quli to be there, so he could undress Abdul and help him sit up. She wanted to make quite sure that Quli saw what was happening—or, rather, not happening—between them. Abdul understood what was going on, and he was also careful not to betray what he felt when the warm body of his woman was so near him.

By the fourth day, Abdul was on the mend. His wound had healed and needed very light dressing. He felt fit again and was ready for action. But he knew he need not move till some news of Hassan arrived. He had heard that Hassan had resumed his march, but not yet reached his destination. Quli and he had agreed that they would let their soldiers recuperate and strike when the moment was more propitious.

Dressing finished, they were with Abhi in his galla. He always brought them up to date with their accounts. They had made more in the raid than they had taken from him, but even so, they would need much more for the next stage. These things needed discussing with Abhi, who had now become their trusted adviser. Quli was the money man.

'Sethji, we expect this campaign to be longer, say six months at least. We will have to buy more guns and ammunition. Soldiers have to be paid and fed. We hope around five thousand will be with us before long. How much would we need for that?'

'If you are buying guns and ammunition in another town, I can give you a note for the merchants we do business with there, so you don't need to carry any money. Will you be going to Vishalnagar?'

'That is closest, but the king there will also need all the ammunition he can get hold of. We hear that Hassan has begun his march on Purana Zilla.'

'It is a big town and it can get supplies from the North. You can buy what you want there. We have a merchant there to pay on your behalf.'

Shivnarayan came in.

'Sethji, there is a messenger who wants to speak to you.'

'Bring him in.'

Vasudev came in. He had been sent by Gulabchand. By now, Gulabchand knew of Abdul's routine in Ranipur. So he thought it best to rely on his daughter and son-in-law to receive the messenger. Abhi saw the need for confidentiality. He asked Shivnarayan to come back later in the morning.

'What is the message? Who has sent you?'

Anamika had heard someone's horse riding into the village square. Curious, she came in where the men were sitting. Seeing Vasudev, she asked, 'Vasudevji, what brings you here?'

'Behenji, Diwanji sent me with a message for your guests.'

Abdul was surprised.

'How do you know who this man is? How does he know we are your guests?'

'Khan sahib, my father is the diwan of Purana Zilla and Vasudevji works for him. He has known me since I was a small child. We did not tell anyone about you but knowing my father, I am sure he knows your every movement as he knows Hassan's plans.'

Abhi decided that he should explain. 'Khan sahib, as you know, for Hindu families, once a daughter is married she cannot visit her parents' home. Nor can she send any messages without her husband's permission. I can assure you that she has not sent any message to her father about you. We would never betray your trust.'

Abdul was not surprised. He knew how Wazir Qaramat Ali got his news from the four corners. He was sure that Gulabchand did the same. What he did not know until now was that Anamika was his daughter. Her boldness and cunning made sense now. He spoke up, 'Tell us what the message is.'

Vasudev opened the small sack he was carrying. He took out a betel nut, a sharp knife and a nutcracker.

'Diwanji said to give you these as his message.'

Abdul was perplexed. Quli was angry.

'Is this the message? Is there no written note?'

'No Huzoor. This is all I was told to bring.'

Abhi looked at Anamika.

'Mika, can you explain what this is about? You know how your father's mind works.'

'Abdul Khan sahib, Murshid Khan sahib, my father is bringing a question to you. If you want to crack the nut, do you use a sharp knife or a nutcracker?'

'A nutcracker of course. So what?'

'The king in Vishalnagar is asking if you would join with him in defeating Hassan. The knife has a sharp blade but it is useless to crack open a betel nut. But the nutcracker has two arms, one with a sharp edge and the other, a solid support, which combine to crack open the nut.'

Abdul was flabbergasted at how quickly she had deciphered the meaning of the message. He also understood why the messenger had been sent to Abhi and Anamika's house. How Gulabchand would have managed to convey the same message without Anamika was something he did not have the time to figure out. Accompanied by Quli, he went back inside.

When they were gone, Vasudev said to Abhi, 'Sethji, there is a note for you.'

He handed Abhi a note. It was obviously written in some kind of cipher. Abhi asked Anamika to bring him a ledger from a distant cupboard. This was clearly not Shivnarayan's work. When Anamika handed him the ledger, Abhi opened a certain page and wrote a note on it. He opened his desk, put away the note Vasudev had brought and took out a piece of paper. He wrote something on it as well.

'Vasudevji, give this to Diwanji. Tell him this will be enough for his purposes.'

Anamika was impressed at the deftness with which Abhi had conducted this piece of business. She well understood that the request was for a banker's order for the king, to be given to bankers in Vishalnagar, for a large sum of money. Devi Singh wanted to make quite sure that he would have the funds to fight Hassan. He was asking for a loan from the house of Rathore Bankers, now run by Abhi to cover his expenses. Abhi only had to give an order to the local bank in Vishalnagar to ensure that. He had already offered this facility to Quli, little realizing that within minutes there would be a request from Vishalnagar. He only had to check their accounts in the old ledger and make out the order, in the short time that he had to keep the transaction a secret from Abdul Khan.

Abdul and Quli came back outside, having made their decision and said, 'Yes, we are willing to join forces. Now can you take the message to Diwanji?'

Abhi was quick to see that Vasudev would not take a verbal message. He looked at Anamika and said, 'Can you help Khan sahib?'

Anamika went inside and came back with an ornate metal box with delicate filigree carvings on top. It was a set for making paan. She pulled out a betel leaf and expertly started putting chuna on it. Abdul and Quli were astonished and Abhi much amused. She put the kattha paste on it. Then she picked up the betel nut, and using the nut cracker, cut some fine shreds off. She put the bits on the paan and then folded it up. She stuck a clove through it to hold it together.

'This is Khan saheb's answer. Vasudevji, take it back.'

Vasudev put the paan carefully in his sack, alongside the piece of paper that the Khans had not seen. Abdul and Quli did not have to ask about the meaning of this answer. The nutcracker had been used to break the nut. The resultant paan was a harmonious, sweet and pungent answer to the original message. Abdul Khan was ready—pungent for the battle and sweet for the friendship. Vasudev's work was done.

'Behenji, give me permission to go.'

It was Abhi who spoke first. 'Tell Diwanji that we are well. Tell Meeraben and Gulabbhai that, as you can see, I am getting better every day and their daughter is happy. Tell them not to worry.'

'Vasudevji, let me give you some milk. You must be tired coming all the way,' said Anamika.

Vasudev hesitated. Again Abhi spoke up. 'Do not worry about old conventions. You can take something at the daughter's married home. I insist.'

Anamika was pleased that Abhi had said that. She took Vasudev inside and gave him a cup of milk. When they came out, Abdul and Quli were again in deep conversation with Abhi. Vasudev left quietly.

'This offer gives us new ideas about what we have to do. Now the campaign can be short and swift if we combine with Raja sahib. We may not need to worry about getting ammunition, as they have the big guns. This may save us some money.'

'Khan sahib, I am not a soldier, but I would say do not make any decision yet. If the Raja sahib has offered you cooperation, he knows he needs you as much as you need him. So he may feel Hassan is a powerful force. Who knows how long the campaign would be, even with the two forces combined? Keep to your original plans, as you never know what might be needed. Better to have more than less. Now, of course, if you want to buy ammunition in Vishalnagar your task will be easier. Do not worry about the money. You still have plenty.'

Abdul was once again listening very carefully to what Abhi was saying. Unlike Quli, he was not worried about money. He was busy thinking about how he would plan his joint campaign with kind Devi Singh. He had the swift troops, while the king had the larger forces and the big guns. This was the combination of the sharp upper edge of the nutcracker and the lower solid support. He now understood the message better. He was expected to be the cutting edge. While he would strike Hassan from the back and make him retreat towards Vishalnagar, the king would attack from an advantageous position.

Anamika could tell what Abdul was thinking about. She knew she could not talk to him in secret any time soon. His recovery would take some time yet, and he had to feel that he had wiped out the disgrace of his failure with Hassan before he could come to her as her lover. She felt she could now take part in the discussion openly.

'Khan sahib, do not worry. As soon as they get your answer, they will get another message across to you, and I am sure it will be sent directly to you and not through our house. They know now you are their ally. Now they will trust you.'

'But I am learning so much about the subtle art of sending messages this way. I wish I could receive more such messages, and Sethji and you could teach us how to read these mysterious codes. I now realize that I was dealing with a Diwan's daughter that day when we came to your village.'

Anamika did not want this conversation to go any further. 'That seems so long ago.'

Abhi picked up on her embarrassment. 'For me it has been a lifetime since that day, and what a different life it has been for me— thanks to you, Abdul Khan sahib.'

Quli Murshid was getting impatient. He wanted to speak to Abdul alone, at length. So he quickly intervened, 'Sethji, give us your permission to leave. We have so much more to do now.'

Abhi understood. 'We will see you again tomorrow.'

Abdul knew that Quli would be reluctant to come again, now that it was known beyond the village that they came to this house regularly. 'No. I am now fully recovered, thanks to the kind and careful treatment I have received from the gracious lady of the house. We will no doubt come and consult you many more times, but not trouble you every morning as we have done.'

'Please, Khan sahib, Murshid sahib. Consider this as one home you are always welcome in. Do come again whenever you wish.' Anamika was careful to include Quli in her invitation.

19. Qaramat Ali

The march back was slow and halting. Qaramat Ali knew that the women of the zenana were reluctant to go back to what would be an idle, long wait for Hassan's return. Or maybe, as they hoped, he would get impatient if the campaign dragged on for too long and call some of them back.

Taking the women back—some in their palkis, some on camel back and others on horses—was a familiar task for Qaramat Ali. The women were angry and frustrated. Rumours were flying as to what had really happened that fateful night. Salma had been spreading poison about Niloufer and Nadya. Laila, meanwhile, was vituperative about Salma, as she did not know that Salma had also been thrown out by Hassan. The women who had been waiting upon Hassan at his dinner were innocent of what had happened. All they knew was that for some reason, their stay in the camp had been cut short and they would not be required for a while. Boredom and frustration faced them.

Qaramat Ali had to pretend to be returning with them. His grandson, his daughter's firstborn, was with him. Qaramat was training the young man to take over command someday. He could well deliver the zenana by himself. Qaramat was itching to get back to the camp. He also was not looking forward to the hothouse atmosphere he would find back in Muzaffarabad. With the king away and nothing else to do, there would be idle time for devil's work. A palace full of women was not his idea of an active life, since the women were not his.

He had already been receiving some strange messages from the palace. Timur Langda had sent a pigeon which told him the Mallika was angry with Niloufer and wanted her arrested along with the other woman who was involved in the attack on the king that night. Thankfully, they did not know her name. Qaramat did not like the sound of this. He knew the facts and even the way Hassan had admitted how much he appreciated his saviour. But all that was a secret. The queen had been misled, and the king would be unhappy if she did something rash. Qaramat had a problem in his hands, but he had already thought of a solution.

★ ★ ★

Niloufer knew she was in trouble. Whatever may have happened that night, what mattered was what the wazir had announced and Hassan had begun to believe as true. She had not been able to prove to Hassan how seductive Nadya could be. He had gone off to war filled with the anger he needed to fight. Nadya was new and a stranger. She also needed defending. Niloufer knew that soon after they began marching back, Salma had gone to see the wazir. Niloufer did not need to know what Salma had said, but it was sure to be against her. But had she also maligned Nadya? Niloufer did not care for herself so much as she did for Nadya.

When the moving caravan halted for the night, Niloufer waited patiently. When she was sure that most people had gone off to sleep, she put on her burqa and walked stealthily to the wazir's tent. As she thought most likely, the old man was praying. There was a Quran in front of him. Niloufer did the minimum she had to for the namaaz. And then she entered the tent.

She came in and salaamed. 'Wazir-e-Alam, can a humble slave request a meeting with you?'

Qaramat Ali was not surprised to hear the familiar voice. Even the burqa Niloufer was wearing was distinctive. 'Please come in, Niloufer begama. Please sit.'

Niloufer was pleased that he had recognized her. She removed her burqa and sat down.

'What brings you here at this late hour?'

'Huzoor, you know everything. I have a young woman in my care. She has pleased our Lord with her fine manners and attractive ways. But now lies and rumours are being spread that she harmed our Lord. I can swear on the holy book that she saved him. She made it possible for him to escape Abdul's sword.'

'So did you, as well. We know that you intervened and stopped Abdul from striking our Lord.'

Niloufer knew Qaramat Ali had his ways of getting information. But even she was surprised how accurately he had described it.

'But who will believe me? I heard what was said in the Huzoor's presence about us two women. This is what they are now saying. We harmed our Lord.'

'I hear that Mallika-e-Alam is not pleased. I hear that she is angry as she has only heard the lies.'

'What is you advice, Huzoor?'

'Can you ride a horse?'

'Thankfully, yes, Huzoor.'

'Can you bear to leave your little pigeon in my care?'

Niloufer was astonished to hear the same words she had said to Hassan about Nadya.

'I can, Huzoor.'

'Can she ride a horse?'

'Yes, Huzoor. My pigeon has been a falcon in a previous life'.

'I advise you to take a horse and go away as soon as you can ride out.'

'Where shall I go?'

'That is a difficult question. You cannot go back to Muzaffarbad, since the Mallika-e-Alam is displeased with you. I do not want you to go back to Huzoor's camp, as there are not any zenana women to look after. I would advise you to seek shelter with your son.'

'I cannot betray the king, Huzoor. I have served the family faithfully all these years and I cannot bear it if people say I have been false to my Lord.'

'You were good to our late king. We owe you a lot for keeping quiet about his last hours. Mallika –e-Alam has forgotten your services to her family. But do not worry. I know the king thinks highly of you. I will tell him myself I advised you to run away. I will also tell him you will never help Abdul to attack him.'

'Huzoor, I will say many prayers for your good health. But what about my little pigeon?'

'Do not worry. I will take her personally back to Huzoor. I think he needs someone of her ability to protect him. She has saved him and may yet do so again. I want to get back to Huzoor myself, and I will guard your sweet girl. I will tell Mallika-e-Alam that you escaped my arrest. She will be angry with me, but I know how to handle that.'

'Your honour, many many shukriyas for your kindness. I will remember it for ever and ever.'

'One more thing.'

'Yes, Huzoor?'

'Get some men's clothes as you ride away. For both you and your pigeon. Tell her to come to my tent as soon as possible. It is best for me to ride in the night back to Huzoor's camp.'

'Yes, Huzoor.'

'Tell your pigeon to keep that dagger with her. It is the proof of her innocence. It will be useful someday.'

'Yes, Huzoor.'

'Come with us till we reach the river. We will then go in the direction of Purana Zilla across the river. You turn towards the west. Your son is camped near the Ranipur village. It will take you a night and a day at least. I trust you have some coins to buy food along the way? Or shall I give you some?'

Qaramat Ali took a small purse and handed it to Niloufer. Overwhelmed with gratitude, she salaamed again thrice, put on her burqa and withdrew into the night.

20. Hassan

The Sreni river ran eastwards from its mountainous origins. It did not flow straight, but bent around itself, quite sharply at first and a little less so again towards its final confluence with the Yamuna, just before the big holy meeting of Ganga and Yamuna at Prayag. The early course of the river ran through Purana Zilla. It then wound around itself, dividing Ramgarh into two regions. Anyone going from Ramgarh to Purana Zilla had to cross the Sreni twice if he was to attack Vishalnagar. Once you had crossed the Sreni from the north-eastern side, where Muzaffarbad was, the country was wooded but flat. There were villages on the Ramgrah side, but they were few and far between. Ranipur was to the west of where Hassan had crossed the Sreni. He had to head straight towards the bank, where he had to cross the river again. The river at that end was quite tricky to cross. At places it ran through deep ravines. It was notorious for battering horses that tried to cross it, and people found it troublesome.

After three days of marching, Hassan had reached the border of Ramgarh and Purana Zilla. It may have been a smaller party than before, but the elephants and camels always slowed things down. The horses had reached earlier, but Hassan had come on an elephant, which suited his dignity. He also wanted time to think through how he would fight his first battle. He camped on the Ramgarh side, twenty miles from the border. He had to plan his campaign carefully.

These two kingdoms had a long history of antagonism. Akbar had pursued a policy of befriending the powerful Hindu kings, especially the Rajputs. He had married a Rajput princess, Jodha, who bore him his son and heir, Salim, who later succeeded him as Jahangir. Jodha's brother, Man Singh, became an important general in Akbar's army. During Akbar's times, the raja of Purana Zilla had been a member of Raja Man Singh's party. This party remained friendly with Akbar's successors in Delhi. Rajput princesses from the party went on to marry some Mughal princes. But many other Rajput families refused to marry their daughters or sons to Muslim princes and princesses, even if they came from the powerful Mughal families. The Rajputs became a divided people. The antagonism had now lasted a long time. Ramgarh had been a Rajput kingdom, but being hostile to Akbar, the raja had lost his kingdom. Akbar had sent his subah to rule Ramgarh as part of the Mughal empire. Purana Zilla was independent but paid a small tribute to the Emperor by way of annual gifts of horses and gold.

When Aurangzeb came to power, the old Mughal-Rajput bond was broken. Purana Zilla became fully independent, as well as hostile. Ramgarh still being part of the empire, its subah was deputed to bring the raja under Mughal control. But despite a fifty-year struggle, Purana Zilla remained undefeated. Ahmad had tried a big campaign, but after a year he had given up as well. A treaty had been signed. Now, of course, both the kingdoms were independent of Delhi and there was no reason to quarrel. Yet each new ruler of Ramgarh coveted the fertile lands of Purana Zilla and wanted to acquire territory on that side of the border.

Hassan's camp was smaller than what it had been before, minus all the women and the hangers-on. It was now a thorough military camp and there was a sense of anticipation about the coming battle. There were men selling horses to soldiers who had lost their own in the surprise raid. Itinerant blacksmiths and sellers of food had all come from nearby locales, since an army always spent money. This was normal for any army that marched at the pace of its slowest movers, which were always camels, guns and elephants. But even so, this was a fighting army and there was less jollity than before.

The battle ahead had to be planned and Hassan was holding his conclave. It was a smaller meeting than what he had had back on the other side of Sreni. The purple tent was still there, but the furnishings were sparser than before. There were ten people with him.

'Zail Singh, what preparations have you made for our attack?'

'Huzoor, we are four days' march away from the Sreni's other bank. We have to ford the river with our horses and our guns. I have already sent the elephants and guns ahead, as they take longer to get there. Crossing the river with them is tricky, but we know places that are easier than others. My men are leading the elephants and the camels with the guns. We have to get the horses and the foot soldiers ready to march tomorrow. Huzoor will have to choose whether to ride an elephant or a horse into the campaign.'

'I will be on an elephant so that every one of our men can see me. I will carry the standard. Have my horse ready, marching along, so I can shift on to that if the battle gets rough.'

Zail Singh already knew this, as this is what kings always did. But he supposed that Hassan needed to spell it out in order to convince himself that he was planning the battle.

'As Huzoor wishes.'

'What news do we have of Devi Singh's army?'

'They have not moved out of Vishalnagar yet. I expect that they want to entice us to move farther into their territory, wait and see how well we can cross the river and then strike us when we have just arrived. They have their big guns ready to fire at us as soon as they get us on the other side. This is what they did in the previous campaign against your father.'

'So why are we repeating our tactics? Why don't we change our plans?'

'How, Huzoor?'

'Let us make them cross the river and meet us on this side. That will save us a lot of trouble. Our guns and elephants won't have to cross the river.'

Zail Singh was surprised at this novel suggestion coming from the king. He had no idea Hassan could think strategically. But he was still skeptical about this idea. 'How do you propose to bring them across, Huzoor?'

'We start attacking every village of Purana Zilla that is on this side of the river. We loot and burn and destroy. When their people run back and complain about us, they will have to come and protect their villages. We will collect a lot of gold and stores. Our men could also enjoy their women. After all, they also need something to boost their morale. Get our horses and foot soldiers ready.'

'Huzoor, the villages on this side of the river are scattered and not very prosperous. This plan will stretch our army.'

'Send out some horses to find out where the good targets are. Let them come back and tell us, and we will send out parties of two to three hundred horses to attack. In the meantime, let the elephants and camels proceed to the river bank. The enemy should think that we are going to cross the river. They will see the elephants coming. We stay back and don't move yet. Let them wait longer for us to advance. Then when we have all the information about the villages, we attack everywhere at once. That will bring them across. We will then have them on this side and destroy their guns.'

A loud cheer went up in the tent. The veteran officers were surprised that the young king had suggested such a new way of fighting an old battle. Every single time before this, they had followed the old pattern and lost inevitably. Now there was a new hope. The new king may yet be the one who conquers Purana Zilla.

Hassan clapped his hands and the meeting ended. He was pleased with his plan. He could see that no one had expected him to come up with a strategy like this. He was now ready for a big fight. The anger was high in him. But here he was all alone. No Niloufer and no zenana to cater to his appetite. He had resolved that as this was his first campaign, he was going to discipline himself. When on the march, his food was to be simple. He would only drink if he knew he was not riding out the next morning. But despite all of this, his anger would not subside this night. He reached for his hookah, which had been primed for his enjoyment. As usual, it had tobacco and opium in a mixture that would relax him. He had a lot on his mind. He had become king only six months ago and so much had happened already. Here he was, all on his own, out to prove that he deserved to be a true successor to his father. He had never expected this to happen so soon.

Contemplation with a hookah had soothing effects on him. A dreamy mood began to descend over him. He had read many works of philosophy and treatises on war. He liked making plans of battles he was going to fight as much as he enjoyed thinking of the pleasures he had had with the many women who had come into his life. Weaving through these thoughts in his mind, he was guided to a half-awake state. The hookah needed refreshing. He clapped his hands again.

He was surprised when, instead of the attendants to refill the hookah, two other people came in and bowed. Trying very hard to wake up from his dreamy haze, he realized that one of the two was his wazir, Qaramat. Along with him was a soldier he had not seen before.

'Wazir-e-Alam, I was wondering how long it would take you to get here. Have you brought what you promised?'

Qaramat Ali took off his turban and bowed deeply, thrice. He nudged his companion to do the same. Hassan was astonished to see that blond head once again, but he was thrown off by the men's costume.

'Huzoor, your humble servant begs forgiveness for defying your orders. But I thought your comfort and happiness required me to be by your side. This young soldier is called Nadeer and he will also keep you company. He is very adept at wielding the knife. He will be your guard.'

Qaramat bowed thrice and withdrew. Nadya was uncertain as to what she had to do. She could see Hassan looking at her. But the lust of the previous occasion was gone, replaced with thoughtfulness.

'You saved our lives the other night. Where did you learn to fight?'

'May it please Huzoor. I was in a team of guards for the prince of Samarkand once. I can also give you pleasure if that is your command.'

'We will have no indulgence till the battle is over. You are our bodyguard. Be alert. Be vigilant. Stay near us, ready to fight for us.'

Nadya was puzzled. She had expected that she had been brought in to be Hassan's plaything. Now he seemed to have forgotten all that. She was to be his guard. He was spurning her charms. She would have to cope with this new challenge. She bowed thrice.

'Huzoor, your slave is ready to obey your every command.'

'What is your name?'

Nadya hesitated. She was about to say what Niloufer had taught her, but that was no longer the game. She bowed again and said, 'Nadeer, Huzoor.'

Hassan clapped his hands. Nadya realized that she would have to find a corner not too far away to sleep. She left Hassan's presence. She knew that it would be a large tent, even if not the small palace that it had been the previous night. She saw a place where soft grass had been spread. This, she decided, would have to do for the while. She undid her belt, put her dagger beside her head and lay down.

She was tired after the ride but could not sleep. She realized that her life was about to change again. She had been bought for her physical charms and her ways of pleasing men. But last night seemed to have changed all of that. Niloufer had told her that they were going to be punished because the king had said something bad about them. But Qaramat had brought her here. He had not explained why she was here. Hassan was now a different man, and she was now his bodyguard. Whatever that entailed, she was sure it would be less physically demanding than what she was usually expected to do night after night. That finally brought sound sleep.

21. Vishalnagar

Devi Singh was sitting on his jhoola. Gulabchand was with him, as was his army commander, Samsher Singh. His master of gunnery, Pierre Drouon, was also there in a splendid French general's outfit, though he had been cashiered a long time ago. Other officers were present, as was Devi Singh's younger sister, Sonal. The family had given her the best education possible in matters of the mind as well as in martial arts. She had just turned eighteen and Devi Singh thought that she should begin to take interest in the royal family's concerns.

The officers were awaiting their orders. 'Diwanji, what is our next move?' Devi Singh asked Gulabchand.

'Rajasaheb, Abdul Khan has agreed to our proposal. We need to tell him what to do. But that depends on your plan of action.'

'My plan is to try and keep Hassan on the other bank as long as he can be kept there. We should lull him into doing nothing by doing nothing ourselves. He will march with his elephants and guns to the river so they can cross where the fording is easy. When we know their guns have got to our side of the river, we ask Abdul Khan to attack him from the rear. Let us hope that he will be forced to rush towards us, and then we can then squeeze him from either side. What do you say?'

Pierre Drouon had to finalize his own timetable. 'Does the Raja's plan require any guns to cross to the other side soon?'

'If we can do it far away from where Hassan expects us to be, yes. I would imagine that he expects us to stay on this side of the river. We should cross over and confront him while he is being pushed back by Abdul Khan. It would be even better if his guns have crossed the river by then.'

Gulabchand was impressed. It was Sonal who surprised them: 'But what makes you think Hassan cannot anticipate this and think differently himself?'

'What do you mean?' asked Devi Singh.

'I don't know much about armies, but when I was taught the Nyaya and Vaisheshika schools of philosophy by Acharyaji, we learned to think logically and debate. If I cannot see your argument before you make it, how can I be ready with an answer? So, the first task of a logical debater is to ask himself: what is my opponent thinking?'

'Diwanji, what do you say?'

'Rajkumariji makes an interesting observation. If the two warriors are looking at each other through a mirror, then each is his opponent's shadow,' replied Gulabchand.

'So what follows?' Devi Singh asked Sonal.

'We make our plans, but we should be ready for our opponent to also do the unexpected,' she replied.

'What might Hassan do that is unexpected?'

'He could wait for us to come across, rather than cross the river as we expect him to.'

'How long can he hold out?'

'As long as he can feed his army.'

'Can he maintain his supplies from Muzaffarabad for very long?'

'He can forage from our side. Remember, the Marathas sustain their armies that way. Why not Hassan?'

'He could destroy our villages then.'

'Why not? All armies do that nowadays. It is not like the old days, when the Delhi Emperor maintained good order everywhere.'

'So what do we do? Do we change our plans?'

'No, we stick to our plans, but stay ready to change if we need to.'

'How?'

'We use our friends on the other side to harass and divert Hassan. He does not know about that part of our plan.'

Pierre Druoun spoke up. His military education in Paris had not been devoid of some philosophical training. His French Cartesian mind was working away as he heard Sonal's ideas. He thought he could clarify. 'Raja sahib, I look at the Rajkumari's ideas in my own French way. There are two strategies; one old and one new. But either side can have them. What we don't know is which side will use which. We could use the old strategy, and so could Hassan. Then we have the same outcome as before—a stalemate. Or we could switch to a new one while he sticks to an old one. That gives us the advantage of surprise and we could win. The reverse is when he embarks on a new strategy we are stuck with the old. We could lose. What the Rajkumari is saying is that both sides might use a new strategy. That is where things are the most unpredictable.'

'Sounds to me like playing chess,' Gulabchand said.

'If it helps you to think that, so be it. Chess is, after all, a game of strategy. We were taught chess at our école. The army said it helps us to be better soldiers.'

'So what follows from that?'

'We need to have a surprise element that is beyond even our own reckoning.'

'Have you any suggestions?'

'Remember that Abdul crossed the river at Devgarh and attacked Hassan from behind. Let us use the ford at Devgarh to transport our guns and cross over, right at the back of Hassan's army. Then Abdul Khan can deploy those guns and we can have an advantage.'

'Can you do that?

'It is easier to move the big gun on water than on land. We have big barges ready on which we have moved Padmini and the small guns before, and we can do so again. Sreni is turbulent at some places, but if we move carefully, we can get there in two days.'

'Would our enemy not see through this move?' Samsher Singh was skeptical of this foreigner and his ideas.

It was Gulabchand who found a ruse. 'Let us spread the news that Pierre Druoun has quarrelled with Raja sahib and walked out with his guns. No one knows where he is headed, but he may join the Marathas or the Nizam.'

Devi Singh was intrigued. Sonal spoke again. 'We need to fool Hassan, but make sure that Abdul Khan does not think we are weakened. We have to send him a message.'

Gulabchand had to think quickly, but Sonal was quicker. 'I have not seen Savitri didi for a year. Can I go and visit her?'

Gulabchand was cautious. 'We have to make sure you are safe and Hassan's army does not capture you.'

Pierre spoke up. 'I have to take the guns across. The guns will be on a barge, but I was going to take a boat along. Rajkumariji can come with me, suitably disguised as a gunner.'

Devi Singh was dubious. He had to make sure his younger sister was not going to get hurt. 'Sonal, are you sure you can do this?

I will spend sleepless nights till I hear that you are safe in Ranipur.'

'I promise you, bhaiya, I will be careful. You have made sure that I can wield arms if I have to. And as I will have a gallant Frenchman guarding me, I will be alright.'

Pierre made a deep bow.

22. Abhi and Anamika

As days passed, Abhi found that his legs were tingling with new life. Everyday, he began to take one or two careful steps while Jibril watched over him. Soon he only had to be carried over the threshold between the bedroom and his galla. The warm bath that Anamika and he now had together everyday was their own private joy. Anamika was thrilled, but worried whether she was pushing his recovery too fast.

One day she decided that she would take Abhi to the temple with her. This was not easy. Jibril could carry him to the temple, but being a Muslim, he could not enter the sacred place. But if Abhi could walk only a few steps, they could worship together. So they convinced the temple's pujari to allow Jibril to come within a few steps of the temple. The pujari had requested all other worshippers to clear a way for Abhi. Anamika then held Abhi close to her as he took each careful step. They were the most difficult few steps for Anamika. She was tense but thrilled as Abhi gingerly touched the ground. It was an eternity before they bent down together in front of Goddess Amba, fierce with her red tongue hanging out, riding her lion and crushing the buffalo demon under the lion's feet with her spear.

They both prayed. They offered their gifts of coconut, sweets and coins. They picked up the sindoor and smeared it on their heads and brows. The pujari forgot to object when Jibril came closer to the temple to pick Abhi up and put him on the horse that had brought them there.

That night was special. Anamika could not stop crying tears of joy at what Abhi had done. He was choked with emotion, too. Then they did what they loved doing. Anamika was bolder in wrapping her legs around him so he could feel her warm body. He hugged her close and put his mouth to her breasts—he knew she loved that. He began to bite like he had never done before—always having been stopped by the fear that she would get too excited and then he would not be able to satisfy her. But now she relished his attentions and let him be bolder with his hands. Soon she felt his legs rubbing against hers. She was thrilled. She spread her legs so he could rub her sensitive areas with his knees. She was crying and kissing and biting him. He was happy exploring the limits to which he could make love to her. It was yet another night of wild love between two young bodies.

'What did you ask the goddess for?' Abhi asked.

'I prayed to Kali for your complete recovery. And I prayed for a son.'

'Will you be Uttara?'

Anamika sat up, worried. 'Don't say that. Abhimanyu died in the war so young and Uttara had to carry his child in the womb all alone. But I want your child and I want you to be there.'

'So you will not be Kunti?'

'No.'

'Why not?'

'Her husband could not give her children. So she got them from the gods. That is not what I would ever do.'

'I know the astrologers have said you will bear a son. But they are often wrong. Will Kali prove them right?'

'You know what Sita did?'

'Got abducted by Ravan.'

Anamika laughed and sat up and gently hit Abhi. 'No. She waited all the years of early marriage and the years of exile. But when those years were finally over, she bore Ramachandraji twin sons—after he became king. She was forty-two years old then.'

'So which kingdom do I have to rule?'

'The one lying right next to you. It will wait till you come and conquer it.'

'But what about Yama? Won't he come and take Satyavan away?'

'Remember, he never did. Savitri will keep Yama away from Satyavan.'

'Can I tell you something?'

'What?'

'Let him come as often as he wishes to, and my Savitri will keep him trapped in her riddles.'

Anamika was astonished at what Abhi was saying. He had figured out her bargain with Abdul. He was saying he was not going to be a jealous husband. Anamika smothered him with kisses as she shed happy tears. They lay intertwined all night.

23. Guns and Camels

Pierre Druon knew that if he was going to shift the guns, he had to make it as obvious as possible, so that even the most stupid of Hassan's spies would not miss his moves. The transport barges had been constructed long ago. Big guns like Padmini were the heaviest weapons they had in use—heavier even than elephants. These big guns came from Europe, as iron smelting and casting in Hindustan could not match the quality that European smelters had. It was different in the old days, when Indians could smelt better iron than anyone else. Now they could make the smaller field guns and the matchlock bandooks, but the big ones were brought in from beyond Turkey by sea and unloaded at Surat. From there they were dispatched to whoever had the money to buy them. Each gun had its own master gunner, most often a Turkish or a French military officer.

Big guns made a decisive difference in wars. The Mongols had seen their use in China and they took the guns with them in their world-conquering campaign across Europe. The Mughals brought them to India. Babur used them against Ibrahim Lodhi in the Battle of Panipat. The elephants of Ibrahim Lodhi had been running rampage until Babur fired his heavy cannon. The elephants panicked and that was the end of Afghan rule and the start of the Mughal dynasty in India. Every king since then knew that if he could afford it, he should have a big gun. The problem was, of course, that big guns moved slowly. Each of them required several camels to drag it, and often the chains snapped on difficult terrain. Moving a gun across land was a difficult task, but that is where the expertise of Pierre and his fellow master gunners came in.

Pierre was moving his Padmini as well as some smaller field guns. The convoy of barges and boats, bearing guns, camels and soldiers, was launched the morning after the decision in the durbar at Vishalnagar. The complication caused by Sonal's decision to go with Pierre meant that her presence had to be a well-guarded secret. Not just because of the false trail they had laid, that Pierre had broken with Devi Singh, but also because a well-born woman could not be seen travelling so openly. Sonal made a fine looking young man with a turban and a soldier's uniform. For good measure, she had even painted on a moustache above her lips. Pierre had to pretend he did not know who this callow soldier, travelling on the same special boat as him, was. This boat was somewhat more luxuriously appointed, with comfortable seating and well-stocked with provisions.

The sailing was smooth, if slow. The boat carrying Pierre and Sonal was in the lead. It was followed by the two big barges, which together held Padmini and ten soldiers to keep watch, in case the waves made the gun slip. Then came the smaller barges with the field guns, and then the camels, that would be needed at the other end to drag the guns overland. Once the boat was on the river, Sonal could begin to shed the pretence that she was an ordinary soldier.

She was curious to learn what she could about how the guns were fired. Pierre was happy to explain. 'The force of the gun comes from how far you can project the shot. The bigger and longer the gun, the more you can pack in it. You need gunpowder, and along with that you can pack any other material such as stones, nails and bricks, which cause damage when they land with tremendous force. You pack the ammunition in and then, at the other end, you light the fuse. You have to move back before the fuse reaches the gunpowder because the gun recoils as it shoots the charge.'

'Why does it do that?'

'If you were to take a heavy stone in your hands and run up and throw it far into the distance, you will find you have been pushed a step or two back. It is what we call Newton's laws of motion. Isaac Newton, an Englishman, has discovered these laws, which now everyone trusts to make their calculations.'

'When did he do that?'

'Just about fifty years ago. He was a real bookish man, but a genius at mathematics. He worked out the mathematics of how the planets, including the Earth, move around the sun.'

'But how can that be? I was taught that the sun moves around the Earth and so does the moon. The planets move and determine our life's chances. We worship the sun and the moon and Shani and Rahu. How can they move around the sun?'

'This is the new knowledge, which is still causing problems in Europe. I am a Catholic and my church does not believe what Newton says. But when you are fighting a war, you have to use science. If you don't, your enemy will, and you will lose.'

'But you have still not told me how the Earth can move around the sun.'

'Newton calls it the principle of gravity.'

'What is that?'

'The example my teacher gave me was of dropping a stone. It always hits the ground. No matter where you are, you can be sure that even if you throw something up, it will eventually fall down to earth. The Earth has the power to pull things towards itself. You can run faster downhill than uphill, because the Earth has the power to pull you to itself.'

'So?'

'The sun is bigger than the Earth, and it pulls the Earth towards itself. But the Earth has it own pull, and so do the other planets. They keep on attracting and repelling each other.'

'I am not sure I understand this idea. I want to go on believing what my teacher told me about the power of god to make things move.'

'You are not alone, Rajkumari. Most people would agree with you, though they may believe in a different god. Even Newton said he had only unraveled God's secret scheme for the Universe. My problem is that if I am fighting a war, I have to understand the laws of motion when I fire a gun. If I don't, my soldiers may die and my king can lose the war.'

'So, is your new knowledge only useful for war?'

'Not just war. But war makes kings listen to the people who think about such things. There was a man many centuries ago—Archimedes was his name. He was able to defend his kingdom from invaders who had come on ships. He ordered that large mirrors be brought to him on the shore. He held up these mirrors and reflected the sun's rays on to the ships. They started burning in the heat of the sun.'

'How did he do that?'

'He had reasoned that the sunrays are a source of heat but as such, they are scattered. By using the glass mirrors, he was able to concentrate their heat and throw it back onto the ships. They caught fire thanks to the concentrated heat of the sun.'

'But even so, this is knowledge that helps us to fight.'

'He also made another discovery that we all benefit from. One day, as he sank into his bathtub, the water spilled out. He pondered over this and realized that the water displaced was due to how large he was. We can take large heavy guns on barges as long as the barges are large enough to displace a lot of water. That displacement is what allows the barge to carry the gun and not sink. If you put the gun on a small boat like we are in, it would sink.'

'Did people not sail before he discovered this?'

'They did, but they did not understand why sometimes you need large barges and other times, just small boats. With knowledge you can take a simple principle and use it in many different ways.'

Sonal was fascinated. Her learning had been in philosophy and the arts. She had little acquaintance with science. This was something even her teachers did not know. It was worrying that the new knowledge allowed guns to be bigger and better. That way lay conquest. She would have to tell her brother to get someone to impart the new knowledge.

Sreni was being kind to them today. There were no large waves, nor any difficult passages. The ravines lay west of Vishalnagar, and they were sailing eastwards and southwards. Pierre kept anxiously looking at the barges that were following with the guns. On the banks of the Sreni, a few people noticed the barges and boats, but none understood what it was that was sailing by.

'I have been to the observatory in our town. I have seen the planets in the sky. But why did I not see their motion?'

'People have been looking at the sky since they were first on the Earth. They made up stories about the planets and the sun and the moon. They devised astrological charts to foretell the future. Then someone developed a telescope and we could see the stars much more closely and map the sky. Still, mapping the stars is one thing and understanding how and why they move is another problem. Mankind slowly learnt how the planets move, their rise and fall, the phases of the moon and the eclipses of the sun and the moon, over many years. Before that, they made up stories about eclipses like you have, about Rahu swallowing the sun.'

'How do we know it does not?'

'We can now observe the sky much better with more powerful telescopes. We can see that the eclipses are caused when the sun and the moon cross each other's paths. That would not happen if they were independent. But in a system of planets, they all move in relation to each other, like in a dance formation. Newton figured this out and then wrote down the mathematics of motion of the planets.'

'I must study that mathematics.'

'Whatever I can teach you, I will be glad to. But right now we have to win this war.'

'With the help of science.'

'Right. With the help of science.'

Sonal was impressed. There was a lot she had to learn about the world and about knowledge. Pierre was very good at explaining, and she liked that he treated her like anyone else. He did not talk down to her or treat her like a little girl. She must find out more about how he came to be in Vishalnagar, she decided. But there would be time enough for that

24. Niloufer

She may have ridden horses before, but that was a long time ago. Niloufer had ridden along with Qaramat and Nadya to the river, but once across, she had to go her own way. As they went straight on to the other bank of the Sreni, where Hassan was camping, she veered to the right. She was not quite sure where she was. Qaramat Ali had indicated the general direction, but as the evening began to end and the night sky came on, she became doubly careful as to where she was going.

Speed was of the essence. Speed and surprise. Abdul had to be surprised by her arrival, as she hoped that would make him amenable to sheltering her. What had transpired that night was her burden. She had saved Hassan and angered Abdul. Yet here she was, fearing that her enemies would punish her for hurting Hassan and helping Abdul. There was no telling what Abdul would do. If he was still angry, it would be difficult for her. He had hardly noticed Nadya, though she stabbed him. Had Nadya been with her, she could have offered her as a temporary tribute. Nadya would not have minded and Abdul could do with a beautiful body next to him. He had no money and no zenana to keep him happy.

Niloufer was dressed in a turban and flowing robes with pajama trousers underneath. A piece of cloth masked her mouth, and little could be seen of her except those luscious almond-shaped eyes that Ahmad used to love so much. She saw some huts in the distance. It looked like a small village. Niloufer was uncertain whether to approach it or skirt around. But before she could decide, a horseman appeared next to her—so suddenly that Niloufer had no time to think.

'Who are you and what are you doing here?'

The tone was not menacing, but neither was it friendly. Niloufer had to think quickly about how much to reveal of her plans. She decided to bluff her way through.

'I am a messenger from Hassan Shah. I am going to the camp of Sardar Abdul Khan.'

'Show me the message.'

'Messages are not written down. I have to speak to Abdul Khan.

If you know where his camp is, take me there quickly.'

The horseman was uncertain as to what to do. He was not a soldier but a village headman. He decided the best way was to pass this stranger on.

'Abdul Khan sahib is a good man. His soldiers do not rob us and pay good money when they get food from us. I can take you to the camp. But now it is too dark. Come and stay in the village, rest tonight and I will take you tomorrow morning.'

Niloufer was not ready to reveal any more of herself than she already had. She was sure that the horseman had not realized he was speaking to a woman. Any overnight stay would blow her disguise.

'No, I have to go as soon as possible. Hassan Shah has bade me to deliver the message as quickly as I can.'

'Follow me then.'

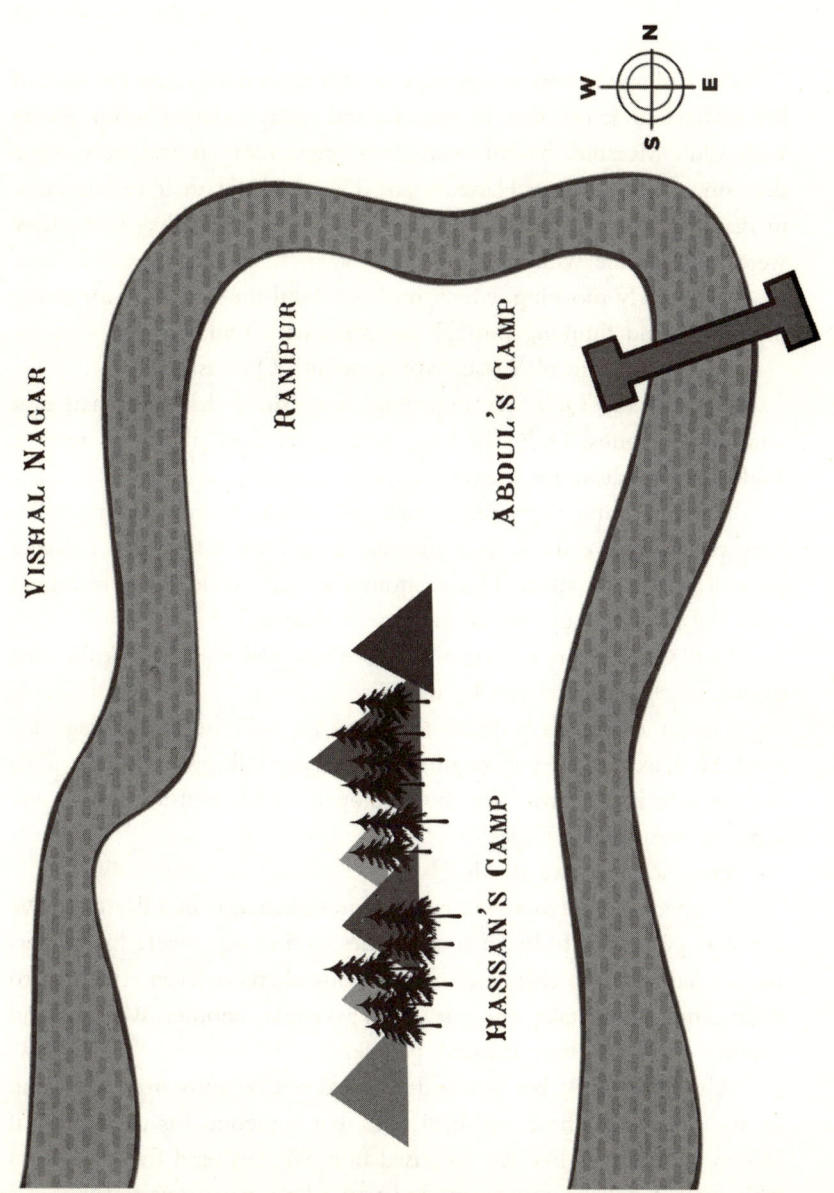

25. Abdul

Abdul had now recovered enough to walk around his camp. He wanted his soldiers to know that he was fit and ready to fight again. Along with Quli Murshid, he surveyed their preparation. It was now some days since their raid on Hassan's tent. They had got their repairs done in Ranipur and had rested. Their morale was high and they knew they were now on the winning side.

It was early morning, which was for Abdul the best time for doing his rounds and thinking through his plans with Quli.

'So, what is the plan you have in mind?' Quli asked.

Abdul knew Quli was impatient. Ever since that lost chance at winning the guns, Quli had been testing his chief about his resolve. Abdul had to show his mettle.

'Hassan is camped by the border and waiting to cross the river. We have yet to receive the second message from Devi Singh. But I expect he will tell us to attack Hassan from the rear while he is trying to cross the river. We can attack anytime it suits us.'

'Can we win on our own? Are we not just the sharp knife that cannot crack the betel nut by itself?'

'Hassan cannot wait there for long. He will need to forage for food. So I expect he will begin attacking the villages of Purana Zilla on this side of the river. We should stop his soldiers from getting any support from these villages.'

'How long do we do that?'

'I expect the message will come from Vishalnagar in a day or so. We can start going out today in small parties to find out where his soldiers are headed and stop them from getting anywhere, or even returning to their camp. I will take one party and you take another. We can send out five more to chase Hassan's people.'

'That may work, but you and I should not be away from the camp on the same day. These are small raids, but someone has to be here if Hassan surprises us like we surprised him. We can send five parties on their own. I will go tomorrow, and you take a party out today.'

Abdul was happy that Quli had noticed he had been thinking about how to attack Hassan. But still, he was impatient for the message from Vishalnagar, as that would trigger the bigger battle.

They saw a soldier approaching rapidly.

'What is it, Suleiman?'

'There is a horseman from the Sitapur village and he has brought with him a messenger.'

'Bring the messenger to my tent. I will see him there.'

Abdul and Quli quickly got back to Abdul's tent. It was not much bigger than any other tent, since Abdul wanted to impress his soldiers with his awareness of the fact that he had not yet earned a king's luxuries.

'I hope the message is easy to decipher and not some riddle again.'

Abdul was astonished when he saw the messenger. He knew immediately who it was. 'Ammijan, what are you doing here? Have you got a message for me from Hassan?'

Niloufer was relieved that his first words showed he was moderately annoyed, not angry. 'I am sorry to impose on you like this Lalla. I need to shelter with you for a while.'

'Is this some trick that Qaramat has asked you to play to find out my secrets?' Abdul knew that Hassan was a simple soldier, and cunning tricks were Qaramat's speciality.

'No. The attack you made that night nearly killed Hassan, as you know. He was lucky to escape, and had Nadya not plunged that dagger in you, you would have killed him. He has not been able to withstand that humiliation.'

Abdul was not sure what all this was leading to, but he was glad that Quli was getting a better account of his valour than he had been able to give that crucial night.

'Ammijan, what are you saying?'

'Hassan has told everyone that he nearly killed you, but we two women prevented him. He is willing to forgive, but the zenana and the Mallika-e-Alam want me arrested. So I have escaped. Wazir-e-Alam advised me that if I hide for a while, I can save myself. I can't go to Hassan's camp, as the army is there for the battle and not for entertainment. I cannot go back to Muzaffarabad. So you are my only solace.'

'My army is also a fighting army. How am I going to look after you while I am out fighting?'

'I can stay in any corner and not be a problem for you. I can help with medicines and ointments for your soldiers if they need them.'

'Ammijan, I do not want any of my soldiers to know you are here or to rely on ointments and medicines. The sight of any woman will disturb them.'

'I cannot go back now to Muzaffarabad.'

Quli knew that there was only one way out. 'Sardar, you know what you have to do. Begam sahiba can hide in Ranipur.'

This was not a surprising suggestion for Abdul. He had been resisting proposing what, for him, was a very attractive option. He did not wish to seem too eager to go back to the haveli. 'It is one thing to go there for dressing a wound. But if Ammijan has to live there, will Sethji be able to accommodate a Muslim woman in his house?'

'You know Sethji and the Lady of the House are honest people. Let us seek their advice.'

Niloufer was perplexed but relieved that there seemed to be some solution to her problem. Abdul was not about to send her back.

'Ammijan, I know you have been travelling and you must need rest. But come with us, and we can ask our Sethji and his lady if they can find a way out for you.'

Quli thought it best to cover Abdul's embarrassment. 'You go. I will stay here. When you get back here I will take out a raid party, and you can lead one tomorrow.'

26. Hassan

Hassan was holding his daily meeting in his tent. Qaramat had already advised Nadya that she had to crop her hair and put on a turban and men's clothes. She had to be as inconspicuous as she could manage, but stay within sight of Hassan. She stood behind him, all alert in her new outfit.

'Zail Singh,' spoke Hassan.

'Huzoor, I am at your command.'

'Are our troops ready for the foraging raids?'

'Yes, Huzoor. I have ten teams ready to go around and find the villages on the other side to loot.'

Qaramat spoke up. 'Huzoor, we have already spent five lakh rupees on the campaign and every day costs us more. I have to ask your permission to get some more money from our bankers if you plan the campaign to go on for a while.'

'Wazir-e-Alam, let us hope when the soldiers return from their raids they bring back enough to help us carry on a bit longer. How soon can we get the money if we need it?'

'Huzoor, I can send someone back to Muzaffarabad, but that will take three days. There are the Rathore bankers in Ranipur. They are always helpful and give us loans against revenue collection. Ranipur is less than a day away.'

'But I hear Abdul has been to Ranipur. Will he not stop our soldiers?'

'Huzoor, if you wish to raise money from the bankers in Ranipur, I will have to go myself. I am sure Abdul Khan will not harm me. Those are the laws of warfare.'

'Let us wait and see what the raiding parties bring. We can decide later. Zail Singh!'

'Huzoor.'

'How many parties can you send out today?'

Zail Singh had already mentioned that, but such trivia was not for kings to recall.

'Ten teams are ready.'

Qaramat spoke up. 'Huzoor, the left side of the Purana Zillla on this bank is hilly, as you know. I would advise sending a larger team there. On the right hand side the terrain is flat, and smaller parties can go.'

'Well said, Wazir-e-Alam. Send six teams to the left and tell them to march together, two teams at a time. Send four to the right separately.'

Ji, Huzoor.

A messenger came rushing in. He bowed thrice to Hassan. 'Speak up. What is the news?' the king asked.

'Huzoor, we hear that Devi Singh has quarrelled with his firangi man, who owns the big gun. The firangi is leaving Vishalnagar and taking his gun away with him.'

'Did you see this?'

'No, I did not see it myself, but one of our men has been watching the other bank from this side. He has seen big barges being loaded with guns and the firangi leaving Vishalnagar. He sends the message to Huzoor.'

'Wazir-e-Alam, what do you make of this?'

'Huzoor, everywhere it is the firangis who are in charge of the big guns. We are lucky that we have our Turkish officers who know about guns. Your father recruited them years ago. But the Purana Zilla has a Frenchman. He is known to be greedy. People say he was sacked from the French army for stealing money. It maybe that he demanded too much and Devi Singh did not give him what he wanted.'

'Could this be a trick?'

'If the guns have been loaded on the barge and sailed away from Vishalnagar, I doubt it is a trick. What we need to know is how many other boats sailed out and how many soldiers he took with him. He may just go off and sell his gun to the Marathas.'

Hassan had to know more. He ordered the messenger, 'Tell our spy to come back here and report to me. I need to hear from him what he saw.'

Ji Huzoor.

Hassan clapped his hands and everyone dispersed, except for the young soldier standing next to him with a sword unsheathed. Hassan turned to Nadya. Now Nadeer. She was no longer just a highly desirable woman; she had to be a killer if required. She was a falcon, not just a pigeon, as Niloufer had told Qaramat.

'Huzoor, you are worried about something,' she said.

'How do you know?'

'I get messages from your lips that are more eloquent than words. I know you have something troubling you. How can I remove your worry?'

Hassan folded his arms and Nadya knew that this was more than a game.

'What do you think, Nadeer? Am I being cheated? Am I going to be surprised once again like that night?'

'Huzoor, what was said about the firangi quarelling and leaving sounded too sudden. We have heard no rumours about his fighting with his raja. Now that you are near the river waiting to cross, it seems the firangi is leaving. Wazir-e-Alam is a clever man, but even he does not see that this could be a trap.'

'I need to think this through.'

'Huzoor, allow me leave to ease your troubles.'

'So what do you suggest we do?'

'If you trust me, Huzoor, allow me to go and find out.'

'Where will you go?'

'To the river. If he is going far away, he will have made preparations for a long journey. He should be travelling with many boats or camels to take his baggage and his food. But he may just be hiding out at the river to fool us. If I go dressed like this, no one will notice. I can ride out early tomorrow morning.'

'Don't get caught. And don't get killed.'

'As Huzoor commands.'

27. Anamika

Now, every day was a joy for Anamika. Abhi was getting more active by the day. His daily bath and his few short steps inside the house were helping him gain confidence. She was careful not to push him too much and to let him rest. He also put on his full 'banker' dress everyday now, with a shirt and a dhoti and a long coat. She put a tilak on his head, with sandalwood paste and vermillion. Then he put on a turban before moving to his galla from their bedroom with Jibril's help. Once there, he took the turban off and put it at his side. This way, he felt like he was being a proper Seth. She herself made sure that she looked her best, with sindoor in her hair and wearing one of her colourful saris, with a matching blouse and a fine petticoat. Sushila and Rajat helped out in the house. Ganga, a Brahmin widow from the village, came to grind grain to fine flour for Anamika. Ganga was also good to have around on special days. She had a young son, Kishan. She let him play with Jibril and Wahid in the village square while she worked for Anamika.

Abhi was at his galla. Anamika had decided to cook a special meal for them, so she was busy in the kitchen. She was mixing the flour with ghee and sugar to make sweets to have with lunch, when she heard the now familiar sounds of horses in the village square. Sensing what it could be, she told Ganga to look after her cooking and, wiping her hands, went into the front room.

As she opened the door she found Abdul standing there, looking somewhat sheepish. With him was a woman dressed in flowing robes and a turban. Anamika saw that the woman was tall and had beautiful almond-shaped eyes.

'Come in, Khan sahib. We have not seen you for some time.'

'Can we go in and speak with Sethji?'

Anamika saw that Abdul was shy about speaking with her in the presence of another person. She sized up the situation. 'Khan sahib, you are welcome, and so is your guest. Please come in. Sethji is at his usual place in the galla.'

Abdul had decided that he would not introduce his mother to Anamika before he had secured some sort of agreement with Abhi to accommodate Niloufer. Abhi was, of course, warm in his welcome. 'Khan sahib, we have not had the honour of your visit for a while. Please come in.'

Niloufer was intrigued that her son seemed to know this Hindu family so well. She was quick to notice that Abhi did not rise to greet them. She was also fascinated by Anamika's boldness in front of her son. She had not seen many Hindu women show such ease in the presence of men, especially Muslim men.

'Sethji, meet my mother, Niloufer Begum.'

Anamika was impressed that the handsome woman Abdul had brought was his mother. She began to look for resemblances between the two, but besides the almond eyes, she did not spot any immediately.

'Begum sahiba, welcome to our humble home,' said Abhi. 'Please sit. Anamika, can you see that Begum sahiba has a comfortable seat?'

Anamika grabbed a cushion and added it to a perch not far from where Abhi was seating. She took Niloufer there and asked her to sit. Abdul preferred to stand, as she well knew.

'Khan sahib, what can we do for you and the Begum sahiba?' Abhi resumed.

Niloufer spoke up. 'Sethji, I am Abdul's unfortunate mother. I have had to run away from Hassan Shah's durbar and need to hide somewhere for a few days. I have no one to turn to but my son. But he is a fighting man. He cannot look after me. So he has brought me here. I do not know you but, he seems to have a lot of faith in you.'

'That should be no problem at all, Begum sahiba. Khan sahib, what would you wish for your mother? We can always find somewhere for her to stay.'

Anamika was pleased with Abhi's response. 'Khan sahib, please consider this house to be yours. Begum sahiba, think of me like your daughter,' she added.

Abdul had to demur, if only for his own honour. 'Sethji, please consider this carefully. I do not wish the village to say that you have put up a Muslim woman in a Hindu house, and so they must stay away from you. I do not wish for you to come to any harm. Find somewhere suitable for my mother to stay in the village and I will be grateful.'

Abhi understood his problem. 'Khan sahib, the village knows you and respects you. They have seen you coming here on good days and when you had the injury. No one thinks of these things. We will look after her as our own mother.'

Anamika saw that Abdul was still hesitant. 'Khan sahib,' she said, 'We can give Begum sahiba her own separate room and her own cook who will look after her. Ganga helps me out and I will ask her to cook for Begum sahiba. When the older Sethji was here, he and my mother-in-law used the big room over there. Begum sahiba can have that room. She will be comfortable there.'

Niloufer was quite taken by this beautiful woman. 'Please do not call me Begum sahiba,' she said. 'My Lalla calls me Ammijan—I shall be your Ammijan.'

Anamika could not help stealing a glance at Abdul, who was as near blushing as she had ever seen a man be. Inwardly, she was savouring their secret, but she kept her counsel. Niloufer staying with them meant that she would see more of him.

Abhi was quick to move to practical details. 'Anamika, Ammijan must be tired. Can you ask Ganga to see that everything is alright for her? She can show Ammijan the room and help her with whatever she needs. I have to tell Khan sahib about his accounts. Then you can put Khan sahib's mind at rest by telling him how well we will look after his mother.'

Anamika saw that Abhi was saving Abdul Khan any further trouble regarding his mother. This way, she could get Niloufer settled in and then see Abdul on her own.

Anamika took Niloufer to her new room. It had been left vacant since Ramdas and Revati departed. She called Ganga to come and help her. Ganga was shy in Niloufer's presence, but Anamika was quick to direct her in the task of preparing the bed and making sure the room was comfortable.

'Ammijan, let me give you some clothes to change into. You can have a bath and put on more comfortable clothes. I only have our style of clothes, but I hope you do not mind.'

'Beti, I have worn all sorts of clothes in my life, so please do not worry. I can be comfortable in anything. Do not put yourself to so much trouble.'

Anamika would not hear of it. She took Niloufer to her room and opened her cupboard to pull out some clothes. Then she had an idea.

In her in-laws' cupboard there were the clothes—particularly kurtas and pyjamas—that Ramdas used to wear. She realized that they would be comfortable for Niloufer and laid them out for her. Soon there was a pile of saris, blouses, petticoats, pyjamas and kurtas on the floor for Niloufer to choose from. Ganga finished making the bed and swept the room clean in the meanwhile.

'Ganga, can you heat up some water for Ammijan to have a bath? Then we must give her something to eat. She must be hungry.'

'Beti, you are very kind. I will have a bath and then I will rest for a while. I have been travelling for two days.'

'Just call me or Ganga and we will get you whatever you wish.'

Anamika left Niloufer to be looked after by Ganga. She thought that would make Niloufer feel more comfortable giving orders to Ganga. Ganga would not mind, as she would get extra money from Anamika for all the work. Anamika came out and found Abdul ready to take leave.

'Sethji, you have explained everything. I do not worry about money, as you know. I will tell Quli how much is still left. But now, wish me luck, because we must go out campaigning.'

'Khan sahib, our prayers are with you. Anamika, can you see to it that Khan sahib is happy with what we have done for Ammijan?'

This was the cue for Anamika to speak to Abdul alone. But they both knew that this was not the time for intimacy. Even so, Anamika took Abdul upstairs to the room of their first explosive encounter. Then she looked up at him. She did not come too close to him. He knew what she wanted to do and say. He did not say anything either. Anamika took Abdul's hands in hers and placed them on her cheeks.

'Lalla, do not worry about Ammijan. She is safe with us and we are happy to look after her. Go and fight your battles with your mind at ease. Come back and you will find me still here.' Anamika was sure that Abdul had noticed that regardless of her actions, her desire for him was still there.

Abdul had to make his problem clear. 'I have to lead my soldiers once more and win decisively this time. Until I do that I cannot rest. But I will return.'

'I know. Ammijan said something about the fight between you and Hassan and how you missed him. Now I know where that wound came from.'

'I have to undo that setback. My soldiers expect me to win when I get out there to fight.'

Anamika gently drew his face towards her and kissed him. It was a deep kiss, but it had affection rather than lust in it.

'Saki knows. She will be ready for her Lalla when he is.'

Abdul hesitated but decided not to linger for more kisses. He squeezed Anamika's hands firmly and turned around. He walked down, followed by her. Once in the front room, Anamika opened the door and Abdul called for his horse.

Shivnarayan came rushing in to the house and went straight to Abhi. 'I see a pigeon on the zarokha. I will get the message.'

Abhi called out to Anamika, 'Mika, tell Khan sahib to wait a while. There may be a message for him from Vishalnagar.'

Shivnarayan came down. The message was in cipher, yet again. Abhi read it while Abdul waited anxiously. 'It is good news. The guns are coming to your aid from Vishalnagar. The Frenchman will join you in two days with them. He is crossing the river at Devgarh.'

Abdul was surprised that the message had, once again, been sent to Ranipur. Abhi saw his puzzlement. 'Khan sahib,' he said, 'they sent the pigeon here because we get messages that way all the time. It says here to let you know. They know that your soldiers are here and so the message can be sent to you anytime. It is quicker this way.'

'Sethji, I better hurry. The battle will commence sooner than I had expected.'

Anamika saw his enthusiasm. He was eager to leave only so he could return to her.

28. The Zenana

Begum saheba was furious. The zenana was back, tired and bedraggled, but when she asked for the wazir, he was not there. Nor was Niloufer or the woman who had been with her son at the time of his battle with Abdul. They had slipped her grasp. No one could explain what had happened to them. With Qaramat absent, there was no one with any authority to tell Fatima Begum what had really happened.

Salma came to the begum the day after the zenana returned. Indeed, the begum had summoned her. She came fearful but determined to have her say. She had taken care to wear a simple white niqab with no jewelry and no adornment on her eyes or lips. Mallika-e-Alam was sitting on her gilded chair in the room where she held her court. Salma entered and bowed thrice.

'Your slave is here to obey your command, Mallika–e-Alam.'

'Tell me the truth. Were you there when Abdul attacked my son?'

'Begum saheba, you know how loyal I am to your family. I had been asked to attend to the Lord, to entertain him. But Niloufer Begum poisoned his mind against me and I was dismissed. She was preparing for Abdul to come and attack the Lord. She is a witch. She has trained another, younger one like her, a yellow-haired woman from Abkhazia. She was sent in and I was dismissed. Within minutes of her going in, Abdul Khan attacked the prince. We were far away—all of us in the zenana. Only the new woman was there, and Niloufer.'

'So what happened?'

'The prince was brave and would have killed Abdul with his sword, but the two women stopped him and let Abdul escape.'

'Can you swear that this is true?'

'Begum saheba, I was out of the tent at the time of the attack, as Niloufer begama had sent me away. But I ran back when I heard the shouting and when I came in, I saw the two women helping Abdul run away.'

'Where was my son?'

'Huzoor was not there. He had struck Abdul and Abdul was bleeding. He must have thought he had killed Abdul. But the women saved him and sent him away. Huzoor did not find out till later.'

'Did you see my son striking Abdul?'

'No Begum saheba, I did not. But I did see the two women saving Abdul.'

'How?'

'The new girl was binding his wound and Niloufer was telling him to run away before Huzoor could come back.'

'Will you swear on the Holy Quran?'

'Begum saheba must forgive me. I am a simple woman. I cannot be sure of what I saw. If I were to swear, Allah might punish me if I saw wrong. Please trust me. I am Huzoor's faithful slave. All I wish to do is to entertain him the best I can. I am sure the two women saved Abdul.'

'You can go. Don't tell any more lies.'

Salma was tearful. 'Begum saheba, I have told you the truth, but I cannot swear upon the Holy Quran. Please forgive me. I am just a simple girl…'

'Go and don't come back in my presence.'

Salma went out as tearful as she had been when Hassan had dismissed her. Fatima Begum clapped her hands. Najma came in.

'Call Laila in my presence,' the begum said.

Laila came promptly. She had been expecting the call, and was waiting just outside the court room. She entered and bowed thrice.

'Begum saheba, your slave is ready to obey your command.'

'Tell me truthfully. What did you see of the fight of my son with Abdul?'

'Begum saheba. It is all the fault of Salma. She was supposed to please the prince. But she quarrelled with him so much that he threw her out and told her never to come in his presence again. As he was angry, Niloufer took advantage and got her new favourite white woman to please the prince. But she was a spy for Abdul. She diverted Huzoor's attention and let Abdul in. The prince was brave and wounded Abdul, but the two chudails helped him run away.'

'Did you see any of this?'

'Of course, Begum saheba, with my own eyes.'

'Will you swear it on the Holy Quran?'

'Have mercy on a simple girl, Begum saheba. I do not see that well at night and I cannot swear.'

'Go away and do not come in my presence again.'

Fatima called Najma again. 'Ask the Nazir-e-purdah to come here.' Najma went out and summoned Timur, who had been impatiently waiting outside. He had been worried that the women from the zenana may say something against him to the Afghani begum. He swiftly entered and made three deep bows.

'Begum saheba has summoned me in her presence. What can her slave do for her?'

'I hear nothing but lies from these women. No one has seen what really happened. How do we know what the two women did? Niloufer beguma has been a faithful servant of our family. Her new woman seems to be liked by my son. What happened that night? Why is the Wazir-e-Alam not here? How did the women escape his grasp? Does anyone know?'

Timur could sense that the Afghani begum had better sources than him about what happened. He would have to come clean as to what he knew. 'Begum saheba, the wazir is back with Huzoor. My messengers tell me that he is advising Huzoor about the battle.'

'Why did he not come back with the two women?'

'Begum saheba, forgive your humble servant. I have some information, but not the whole truth. My messengers tell me that Wazir-e-Alam took the young woman back to Huzoor for his pleasure.'

'Are you sure?'

'Yes, Mallika-e-Alam. My people have sent me a pigeon saying she is with Huzoor every night. He likes her very much.'

'Where is Niloufer?'

'No one knows. I think Wazir-e-Alam may know but he is hiding her.'

'Why?'

'I had sent a message that Begum saheba wanted the two women arrested and punished. Wazir-e-Alam allowed Niloufer to escape and took the other one back to Huzoor.'

'Does anyone know what happened that night? Who escorted the zenana back if the Wazir-e-Alam was riding away to my son's camp?'

'Wazir-e-Alam gave the charge to his grandson, Salamat Ali.'

'Isn't that his daughter's boy?'

'Yes, Mallika-e-Alam.'

'Ask him to come see me. I must know the truth.'

Timur saw that now was not the time to go any further with the conversation. He had to obey the Afghani begum in her angry moods just as he did when she felt lonely. It was worse when she felt both lonely and angry.

29. Battle 1

Quli had a good day chasing Hassan's soldiers. The border between Ramgarh and Purana Zilla was nearer to Ranipur than where Hassan was camped. His soldiers had ridden half a day and more before they came across the border. Quli had anticipated that some would come north towards where he was waiting for them. He had sent more of his troops in the southerly direction, to catch as many of Hassan's men as they could. They had to be careful not to drift too close to where Hassan's main camp was. But that lay farther to the southwest and within the borders of Ramgarh.

When they met up face to face, Quli saw that the soldiers were from Abdul's old army. Before they could start fighting, he called out his name and told them he was recruiting for Abdul's army. The soldiers were surprised to find Quli Murshid waiting for them on the other side of the Ramgarh border. They were expecting to find villages that they could check to see how much they would yield if raided, not a fight with rival troops. They stopped and got off their horses, and so did Quli's men. They embraced each other like long lost friends. Quli also embraced them and shook their hands. He told them that there was money ready to pay them, as well as food and shelter. They could come with him and join Abdul's army. If not, they would all get back on their horses and fight.

The soldiers had been missing their old comrades and immediately chose the path of least resistance. Quli was soon riding back with them. The other companies he had sent out had similar experiences. For some reason, Hassan had chosen the soldiers from Abdul's old army to do the work of foraging and searching. These were soldiers who had little loyalty for Hassan. They had been there that night and seen how swiftly Abdul could strike and upset Hassan's plans. Here was an opportunity to switch. By the time Hassan would find out, there would be nothing he could do.

The happy troops coming back that day were a pleasant surprise for Abdul. Quli had gone out with a hundred and returned with three hundred. There was much celebration as old comrades met each other.

The returning soldiers did their salaams to Abdul, who also greeted them warmly.

'Welcome back to your old family, my braves. We are together again like in the old days. Allah willing, more of our comrades will join us as you have done. We shall defeat Hassan and take over the throne of Ramgarh, which rightfully belongs to me.'

They all cheered and soon fires were lit and food was being prepared. Quli went around discreetly paying the newcomers a part of their salary, which would keep them there. The first day of the new battle had been a good one. As they sat around the campfires, eating and relaxing, Abdul asked them what they knew of Hassan's plans. The soldiers did not know much, but they did tell him that many parties had been sent out to scout what villages could be raided by Hassan's army for food and money.

Quli understood the strategy, as did Abdul. Hassan was going to run short of food and fodder for his large army. The further his army went from Muzaffarabad, the more his supply lines got stretched. This was a good chance for Abdul's army to keep enticing Hassan's soldiers away from him, as they had better supplies thanks to their kindness in Ranipur.

So, early next morning, Abdul was happy to lead his troops. They knew that some of Hassan's troops were going further out west to where the hillier parts of Purana Zilla were, on this side of the river. If he was to reach there in good time, Abdul had to start early. It felt good to be in harness again. Abdul was looking forward to a battle. He did not expect that he would have it as easy as Quli, though one could never be sure. He, along with his hundred men, had to cross the border and fan out towards the southwest to see what troops of Hassan they could take on.

The villages on the other side were west of the small hills that separated Hassan's camp from the border. Here, Hassan's men would have to cross the hills and then begin to explore the villages they could raid. Abdul's troops were riding on the plain, but they had to turn left and make a semicircular detour to be ready on the other side of the hills, from where Hassan's men would descend. They would have the advantage of speed as they were rushing downhill, just as Abdul's men did the night they attacked Hassan's camp. But they were not expecting an army to fight, so Abdul's men had the edge of surprise.

The battle began soon enough, after three hours of riding by Abdul's men. As Hassan's troops rushed down the hills, Abdul took no chances and began firing. The surprise was effective. Abdul's army were able to rush towards the incoming troops and soon there was hand-to-hand combat alongside the heavy firing. Abdul was in the lead and relishing every moment of this battle. He had anticipated well—none of these troops were from his old army. They were hardy men, but unprepared for battle.

The fight lasted only two hours, and at the end, a few of Hassan's troops were able to retreat. But many had died and some were wounded. Abdul's men managed to capture their horses and guns. They asked the wounded ones if they wanted to join Abdul's side. The soldiers saw little choice, and rode back with Abdul's troops. They had lost five of their men, but Hassan's troops had lost many more.

As he rode back, Abdul felt he had begun to erase some of the disgrace that had been attached to him since that fateful night when he had missed the chance to kill Hassan. He was looking forward to how Quli would regard his return to active duty.

30. Niloufer

It did not take Niloufer and Anamika very long to become close to each other. For Anamika, Niloufer was like the mother she had not had for over a year. For Niloufer, living in an ordinary home with a married couple young enough to be her own children was a special joy. After a long life in zenanas, she was finally able to savour what she could have had, had she not been snatched away at the age of seven. It was not long before Anamika told her not just about Abhi's accident, but also, very proudly, how Abdul had changed the prospects of Abhi's recovery. Niloufer could see that Anamika's attachment to Abdul was special. With her experience of the variety of sexual relationships, she guessed that there had been more than handholding between her son and this beautiful young woman. But she did not reveal her thoughts.

As soon as Niloufer understood what had happened to Abhi, she was ready to help. Her long experience with aphrodisiacs and ointments for restoring vitality in the sexual organs was now more useful than ever before. As the two women now talked frankly, Niloufer could tell Anamika about men's bodies and how they functioned and broke down. She told Anamika about her experience with Ahmad. Of course, Ahmad was neither hurt nor maimed. But the malady was not all that different. The question was of reviving the moribund sexual organ so it could do what it was meant to.

As Anamika told Niloufer about Abhi's recovery, Niloufer could see clearly what to do next. She had seen many horsefall injuries in her time and had watched as hakims and bonesetters worked away to restore the broken bodies. This, however, was not so much about bones as about nerves and muscles. Her books had been left behind in the palace at Muzaffarabad. But her memory was good. She discussed with Anamika what had to be done.

'Beti, don't worry. You and Abhi are like my children. But even so, no man likes having a woman see his weakness. I can prepare the mixture with my own recipe. If you will let me, I can even apply it on Abhi. To save his blushes, I will put on a blindfold, but my hands can reach where he needs to be treated. If he does not like that, I will teach you how to do it. But it will take a bit of time before you can do what I do.'

'Ammijan, what would you need for your preparation?'

'Ghee and nutmeg and cinnamon, with some gold leaf and honey. It helps to have turmeric, since it has soothing properties. Almonds and saffron, as well as some ground fenugreek. We have to avoid anything that irritates the skin or causes bleeding. But if I can get to massage him and apply my ointment once a day, I am sure he will be better soon.'

Anamika was quick to find out whether Abhi would agree to Niloufer treating him. That night she sidled up to him in bed and said, 'Remember how Lakshmanji got hurt while fighting in Lanka?'

'Yes, what of that?'

'Hanumanji had to fly out and find the medicine for him. But he could not decide which plant was right, so he brought the whole mountain—so they could choose whatever would cure Lakshmanji.'

'Why are you telling me this story?'

'Khan sahib has delivered the mountain, with all the medicines to cure all our problems.'

'Are you sure?'

'Yes, I am sure. Ammijan can work miracles.'

'Let us hope so'.

Next day onwards, Ganga was put to work grinding the spices and mixing the ingredients under the watchful eyes of Niloufer. She was not to know why she was doing all this, only that it was a medicine for someone. Maybe for Niloufer herself, she thought. Her only job was to do what Niloiufer had asked her to, and to do it well. She had begun to like this beautiful woman. Niloufer had also realized that as a young widow, Ganga had her own dreams, which would need to be fulfilled someday. Niloufer decided that once she had taken care of Abhi, she would take Ganga in her hands.

31. Hassan

*H*assan was beside himself with rage. He had already heard reports about the troops he had sent out the previous day. All four teams that had gone northwards across the border had defected to Abdul. None of the soldiers had come back except for one lone person who had once quarrelled with Abdul and was scared of going back under him. Now Hassan was being told how his hill-bound crack troops had been set upon by Abdul and his men and decimated. A few stragglers had just come in. Hassan had not anticipated this quick attack from Abdul. He had certainly not suspected that among his troops were disloyal units who had previously served under Abdul.

'Zail Singh.'

'Huzoor?'

'What has happened to our troops? Can they not fight or are they all Abdul's men betraying us?'

'Huzoor, it seems Abdul has been waiting for our troops and has spies who tell him where we are going.'

'How many troops does he have?'

'Huzoor, we think he has no more than a thousand. After all, he has no money to pay them. His people did loot us that night, but then, after you wounded him, they rushed off. Maybe another hundred have now joined him from our side. But he has no elephants or camels.'

'Wazir-e-Alam, what is your view?'

'I believe, Huzoor, you should ignore Abdul. Let us defeat Devi Singh and get his territory. Abdul's soldiers can harass us away from foraging, but he is a small fry. He should not be allowed to distract us from our main mission.'

'But if our armies cannot loot the villages on their side, how do we entice Devi Singh's troops to this side of the river?'

'Huzoor, if he has lost his big gun, we can cross the river and attack him. Our elephants and camels are at the riverside already. You give the command and we can begin to cross the river tomorrow. There will be fodder enough on the other side once we attack Vishalnagar.'

'Zail Singh, what do you say?'

'Huzoor, Wazir-e-Alam is a wise man and he has a lot of experience in such matters. As your faithful soldiers, we are ready to carry out your orders. It seems that the big guns are gone. If so, we have an advantage until Devi Singh calls for help from the Marathas or the Rohillas.'

'But can we be sure the firangi has left Devi Singh? Has our spy come back to tell us?'

'He is waiting to be asked to come in your presence, Huzoor. He is outside.'

'Call him.'

A soldier came in, accompanied by a man dressed in simple clothes, like a sadhu. He bowed thrice before Hassan.

'Tell us what you have seen.'

'Huzoor, I was on our side of the river and I saw the big gun being loaded on a barge with some soldiers guarding it. I saw the firangi get into a boat that was at the head of the convoy. The firangi was travelling with only a few soldiers. There were ten other barges with camels and smaller guns.'

'How many soldiers?'

'Not many, Huzoor. It seemed like he was going away in anger and no one was going with him.'

'Which direction did he sail in?'

'Huzoor, he was sailing northwards as the Sreni moves, towards the Yamuna.'

'Good. Zail Singh, make sure this man is rewarded.'

'Huzoor, it shall be done.'

Hassan was still not sure. He did not quite trust the spy, who seemed to him a simple man who had seen only what he had been meant to see. Hassan was thinking about Nadya and wondering why she had not yet come back. She had left early in the morning, while it was still dark. It was now getting dark again. Hassan knew she could ride, and disguised as a man she would be safe. But he had to know what she had seen.

'Wazir-e-Alam, Zail Singh, we have decided that we need to think about these things a bit more,' he said. 'We know that Gulabchand is a clever man and his mind can think of various tricks. Our spy has no doubt seen only what he was meant to see. There seems to have been no secrecy in the way in which the firangi left Vishalnagar. This puzzles me. We will not decide yet, but wait till the morning to give our orders.' He clapped his hands and everyone began to withdraw.

'Wazir-e-Alam, I have other matters to discuss with you. Stay behind.'

'As Huzoor commands.'

Qaramat Ali's shrewd eyes had noticed that Nadya was not there behind Hassan. There had to be an explanation. He hoped she had not met with some violent accident—not unknown for zenana women. He was getting rather fond of Nadya, as she was resilient and charming too.

'Wazir-e-Alam, we may need to discuss the matter of money. If we cannot get food and fodder from the villages of Purana Zilla, we need to rethink our plans. You were saying you could get money from a money lender nearby.'

Qaramat Ali sensed that Hassan was dawdling for time. He was worried about something, which he was not ready to talk about. Maybe it was Nadya. Qaramat realized that this conversation could not be hurried.

'Huzoor, there are several ways. I could send some trusted soldiers back to Muzaffarabad, where we can get money from our Khazanchi. We have plenty. I was mentioning another possibility to you two days ago. The Rathore bankers are an old family and they live in Ranipur, which is in Huzoor's domain. I could go there myself and get money from them if Huzoor so wishes.'

'But is it not where Abdul's camp is sited? I heard you say that Abdul had visited the village and they had fed him. Has he taken the village over from us?'

Qaramat realized that he had underestimated Hassan. Hassan had a good memory. He remembered what he had been told two days ago about Abdul. Qaramat would have to be careful.

'We do not have that information yet, Huzoor, but I could send out my messengers to find out. But if you allow me to go, I am sure Abdul or his men will not stop me.'

'There is another way, perhaps, to change our plans.'

'What would that be Huzoor?'

'We attack Abdul's camp ourselves, and that will take us to Ranipur, where we can rob the banker as well. Tell me if you see any obstacles in that plan.'

'Huzoor, that is a clever plan. But it will delay our attack on Vishalnagar. It may also give Devi Singh the time to get some big guns from other kingdoms. After all, though there are Rajput kingdoms who don't acknowledge his top status, they are still his relations. If he were to tell them he has lost his guns, they may come to his aid.'

Qaramat Ali knew in his heart that he was being disloyal to his king. But he had sent Niloufer to Abdul, and the last thing he wanted was any attack where Niloufer could die. Abdul would suspect that she was a cuckoo in the nest. But before he could say anything more, Nadya came in, disguised as Nadeer in a turban, a tunic and trousers. She still looked fetching, with her green eyes and tall build. She was out of breath, as she had been riding hard all day. Hassan was relieved to see her back. She bowed low thrice to Hassan, and then to Qaramat Ali. He put a fatherly arm around her shoulder and let her catch her breath.

'Nadeer, what news have you brought us?' asked Hassan.

'Huzoor, I rode out to the river and went along the bank across from where our camp was, and then a bit more towards Vishalnagar. At the Devgarh crossing, I saw the firangi's convoy. He was on this side of the river. They were unloading the gun.'

'Are you sure?'

'Huzoor can take my life if I lie. I saw with my own eyes. All the barges had stopped and the boat in which the firangi had come was also there. He had taken no supplies with him for the camels or for the soldiers, as far as I could see. He is coming ashore at Devgarh.'

'Wazir-e-Alam, what do you say now?'

'Huzoor, I have to say Nadeer has found out the truth. We have been deceived by Gulabchand once again. The quarrel is a ruse to send the guns behind our armies so they could attack us from both sides.'

'Nadeer.'

'Huzoor.'

'If what you say is true, then you have saved us from a terrible defeat. We have to think quickly on how to change our plans. Call Zail Singh.'

Nadya went out to fetch Zail Singh. While she was out, Hassan had to confide in Qaramat. 'Wazir-e-Alam, you were clever to bring this soldier here. We will reward you for that.'

'Huzoor is very kind, but I think you should reward your favourite soldier.'

Zail Singh came into the tent, followed by Nadeer.

'Zail Singh, we have changed our mind. Bring the big guns back to our camp. Let the elephants also come back here. We need them here.'

'Is Huzoor sure? I can give the command now and they will begin their journey back early tomorrow morning.'

'See that it is done.'

'What is our plan, Huzoor?'

'We will attack Abdul Khan's army before we tackle Devi Singh.'

'Do we need the big guns back for that, Huzoor? It will be difficult to take them back to the river later if we are attacking Vishalnagar.'

'We have been deceived, Zail Singh. The firangi has landed at Devgarh just a few hours ago. He will be joining Abdul Khan. This is Gulabchand's clever trick.'

Zail Singh was dumbfounded. How had the shah come to know of this? But he had no choice. 'It will be done as Huzoor commands,' he said.

'How long before they reach us?'

'Two days, Huzoor, if all goes well—but maybe three, since the camels dragging the guns are often slow.'

'Hasten them. Also get the army ready for a big battle. There is not much time to lose now.'

'As Huzoor commands.'

Zail Singh left, still unconvinced that Hassan was doing the right thing. Qaramat stayed behind, because he knew there would be more for them to discuss. He was not wrong.

'Wazir-e-Alam, we now need to fight a very different battle. We set out to defeat Devi Singh and take over Purana Zilla. But it looks like we have a fight coming within our own territory with Abdul. If Abdul has made a treaty with Devi Singh, then we have to prepare for a battle that may have two fronts. What is your advice?'

'Huzoor, you cannot fight battles on two fronts at the same time. You have to choose which enemy you can defeat more easily. You were prepared to fight Devi Singh. You thought you may be able to entice him to come across the river, but he has guessed your plan. He has recruited Abdul to keep your troops from foraging and to tie you down. He maybe preparing to come across.'

'So what do you advise?'

'I have to think a bit more about this. As it is, the firangi will be bringing his guns across from Devgarh, and it will take him one to two days to reach Abdul's camp. It will take our guns two or three days to reach here. The question I cannot answer is whether Devi Singh will also start moving across the river soon and join Abdul, or will he wait to see the outcome of our battle with Abdul. So, we need time to plan our battle. If you give me permission, I will now retire, and I can give you my answer tomorrow morning.'

Qaramat was well aware that Nadya was standing there tired after a long day's ride. She needed rest, though he was not sure whether Hassan would let her be. In any case, he had to withdraw so they could get on with their lives. The time was approaching for prayers, and he was keen not to miss.

'Permission given. But I want to see you early tomorrow morning before anyone else.'

'It shall be as Huzoor commands.'

Qaramat Ali bowed thrice and went away. Nadya had been waiting for this moment, but she was not sure what would happen next. Hassan spoke up first.

'We have to reward you for your bravery and for the information you have brought us. What should we give you?'

'Huzoor knows that his pleasure in my work is my reward. I am happy to have done what Huzoor asked me to do.'

Hassan looked at Nadya. She was very tired. Her clothes bore the dust of two days' riding. Her face looked strained. He knew what he could do with her. But he resisted. He had decided not to indulge, and that he meant to keep to. Just for his own sake—just to show that he could control himself. But he still had to reward this highly desirable woman who now happened to be a guard.

He summoned his servants. They came running.

'Prepare my bath for me. Bring me some new clothes.'

Nadya rose and said, 'Huzoor, give me permission to go.'

'Stay here. I want to reward you.'

Nadya was intrigued. The iron bath tub was brought, and along with it a large pitcher of hot water and two of cold water. There were large crimson towels and some clothes for Hassan.

'I know you are tired, Nadeer. I know you have been in these clothes for two days. I remember who you are. I have ordered this bath for you. I will pour the water for you and then leave you to enjoy your bath. There are some clothes for you. They are mine, but even so, have them.'

'Huzoor, you are putting me to shame. It is I who should be bathing you.'

'What you have done today deserves my gratitude. You were brought to me as Nadya. You saved my life. Today, as Nadeer, you have saved me from certain defeat. Till I win this battle, you are my guard and counsel. Let Nadeer have this prize.'

Nadya was astonished. Hassan got up and poured the hot water in the bath. Then he added the cold water. He tested the water for warmth, then, before she could say anything, he picked her up and put her, clothes and all, in the bath. She screamed and laughed. Then he went out of the tent. Nadya decided that she may as well enjoy this surprise gift. She had not had a hot bath since they left the Muzaffarpur palace. Left alone, she began peeling off her clothes. Soaking her bare body in water was a rare pleasure. She needed it. Her fatigue was palpable.

This was another change in her life. What was she to think of what Hassan had done for her? She had been a favourite mistress once or twice, and had been showered with gold and jewellery, but seldom had any man showed her real kindness. She had to be careful, though. She had to remember that she was still a slave woman and he owned her body.

Bath over, she got out. Hassan had arranged towels for her, and clothes. It felt strange to wear the kameez and pyjama Hassan must have worn at some other time. She was tall for a woman, so the clothes did not fit too badly. She dawdled for a bit and sat down on the divan where Hassan had sat before. Before she knew it, she fell asleep.

She woke up when she felt an arm around her and a warm body close to her. Nadya was surprised. Hassan had come in, and instead of waking her up for his pleasure, he had quietly lay down next to her. Nadya sat up.

'Forgive me Huzoor. I should not be sleeping on your divan. I do not know what came over me. Permit me to go.'

'No, stay. I need you by my side. I have been thinking about what you told me. Then I listened to my wazir and my general. I do not know that they understand my problem. I want you to listen to everything they say to me. Tell me if you think they are right or if they are deceiving me. You are now my guard and my counsel.'

'Huzoor, I am just your humble servant. I am happy to do whatever you ask me to do.'

'I have had an easy life. My father was brave. He won battles and became the shah. I had no idea he would die so young. Here I am in my first battle. I realize that my generals and advisers are simple people. My enemy is shrewd. What am I to do?'

'Huzoor, you are one and they are two. You have to find ways of dividing them. Or at least taking them on separately.'

'After what you found out, I wonder whether I have any chance. It is my first battle and it could be the last one.'

Nadya looked at Hassan. For the first time she realized how young he was. He was worried. Nadya felt a concern for him that she had never felt before. She had to perk him up. She sat up. It felt absurd to be in Hassan's clothes, but she knew that this was not the time to turn back into the woman Hassan had seen before.

'Huzoor, you are worried. I can feel you are restless. Let me do what I can to relieve your worry. Allow me.'

Nadya began gently massaging Hassan. She was well acquainted with men and their fears and weaknesses. She knew Hassan was very frightened. He was facing defeat and possibly death. She could not change much in the situation they were facing. But she could help him relax. She began with his shoulders and his back. Hassan did not resist; he submitted to her expert hands. She turned him over and rubbed his chest and arms. He sighed, then sat up and took his kameez off. Now her fingers could rub and knead his knotted muscles. She began to work his body over. She had done this before, many times. She had seen brave, even cruel princes crying in her arms when the world had become too much for them.

Hassan began to unwind. Slowly but surely, his tension began to go away. But there was still that fear in him. He had lost his gamble with Abdul. Nadya sensed that Hassan was contemplating his second defeat at Abdul's hands. She had to try something else.

Nadya stood up and took off the clothes she was wearing. She was no longer Nadeer. Hassan was startled. There was the woman he had seen in his tent before. Once again she was naked but for the Cross around her neck.

'Huzoor, shall I dance for you?'

Hassan sat up. His resolve to starve himself of pleasures of the flesh was gone. 'Who are you? We don't know your name.'

Nadya was pleased that the game was on. She was ready to play. 'Huzoor, simple creatures like me don't have names. Call me by whichever name it pleases Huzoor.'

'You are Nadeera. Why have you come?'

'Huzoor, I am here to do whatever you want. Your wish is my command.'

Hassan kept on looking at her. Nadya could see that his troubles were not yet over. He was not the lusty prince she had entertained before. She began moving around the divan while cupping her breasts in her hands. She climbed on the divan and put her arms around him, bringing her breasts to his mouth.

'Huzoor, I have been a bad girl. You must punish me. Devour me, hurt me, kill me. I am your slave.'

'Where is my wine?'

Nadya laughed. There was a surahi by the side of the divan as always, with a silver cup. She poured out some wine in the cup and offered it to Hassan with both hands. She was not sure what would happen next.

'Drink,' ordered Hassan.

Nadya knew what this meant. She had to redo what had happened that interrupted night. She splashed the wine on her breasts, then laughed and went around the divan displaying her charms. She had to give Hassan what he had missed that night. He lunged at her. She was easily caught.

'Drink, Huzoor. Nadeera is thirsty for your kisses.'

Hassan drew her closer and began sucking at her breasts. She kept laughing. But he did not persist.

'What is the matter, Huzoor? Does Nadeera not please you?'

Hassan drew her in and said, 'I need you tonight. Just as you are.

I am not a prince tonight and you are not my slave. I am a troubled man. Soothe me.'

Nadya knew what this meant. She lay him down and snuggled next to him. She began rubbing his body with her arms. She let him feel the comfort of her breasts. He began to calm down. She drew his hands to her body so he could explore every bit of her. He began to respond, and she let him do what he wanted. He kissed her—a kiss like she had never experienced before. Sad but intimate. Nadya knew then that Hassan wanted comfort, not conquest. She wrapped her legs around him and moved as close as she could get. He was not aroused. She put her hands around him to see if she could get him up. He drew her to him and kissed her again. The message was clear. They were going to spend the night talking with their bodies, but gently, very gently.

Nadya was happy when Hassan fell asleep. She usually woke up, as was her habit, when she had to entertain. The king would always wake up and want more—a new trick, another woman. But here she was doing something she had not often done. What was happening to her? What was she now? A friend, a companion, a favourite, or a slave like she had always been? She had realized that she was older than Hassan and more mature. She had seen more of the world than he had. He had appreciated that she was cleverer than his officers. Was she now no longer a creature of pleasure, but a trusted counsel? She had no illusions. In a hard life traversing many countries, her body had been her only asset that anyone wanted. Maybe Hassan would want her body again someday soon.

Just then, Hassan woke up. He sat up, as did Nadya. 'Huzoor, what is the problem? What can I do to give you more sleep?'

Hassan looked at her. The lovely naked body was nothing to him. He had woken up aware that the problem he had had no solution. He had to talk again to this woman who could take on so many names. He found the tunic, Nadya's discarded tunic, on the divan and put it back on her. Nadya buttoned up.

'I need to talk to Nadeer.'

Nadya knew what she had to do. She put on all the garments she had shed. Hassan was oblivious to her dressing up. He was troubled.

'How do I do it?' he asked.

Nadya knew at once what he meant. He was still thinking about the battle and how he had been outsmarted and now faced defeat.

'Huzoor, you know I have been in other places before. I can only tell you what I have seen there. That may help. Once I was in another kingdom. My king there was a very nice and kind person. He was about to fight a battle that he knew he would win. His brother was with him, with a large army. His enemy had a much smaller army. Then, on the day of the battle, his brother turned away and did not fight. My king lost the battle and lost his life. I had to be with his brother then. I found out that the enemy had promised his daughter in marriage to the brother. And thus he divided the brothers.'

'How does that matter to me?'

'Huzoor, you have to divide Abdul and the raja of Purana Zilla.'

'How do I do that?'

'If it is true what they say—that the firangi is greedy—you could bribe him to change sides and defect to yours.'

'But if he joins us, Abdul will attack him before he gets here.'

'Huzoor, Abdul need never find out.'

'What do you mean?'

'We give the firangi money to stay where he is. Let Abdul think he is a friend. When the battle starts, the firangi will begin to fire on Abdul's soldiers. His big gun will win the battle for us.'

Hassan was astonished. Here was this woman, brought before him as a slave for his pleasures. By some chance, he had never managed to enjoy her body. But she was solving the biggest problem he was facing.

'We need a lot of money.'

'Huzoor, Wazir-e- Alam can go to the banker in Ranipur, as he was saying. Command him to go tomorrow.'

Hassan drew Nadya close and caressed her. She knew he was still confused. He kissed her. It was just like his last kiss—deep and intimate.

'How can I reward you? Let me make you an officer in my army.'

Nadya knew better. She did not want to delude herself into thinking that she was different. She knew he was still haunted by that night. She drew him closer and offered him her breasts.

'Huzoor, my reward is your pleasure in me. Devour me. Take me. I am yours. You can kill me tonight if you like.'

She knew he was now untroubled. She bent down and took him in the mouth. He was excited. He shoved her away. She laughed. 'Don't be so cruel, Huzoor. Nacheez is hungry for your love.'

The word Nacheez was the trigger. Nadya knew the psychology of men. Hassan had to have his interrupted night back. He got the message. He drew her closer and slapped her. She laughed. 'I am all yours, Huzoor. Command me. Shall I dance?'

Hassan was impatient. He was on her and around her. She directed him where she knew he wanted to be. He sucked and bit and squeezed her breasts. She lay down and invited him to explore her further. He was all over her. She knew he was now in his element. He had to be made to feel masterly. She spread her legs.

'Huzoor, Nacheez awaits your kisses everywhere.'

That did the trick. Hassan went at her, eating her up, and she went on laughing and egging him on.

'Please be harsher, my Lord. Nacheez wants to be punished. She wants your dagger through her heart.'

Hassan could not wait any longer. He entered Nadya while she kept him excited. She bit his ears, whispered obscene messages. She was no longer his guard, nor his counsel. She was his slave, the body bought to give him whatever he wanted. His lust was now unstoppable. Any idea of abstinence was forgotten. It was a night for him to remember.

Later, Nadya looked at the man now asleep in her arms. She knew Hassan had exorcised the bad nightmare of Abdul's attack that night.

32. Sonal

Abdul and Quli were getting their army ready for yet another round of chasing Hassan's foraging troops. They also knew that the arrival of the guns was imminent. What they did not expect was two swift horses arriving so early in the day. Abdul could sense that they were from Vishalnagar. The tall Frenchman was easy to place as Pierre, the artillery master. But with him was a youth he could not recognize. Quli did, and he was astonished. 'Rajkumari, what a surprise. We did not know you were coming.'

Quli had known Sonal since she was a child, back when he lived around the palace of Devi Singh's father. He had seen her growing up from a baby into a little girl. But it had been five years since he had left the Purana Zilla, and, after that, a year of drifting around before he joined Abdul. What he now saw was a fine young woman, dressed as a young man with a sword and a gun. 'Sardar,' he said, addressing Abdul, 'this is Pierre, the master gunner for Raja Devi Singh, and this is Rajkumari Sonal Devi, the raja's sister.'

'You are both welcome. Tell us the news.'

Pierre knew he had to explain everything at once. 'The guns have been offloaded near Devgarh. The camels are bringing them along with some soldiers. We thought we had better ride ahead to bring Rajkumari to the camp. I will take your orders as to where to place the guns, and then I will ride back to escort them here. It will take two days to get them here. But then we will be ready for the big battle.'

Abdul now had to deal with the young woman who had landed in their midst. 'Rajkumari, what can I do for you?'

'Please do not worry about me. I have come to learn about guns and battles. I have had some training in the martial arts, but never witnessed a battle. I am willing to fight and learn about gunnery. I will be alright. But there is one thing I would like to do.'

'What is that?'

'Before the battle starts, I would like to visit my sister in Ranipur. You know them. The Rathore family.'

'That should be no problem at all. When do you want to do that?'

'The best thing would be to do it as soon as possible. If someone can show me the way, I am willing to go now. Then I can be back by the evening and get to know the way I have to live for the next few days fighting the battle.'

Abdul could command his mother to go away, but this young woman was a princess in her own right and he was not about to tell her what to do. He could see that Quli was the right person to escort her, as he knew her well. She would be better off with him. He also did not want to seem too eager to go to Anamika's house. 'Rajkumari, Quli Murshid, whom you know well, will escort you to Ranipur. It is not very far at all. We will have a tent ready for you when you come back.'

'Yes, I know Quli sahib. He will take good care of me.'

Quli could see that Abdul wanted to discuss things with Pierre. 'I will get my horse and come with you. It is not very far at all.'

Abdul turned to Pierre and said, 'Let us go into my tent. You can explain to me what you have brought with you and how we should best use it against Hassan.'

Pierre and Abdul withdrew into the tent. Quli was now ready for Sonal and joined up with her as they rode towards Ranipur.

'Do you remember how you used to scold us if we made noise?' Sonal asked.

'Rajkumari, all I was trying to do was make sure that your father was not woken up from his afternoon rest.'

'We all used to be afraid of you because you were always carrying your gun. For us young girls, you seemed so big and tall and forbidding.'

'As you can see now, I am just an ordinary soldier.'

'Diwanji thinks a lot of you. He was saying how he remembers your service for our kingdom.'

'I am happy that Diwanji remembers me.'

Quli was a shy person when it came to women, and this one was a very attractive woman. He had barely managed to speak to Anamika, but then she was a married woman and that made it easy. This woman was young and of a royal household. Quli did not quite know how to relate to her.

'Pierre has been teaching me about the big gun. I hope I can learn from you the art of fighting on horseback.'

'I will do whatever I can, Rajkumari.'

If he had his way, he would have told Sonal to stay out of the battle and stay at Anamika's place like Niloufer. But how was he to tell a princess that she was not wanted on the battlefield? It was going to be an extra task for him to make sure that she was safe.

33. Afghani Begum

Salamat Ali was waiting patiently outside the Afghani begum's rooms. Timur had brought him, but Timur knew his place. He would speak only if spoken to. Salamat Ali was the wazir's grandson. Since the wazir had no son, Salamat Ali was also going to be his successor. The boy was only fifteen and, as yet, had not even sprouted much of a moustache on his fair cheeks. His green eyes were his mother's and his strong build was like that of any Persian nobleman. He was dressed carefully, in a soft green achkan and a churidar pyjama. Qaramat was a rare Persian in the Sunni court of Ahmad and Hassan. There could be much enmity between the Afghans and the Persians, but Qaramat had managed to stay on everyone's right side.

Najma came to summon them to the presence of Fatima Begum. She brought them in and withdrew after the customary three bows. Fatima Begum was sitting on her divan as usual for her afternoon session. Timur was familiar with the setting. Today, however, he was merely bringing Salamat to the begum. The begum saw them come in and gestured to her attendants to leave them in peace. Salamat and Timur bowed.

'Nazar-e–Zenana, you can go,' the begum said.

Timur knew this was coming. He bowed again and left.

'Are you not Ayesha's son?' she asked Salamat.

'Yes Begum saheba, I am.'

'How is she?'

'By your grace, she is well. And sends you her salaams.'

'Come closer to me. Come behind this pardah. I need to look at you properly.'

Salamat Ali came and stood nervously in front of the beautiful, imperious woman. He was not quite sure what was expected of him.

'Not like that. Come and sit next to me so I can see you properly and check if you have inherited your mother's good looks.'

Salamat sat down on the edge of the divan. Fatima drew him closer to her. She took a puff on her hookah.

'Tell me, what do you do? Are you commanding an army?'

'Begum Saheba, I am learning how to do that. Abbajan has given me the charge of his thousand horses and I am to lead them in a battle when he needs me to.'

'Why is he not here?'

'Abbajan said to me when we were coming back from the camp that he had to go and deliver something precious to Huzoor. He asked me to look after the zenana and make sure everything was brought back safely.'

Fatima found the sweet boy too much to resist. She drew him even nearer to her and began caressing his head gently, flicking her fingers through his hair.

'So do you know what happened that evening?'

'Abbajan told me what happened. He said you may summon me and ask me. So I was to tell you everything just as he saw it.'

'I am very troubled about what happened. You see my neck and my back. They begin to hurt if I start worrying. Ever since that day, when I heard what had happened, my neck and back have hurt constantly. See if you can press them with your hands as you tell me, beta.'

Salamat Ali had heard about the Begum from his mother. Qaramat had hinted that she was a woman who could become troublesome. Salamat thought it best to comply with Fatima's request. He was no stranger to zenana manoeuvres, even at his young age. He began gently massaging Fatima's back.

'Abbajan says that Huzoor had told everyone to enjoy themselves that night, as they were marching the next day. Everyone was happy and Huzoor was having his feast and entertainment. Salma had managed to make him angry somehow, so she had been sent away. Niloufer begum had brought a woman from Abkhazia. She thought Huzoor may like her. But Abdul had planned an attack. So Abdul rushed in when this woman, Nadya, was entertaining Huzoor. There was a fight. Huzoor was hurt by Abdul.'

'No one told me my son was injured. Are you sure?'

'Yes, Begum saheba.'

Salamat had stopped massaging Fatima's back to make sure he did not get caught saying the wrong thing. She took his hands and put them back where she wanted and sidled up closer to him.

'Tell me the truth.'

'Begum saheba, I am willing to swear on the holy book. Abbajan said he had talked to the musicians who were sitting behind a curtain in the tent, and they saw everything. Huzoor was hurt in his right hand. Abdul was about to plunge his sword into Huzoor when Nadya plunged a dagger into Abdul's back. Niloufer then managed to stop Abdul and Huzoor was saved.'

'Oh, thank Allah miya that Hassan was saved. See, my heart is thumping so hard when I hear what you are telling me. Stay here for a bit longer and tell me more.'

Salamat Ali realized what he was being asked to do. It would not do to refuse or resist the grand woman. He knew that in his life he would need all sorts of experiences, and this one was sure to earn him some gratitude in a very high place. He placed his hand where he was being commanded to. Fatima took one deep puff from her hookah. The afternoon was going to be alright.

34. Niloufer and Anamika

They had finally worked out a routine. Everyday, after their bath, Anamika would dry Abhi and take him to their bedroom. Niloufer would be ready with her recipe, which was to be applied to the sensitive parts of Abhi's body that had been mangled in the fall from the horse. After much discussion, Abhi had insisted that it was he who would prefer to be blindfolded. He did not want Niloufer to be blindfolded lest she miss something and do damage. Niloufer knew that even though he was agreeable to her treatment, Abhi was a worried man. She had to be gentle and reassuring. She needed Anamika to be near her at first.

The daily ritual became a pleasure for Abhi. He was happy that something was being done to his most sensitive injuries, and that too without having to leave the house. Niloufer had indeed become like an elder sister, if not a mother. She was gentle and reassuring. She kept narrating stories of her life in the zenanas as she deftly applied her smooth and aromatic mixture. Anamika watched carefully, as she wanted to take over the task. She knew that Niloufer would soon go back to either Abdul or Hassan as the battle progressed.

The daily routine gave Abhi confidence. When they cuddled up at night, he became bolder in his exploration of Anamika's beautiful body. They both knew what the destination was. But they were also willing to let the journey take as long as it needed. There was much to enjoy in their life together. Their love was becoming deeper by the day. Even in the midst of an impending battle, somewhere in their vicinity, they were confident that they were safe.

After the bath and the application, Abhi would dress and sit at his galla. That was how the rest of his day was to be spent. He would be kept busy. The usual trade in cotton and textiles had to be carried on. The banking business also went on. Traders needed his help, as did the kings in the area. Rathore was a famous house. They discounted the bills of other bankers and sent their own bills to be discounted at distant centres. Abhi managed to send money to his parents via a well known banking contact of theirs in Kashi. He knew that his father would visit those houses and renew acquaintances.

Anamika was with Niloufer, learning a recipe for baklava, when she heard the now familiar clatter of horses' hooves. She went to the front door and opened it. She could not believe her eyes. There was Quli, of course, but with him was a familiar face, though dressed as a boy soldier. As Sonal got off her horse, Anamika rushed out and embraced her.

'Sonal, Rajkumari, what brings you here? Murshid Khan sahib, how did you fetch my little sister all the way from Vishalnagar?'

'Quli Murshid sahib is very kind. He only brought me here from their camp. I came along with the Frenchman Pierre and his big gun. We are joining Abdul Khan sahib's campaign, as you know. So I thought I wanted to see how the guns work and also how my big sister is doing. So here I am. How is my brother-in-law?'

'Come and meet him. He is in his galla. Murshid Khan sahib, come in. You don't have to be shy. This is as much your house as Sonal's.'

Anamika could see that Quli Murshid was feeling a little out of place in this hearty meeting of two women who had known each other for a long time. Thus far, he had not conveyed to Anamika that he had seen her as a young girl as well. She was now a married woman, and his reserved nature would not allow crossing certain boundaries of good behaviour. His usual place would be with Abhi in his galla. But he had to linger a while, as Sonal had rushed in.

Niloufer came out, as she also heard the voices. She greeted Quli. 'How are you, Quli sahib?'

'Begam sahiba, I am just Quli for you; not a sahib of any kind. I am well thanks be to Allah. Sardar Abdul Khan is also fine and looking forward to our battle.'

Quli knew that she would be more anxious about news of her son than about him.

'Come and see how nicely I am living here so you can tell Lalla all about it,' said Niloufer. She knew instinctively that she had to leave the two women and Abhi to carry on with their stories for each other. She also had to get Quli out of the way.

Abhi was surprised when Sonal came in and touched his feet. 'Rajkumari, what are you doing? I should get up to greet you.'

'How can you say that? You are my big sister's husband. I know my place is at your feet.'

Anamika was quick to join in the banter. 'She has come to join the battle. She is now big enough to fire the big gun. Or at least that is what she tells me.'

Sonal became serious. 'I told bhai sahib that I am now old enough to take interest in the way the kingdom is ruled. Here is a big battle that is important for Purana Zilla. I have been taught some martial arts, but no one thought that I wanted to do more. So I have come along with Pierre Drouon and his gun. I am learning a lot, as he explains everything to me like a good teacher.'

Abhi was astonished. 'Are you joining the battle then?'

'That is my idea. I am going to be in our tent along with Abdul Khan and Quli Murshid Khan. I will try to be helpful, not a nuisance. I want to learn how the gun is deployed and how we can fire it.'

'Are you sure? What if you get hurt?'

'If I was a man you would never worry like that, would you?'

Anamika had to interject. 'Even so, I do not wish to see you injured or worse. Can you not wait till the end and then learn about what happened?'

'No, I am a Rajput woman and sooner or later I may be married to a raja. He will appreciate it if I can tell him that I understand battles and guns.'

'I wish we had found the lucky man sooner. I doubt he would have allowed you to do this.'

'Well, in that case, he would not have been the right person for me, would he?'

Abhi was much amused. 'Anamika, you two are exactly alike. You don't listen to anyone when your mind is made up. Why should Rajkumari?'

Quli Murshid Khan was hovering at the door to the galla. 'Rajkumari, give me leave now. I will come and get you when you are ready to come back.'

'Murshid Khan sahib, you can't go just yet. I must give you something to eat. It is bad luck to let you go hungry from our doors,' said Anamika.

'Behenji, there is no need to take any trouble like that.'

'Now that you have called me behenji, there is no way I can let you go.'

Being close to women, let alone relating to them, was a strange experience for Quli Murshid. But when Abdul got involved with Ranipur and the Rathore family, he had to deal with Anamika. It was worse when Abdul got hurt and Quli had to help Anamika dress him. Even so, he managed to do whatever he had to do without having to speak to her directly. He had barely said a word to Anamika directly till now. Being with Sonal had further shaken his serenity, and here he was speaking to Anamika as a sister.

Anamika saw that this had been a big step for Quli. She decided to leave him alone so he could catch his breath. She knew he would be happy discussing accounts with Abhi—a simple man-to-man conversation to regain his composure. She dragged Sonal quickly into the kitchen. They had not really had a moment together. In the kitchen, she hugged Sonal closely for minutes, tears in her eyes. 'I am so happy to see you and so afraid at the same time. What are you doing here Raju?'

'I came to see my big sister. That is what I told bhai saheb. I also want to see something of the hard life these men live. I do not want to sit in the palace and wait till I hear the bad news that my brother or my husband is injured or dead. I need to understand why they do what they do, and how. So here I am being introduced to big battles and seeing my big sister.'

'Right now I see you troubling your escort. Quli sahib is usually so somber, but now you have come and he does not know what to do with himself. Let me put him at ease.'

Anamika opened a cupboard and began taking things out. Soon, she had filled a thali. There was a small metal lamp with a wick and oil, which she lit. There was some sindoor and some pieces of barfi. She went back into Abhi's galla. Quli and Abhi were engaged in some frantic whispering.

'Quli bhai, you are from this day my brother. Let me tie a rakhi on your wrist.'

Quli was blushing now. Anamika first swung the thali with the lit lamp around his head, doing an arti. Then she took out her rakhi and asked him to present his wrist. Sonal was watching all this. She took the thali from Anamika's hands while she tied the rakhi. Then she presented the thali back to Anamika. Anamika took a piece of barfi and gave it to Quli.

'You have to eat this. We believe that good occasions should be celebrated with a sweet dish. This is a big occasion for me. I have never had a brother. You are now my brother and my rakhi will protect you.'

Abhi was watching all this with amazement at what his wife was doing and amusement at Quli's blushes. He diverted attention from Quli. 'Why is no one giving me any barfi? And no one is tying any rakhi on me?'

Sonal saw the humour in what Abhi was saying. 'Here, bhai saheb. I will be your sister and tie a rakhi on your hand. And give you two pieces of barfi.'

It was time for Quli to extract himself from this emotional situation. 'Sethji, give me leave to go now. Sardar will need my help with the guns. I will come back in the evening to escort Rajkumari back.'

'Quli Murshid sahib, do not worry about coming back for Sonal. We will send Jibril along to escort her back.'

'I better come back. Sardar will not like it if Rajkumari had any difficulty in returning. I will come and fetch her myself at sunset.'

Anamika understood what had happened before Sonal or Abhi saw it. Quli was enthralled by Sonal's company and was not about to give up the privilege to anyone else. This was going to be interesting.

Anamika and Sonal saw Quli off. As soon as they had shut the door, Anamika hugged Sonal again and lifted her up and swung her around.

'What are you doing, didi?'

'I think you have a conquest on your hands.'

'No. please do not even think about it. I respect Quli sahib. He is a man of honour.'

'Of course he is. That is why he was blushing so hard when you were there with the barfi and I was tying the rakhi.'

'I hope he is a good brother to you. Nothing more.'

'We shall see.'

They went back into the galla. Abhi was tidying up his account books and laying them aside in a pile.

'Come, let us leave Abhi alone. Come into the kitchen'.

Abhi saw how happy Anamika was to have Sonal for company. 'I hope there will be some food cooked today while you are both talking your hearts away.'

'There is a lot of barfi if you get hungry. I have to talk to my little sister.'

'It is not just me, you know. Ammijan will be done with her prayers soon. Don't forget her.'

'I am going to introduce Sonal to Ammijan so she can teach her some secrets of life.'

Sonal was intrigued by this talk of Ammijan.

'Ammijan is Abdul Khan saheb's mother. She will be living with us for a few days while the battle goes on. Come, meet her,' said Anamika.

35. Afghani Begum

Fatima Begum woke up with a start. It was late. Salamat Ali had removed himself once he saw that the begum had succumbed to her opium hookah. He had acquitted himself well, had broken no rules of decorum and had given the begum no reason to be displeased with his performance.

But now she was in a panic. She was sweating profusely. It was probably a nightmare, but even so, her memory was clear as to what the handsome boy had told her. Through the haze of opium and a faulty memory, she recalled that Hassan had had a duel with Abdul and nearly lost his life. All the stories she had been told were false. They all made Hassan look better than he had been. Niloufer and that woman Nadya had indeed saved her son's life. How foolish she had been to suspect them—and now she had no idea where Niloufer was. At least Nadya was with Hassan, as far as she knew. But then, would she be able to save Hassan if Abdul attacked again?

She had been a foolish, self-indulgent mother. Her son was in danger of being killed, and she had done nothing to prevent this horrible event from occurring. She had to do something about Hassan's life. But what?

She summoned her servants. Two of her maids came in with their fans. They knew not to disturb her if she had a visitor. They would not know if the begum was ready for their services until she summoned them. They began to fan her.

'Bring me some water. I am hungry. Get some things to eat.'

Ji Begum saheba.

Fatima needed time and a clear head to think about what she could do. She had to help her son. He had been brought up in luxury. He had never done any hard work, and she had prevented Ahmad from being too strict with the boy. So he had seen little of the hardship of battles and long campaigns. He knew he was going to succeed to the throne. But they had thought that Ahmad would have a lot of time to train his heir. His sudden death had catapulted Hassan onto the throne long before he was ready. Then, of course, he thought he had to show he was capable of being a king in his own right. This is why he had embarked on the campaign. Abdul had all the advantages of his humble birth and had trained hard for many years. Hassan was no match for Abdul. She had to save her son. But how?

She lay back. The maids had come back and placed salvers of food and a pitcher of water, along with a silver cup, for her. She had to think this one out for herself. She could not ask Timur about this, and Qaramat was not around to be consulted. A long and deep drink of cold water felt good. She had been thirsty. She began to eat the kebabs. This was her first meal in twelve hours, and she began to feel better. The palpitations of her heart eased and she could now think clearly about what she had to do.

She had to stop the battle from taking place. Once the fighting began, Hassan stood no chance against Abdul. That much she had no doubt about. Much as she loved her boy, she knew he was not a soldier like his father. She picked up her beads and began to turn them over in her hands, praying silently at the same time. Then the answer came to her. She called out for Najma. Najma was her special maid—not one for fetching water or food or for fanning her. She could entrust Najma with delicate tasks.

Najma came and bowed thrice. 'Begum saheba has called me. What can your slave do for you?'

'Find Nazar-e Zenana. I want to ask him something.'

Night or day, Timur had to be available for Fatima whenever she wished. Najma knew what was coming. She was surprised, as Timur usually came in the afternoons, not at night. She could not be sure that he would be in his rooms and not with some distressed member of the zenana.

'Ji Begum saheba.'

Najma knew her man. As she had suspected, he was not in his chambers but with Laila, who had been removed from her perch as Hassan's number one favourite woman. She had never forgiven Salma for this. It had to be her fault, because she had angered Hassan and he had then gone for the new woman Niloufer had brought in. This would never have happened if Salma had been good at pleasing Hassan.

Timur was trying his usual devices to cheer up Laila. Her excuse was that she wanted to become a more seductive singer to capture Hassan's attention again. Timur could still teach her a thing or two about the way songs are sung. In between, there was no telling how many times their lips met or his hands were allowed to wander all over her.

But Laila was not like the Afghani begum. Her needs were different and Timur could only go as far as rousing her, not providing repose. He was not much put out when he heard someone stop outside the curtains and call his name. He signalled to Laila to keep quiet and tiptoed out.

'Najma, what is it now?'

'Begum Saheba has requested your presence immediately.'

Laila heard that, as Najma had made quite sure that whoever was with Timur should understand that his services were being taken elsewhere. Timur did not have to duck back and bid farewell to Laila. He knew she would understand. This was always the furtive way in which the women could avail themselves of Timur's charms.

He tidied himself up as he hurried after Najma. He would have liked to freshen himself up with attar and change his kurta. But Najma's tone had made it clear that there was no time for such indulgences.

'Begum Saheba, your slave is here. Give me your command,' he said hurriedly after entering the begum's presence and bowing thrice.

'Where have you been all this time? Who was it tonight?'

'How can you say that, Begum Saheba. I am always ready to be at your call. Tell me, what can I do for you?'

'Do you know where Pir Muzzarfarshah Saheb Jalalabadi is these days?'

'In winter months he is usually at Sangampur, on the banks of the Sreni near its confluence with the Yamuna. Would you like me to call him to your presence?'

'How can you say such things? I will go to the Pir saheb myself, with bare feet if necessary. Make preparations for me to visit him.'

'When would Begum Saheba like to travel?'

'As early as possible—tomorrow morning. Make all the arrangements so I can get there as soon as possible. There is no time to be lost.'

Timur was astonished. What had propelled Begum saheba to rise from her opium laden pleasures and rush to the holy man? But he knew his night was now lost. He would have to run around organizing for the begum and her usual party of twenty-five women and men, along with soldiers and palanquin bearers and cooks. There was not much time.

'*Ji Begum saheba.* Your wish is my command.'

Fatima Begum had decided that only the Pir could resolve her doubts. Would her boy win or Abdul? Would the Pir help to stop the battle? Was there a way to stop the many deaths and the damage that would no doubt happen? All these years, Fatima had grown up in families where fighting was a way of life. That was what men did and that was how they won wealth and women. But, in a way, all that had been remote for her. Men went off to war leaving women in their homes and zenanas, and came back flush with victory. Or the men who had defeated and killed these other men became the women's new masters, and life resumed with new kings enjoying the women of the zenana. She was of noble birth, so she may have been spared had Ahmad ever lost out to another king. But when it came to her son, she was no longer sure. Having heard about the encounter between Hassan and Abdul in detail, she began to visualize the bloody ways in which her son could die. It would be all her fault if that happened and she could not prevent it. Niloufer had done her another big favour now by saving her son. The least she could do was not let that favour be in vain.

36. Hassan

The long sweet night of lovemaking was over. Hassan had to now think of the battle ahead. The woman lying next to him had given him a great gift by uncovering the Gulabchand's plans to encircle him from the opposite side. She had also given him an idea about dividing his enemies. Hassan was not quite sure how it would work, but he knew there was no other way. The battle now had to be thought through again. Hassan had not spent much time fighting. He had however acquired a habit of reading and he had read about many battles of the past. He had read the memoirs of the great Mughal king, Babur, and accounts of Akbar and Jahangir penned by their courtiers. He had thought a lot of what he would do when he would have to fight. Here was his first big opportunity. Abdul had surprised him in his camp on the other side of Sreni that night. This time around, he would not be surprised. He had a fight to win.

Nadya felt Hassan waking up and sat up. He looked at her and kissed her once more. This was a kiss saying hello and signalling the change of persona she would have to go through. She smiled and gathered her clothes and left to change in her own little tent which was next to Hassan's big one. Hassan clapped his hands, summoning his servants.

They came with a bowl of water and a fresh set of clothes which they had kept aside. He began to wash and clean himself. He was not one for praying, but he was aware that this was the time of the morning namaz and he had to be clean before God. He bowed towards Mecca and recited the few verses of the Holy Quran he could remember, and that somehow made him feel better.

There was no time to be lost. He clapped his hands again. His faithful bodyguard was present, now dressed in a soldier's outfit. Nadya knew that she would be needed at Hassan's side from what had transpired the night before. She was ready. She came and bowed thrice.

'Huzoor, you called.'

'Tell Wazir-e-Alam we want to see him.'

Nadya bowed again.

'As Huzoor commands'.

While she was gone Hassan called for some breakfast. Baskets of fruit were brought along with some hot food. Soon Qaramat Ali appeared as Hassan was eating some dates. Nadya placed herself in her usual spot behind Hassan.

Qaramat Ali bowed thrice to Hassan. He seemed to be in a thoughtful mood.

'Wazir-e-Alam, what is your advice?'

'Huzoor, there are risks in fighting on two fronts. If we can make a quick dash for it, it is best to fight Abdul first. We do not know when Devi Singh's troops will cross the river and come to his aid. Even so, we can risk a quick strike now. But…'

'Why are you hesitating, Wazir-e-Alam?'

'Huzoor, I walked around our camp after my prayers last night. I find the soldiers are unhappy. They have not been paid and there are difficulties in getting food for them and their horses.'

'Why have I not been told about this? Call Zail Singh.'

Nadya promptly left to find the man.

'How widespread is the dissatisfaction?' Hassan asked Qaramat Ali.

'Huzoor, your soldiers are loyal to you. They will fight if you command them. But they will be happier if they know that we can provide them with better food and that they will be paid their daily dues.'

Zail Singh came in and bowed to Hassan. 'Huzoor, have you summoned me?'

'Zail Singh, Wazir-e-Alam says there is a lot of grumbling among our soldiers. Is that right?'

'Huzoor, I cannot deny that there is some dissatisfaction. But we can still command our troops to fight.'

'But will they be happy fighting?'

'Huzoor, they will fight better if we can find them food and some money to make them feel better. I hear that the camel drivers and elephant mahouts are keen that their animals get proper feed before battle.'

'But why did you not tell me before that my soldiers are unhappy?'

'Huzoor, we had been expecting our raids to get us some food and money, but our soldiers have come back empty handed because of Abdul's attacks… If we march today we may just manage, but not otherwise.'

'Wazir-e-Alam, what is your advice?'

'Huzoor, I have been thinking that the best plan is to get some more money. I can send a message to Muzaffarabad but it will take three days for the money to reach us. Or I could go to Ranipur and ask the Rathore bankers to lend us money against a surety. I await your decision.'

'How soon can you come back with the money?'

'If I start now, I can return late tonight riding on horseback.'

'How many men will you need to guard you?'

'Huzoor, if there are soldiers with me it will attract Abdul's hostility. I say let me go alone and I will negotiate my way back.'

'But how much can you bring back?'

'Enough, Huzoor, to get the battle going.'

'Zail Singh, what do you say?'

'Huzoor, if Wazir-e-Alam can get us some money that will help us. The soldiers need to feel that their stomachs can be quickly filled, and that there is even more waiting for them in the future. The food-sellers are always willing to bring their goods if they see ready money.'

'Wazir-e-Alam, you can go and may Allah help you in your mission. Bring back as much money as you can, safely. But how do we divide the enemy?' asked Hassan

'Huzoor, I would suggest that we tell Gulabchand we are not his enemies. We do not covet Purana Zilla.'

'Then?'

'I could negotiate a truce with him so he stays away while you fight Abdul.'

'But he has sent his big gun already with the firangi. Why would he abandon Abdul?'

'He just wants to save his kingdom from attack. Once he knows we are not attacking him, he will recall the firangi.'

'Wazir-e-Azam, I don't know if that will work. Do we have the time to negotiate a truce with him and then for him to withdraw the firangi? Abdul can offer him money to stay. If he defeats us, he will be the shah and he will have plenty of money.'

Qaramat was surprised. He had never credited Hassan with any ability to think about battles. Who was advising him?

'Wazir-e-Alam, I have a better suggestion. Why don't we bribe the firangi to come over to our side?' asked Hassan.

'Huzoor, if he began to move his big gun away from Abdul, surely he will be stopped or killed.'

'There is no need for him to come over. He can stay where he is. Just when the battle starts, Abdul will find out the big gun behind him is firing at his army.'

Qaramat knew this could not be Hassan's idea. It did not take him long to realize that in Nadeer they had found more than a beautiful body. Yesterday, she had found out about the big gun landing. Today, Hassan was telling him something that he should have thought of himself. Qaramat realized that now there was someone close to Hassan who may outwit Qaramat himself one of these days. That would be the end of his position. He had to think about this challenge.

'Huzoor, I salute you once more. You have made your father proud today. He would have thought of something like this. I am ready to implement Huzoor's idea. What are my orders?'

'We need to get a lot of money from the Rathore bankers and send a message to the firangi that we can make him very rich indeed.'

'Huzoor, if you allow me, I can take Nadeer with me. Then there will be just two of us, but we can get as much money as needed.'

Nadya was surprised by Qaramat's request. Hassan was also intrigued. He could see that Qaramat did not want a big party of soldiers. But taking just Nadya along was risky as well. Abdul could not have forgotten what Nadya did to him. But Hassan could see that Qaramat had devised some devious plan. He could always rely on his wazir to do the clever thing.

'Permission granted. But return by nightfall. Take some food with you, as you will need it.'

Saying this, Hassan waved his hands at the spread in front of him. He clapped his hands and servants came in. He gestured at them to pack some stuff for the two travellers. Qaramat was struck by his thoughtfulness.

'Huzoor's wish is my command.'

Qaramat signalled to Nadya and the two of them went out. Zail

Singh was intrigued; he knew that the young Nadeer was more than just a soldier. But Zail Singh himself was just a simple soldier and did not wish to delve into the mysteries of the king's favourite.

'Zail Singh, send a message to the camel drivers and the elephant mahouts that they will be looked after. Let them buy the food with this purse I am sending them.' Saying this, Hassan took out a bag of coins from underneath his divan. He had anticipated some such demand and had been ready with what he could spare. Zail Singh was grateful.

'Huzoor is very kind. Your army will appreciate Huzoor's kindness.'

'And we will walk among the soldiers this morning and talk to them. We want to tell them that we know their hardships and we will get them better food and more money. Come, let us go.'

37. Vishalnagar

*D*evi Singh was anxious for Gulabchand to arrive. He had been sitting on his jhoola since morning. He had been thinking about his sister, out there with Pierre Drouon and the big guns. He was sure the battle would not be long delayed. They had to make a move as soon as they could. What had Gulabchand planned?

When Gulabchand came in, he was his usual calm self, he saluted his king. He could anticipate what was on the king's mind.

'Rajasaheb, we have to start moving our soldiers across the river. I have heard from our spies that Hassan has given orders for his guns and elephants to be moved back to where his camp is. This means he has found out that our guns have reached there. We have to back up Abdul Khan with our forces.'

'I am glad you think that. I am worried about Sonal Devi. She is impetuous and before she gets into any sort of adventure I need to be there. This is going to be a decisive battle.'

'So it will be. But on previous occasions we did not have an ally on the other side of the river. Now we do, so Hassan Shah faces two armies, not one.'

'How are you moving us?'

'Rajasaheb, the barges and boats are back. The barges will make a bridge across the river. We will move our horses and smaller guns with their help. That way, we can move the army swiftly. Some troops will ford the river down stream.'

'Where do you think he will take up his position?'

'I expect he will come to our side of the border rather than fight on his territory. That way, we suffer collateral damage from the battle and he can withdraw to his territory if he is losing.'

'Can we get across the river quickly enough to stop his guns from reaching him?'

'How do you propose to do that?'

'We have horses and camels with mounted guns. If we take them across quickly, we can intercept them before they reach Hassan Shah's camp. That way, Abdul's small army and our guns can match Hassan

Shah's ten thousand men.'

'Samsher Singh is ready with the troops and we can move as soon as you give your command.'

'Come with me. We will seek our blessings from Goddess Kali before we fight.'

38. A Banker's Duty

Before the dark evening could descend, Quli Murshid Kahn was back at Ranipur. They had anticipated this, and Sonal was all set to take leave of Abhi and Anamika. Knowing how embarrassed Quli would be with all the emotions on display, they had managed say their farewells to each other before Quli arrived. Anamika embraced Sonal one more time and told her to take care. Soon, they were off on their horses as Anamika carefully closed the doors.

Now they were on their own. Niloufer was there, of course, but she had now become part of the family. She was helpful in arranging the day for Anamika and when on their own, she gave her a lot of good advice. Anamika was learning much from Niloufer, mostly about ointments and mixtures that were good for health.

They were talking in Niloufer's room while Abhi was tallying up his books, when yet again they heard the sound of hooves. These horses had been rushing to Ranipur, as far as Anamika could tell from the noise they made. So she immediately went to the front room. Niloufer followed at a short distance, curious as to who it could be.

Anamika opened the door. There stood before her a dignified looking old man—clearly someone important. Along with him was a younger person, very fair in complexion and with lovely green eyes. Anamika wondered who they could be, when Niloufer spoke up.

'Wazir-e-Alam, welcome. How did you know I was here? Nadya, come hug me at once.'

Anamika was astonished. Niloufer seemed to know them, and yet again on this strange day, a boy soldier turned out to be a young woman. Niloufer hugged Nadya tight while Qaramat Ali stood by, waiting to greet her.

'Anamika, let me tell you who these people are. This is the Wazir-e-Alam of Ramgarh and this is my pretty pigeon, Nadya, who is the delight of many of us, but the favourite of Hassan Shah.'

'Niloufer Begama, I hope you are well.' Qaramat Ali spoke first. 'You must forgive us for coming to your house without announcing our arrival, but we are here on some business with Sethji. I had to come see him. I had guessed Niloufer Begama would end up here, and so I took the liberty of bringing her favourite person with me. This is Nadya.'

Nadya made her usual salaams to Anamika.

'I am not someone you need to salaam at all. If Niloufer Begama likes you, you are my friend as well,' said Anamika in response. 'Come and take some rest. Wazir-e-Alam, you wish to see my husband. Let me take you to him.'

Anamika took Qaramat Ali to the galla. Even at the end of a long day, Abhi was alert and had already realized that new visitors had come. Anamika was brief.

'Abhi, this is Wazir-e-Alam of Ramgarh. He has come for some business. I will bring some water and refreshments for Wazir sahib.'

'Please Sethaniji, do not give yourself any trouble. We are not staying for long.'

'My house should not be known as a place where we send guests away without refreshments. I will be back soon.'

Abhi realized the seriousness of the visit.

'Wazir-e-Alam, what brings you here? Is it something we can help you with?'

'Sethji, you know why I would come riding all the way across from our side. We need your help. We need to borrow money from you. I can give you a guarantee of repayment against our revenues.'

'There is no problem. I know the wealth of Ramgarh is sufficient to borrow any amount. How much would you like?'

Anamika came in at this point with a jug, a silver cup of water and a plate with some sweets. She left them and withdrew.

'Sethji, we need five lakhs immediately. I will sign a promise on behalf of the shah.'

'How would you like the money? In sacks of one lakh each or will you take a box back with all the money?'

Qaramat was impressed. He had not had dealings with this young man—only with his father. He had heard that Abdul had sent the father away and that the young man was paraplegic. So he had not expected such an alert and quick response to his request.

'Sethji, that is very kind of you. I hope you do not have any trouble with Abdul Khan.'

'Wazir-e-Alam, my business is to lend money to whoever I can trust to pay me back. I have to make my own judgments and then face the consequences.'

Qaramat had to think carefully. Five lakhs was a lot to carry through a lonely countryside for just the two of them. He had a solution.

'Sethji, I will take two bags of fifty thousand each. Give me the other four lakhs in a hundi note. The two bags we can take on our horses. I have a soldier with me who can share my burden.'

'As you wish, Wazir-e-Alam. If you like I can give you four hundi notes of a lakh each. Then you are free to spend them as you wish.'

Qaramat saw why this family was so trusted. The young man had thought ahead. He quickly agreed. 'That would be even better, Sethji.'

'Anamika, can you come here?'

Anamika heard Abhi's call and immediately went in.

'Wazir sahib needs two bags of fifty thousand filled in. I do not want Shivnarayan to be here. Can you get the money out?'

'Yes, of course.'

Qaramat was astonished at how swiftly Anamika took the keys from Abhi and knew which cupboard to open. She brought out two leather sacks first. Then she opened what seemed to be a secret door hidden in a wall. She began to take smaller bags of coins from the large cupboard. Qaramat could see that she knew how much there was in each bag, and Abhi was watching her very carefully. It did not take very long at all, and Anamika put the bags in the large sacks one by one. She did not close the bags—she knew what she had to do. She brought them to Qaramat and then left the room.

'Wazir-e-Alam, please make sure you have the right amount.'

Qaramat stood up and saw that each of the two sacks had five bags each. He did not need to count. He could feel the weight of each bag and judge for himself how much money each had. He had no doubt that the right amount had been given to him.

'Let me sign my promise, Sethji.'

Abhi opened his ledger and turned to a fresh page. He wrote something and gestured to Qaramat to sign there. Qaramat went up to where Abhi was sitting, took the qalam from him and signed his name in Persian with a flourish. He took a ring off his finger and put a stamp on the page where he had signed. Now Abhi had the wazir's signature stamped with the Ramgarh seal.

'Sethji, please give me leave to go. I have to get back to my shah's camp.'

Abhi called Anamika. 'They have to go. Could you give Wazir-e-Alam something for their journey back?'

'No, please do not take any more trouble. It is best if we hurry back, because the journey will be long and it is getting darker as we speak,' the Wazir interjected.

Anamika was aware that Qaramat wanted to avoid Abdul's army as much as possible. She brought him out into the main room, where Niloufer had been talking with Nadya.

'Niloufer Begama, I wish I could leave your pigeon with you in this friendly house, but she has to be the helper of this old man today. Hope you keep well, and we shall soon see you back with our Huzoor,' Qaramat said.

'Please give my salaams to Huzoor and tell him that as ever, I am his servant. He can call me whenever he likes and I will come. Take care of my pigeon,' She replied once again embraced Nadya and then bowed to Qaramat thrice. Anamika had not had a chance to speak to Nadya but she could see how affectionate Niloufer was with her. She had heard Niloufer narrate the incident when Abdul got hurt. She could not believe that this stunningly beautiful woman could also be such a brave wielder of the dagger.

'Nadya behen, I have failed in my hospitality and you are going away so soon. Do come back whenever you can. You will find Ammijan here and we will look after you better next time.'

Nadya did not know how to speak to this respectable housewife, as she had had little contact with such people. She bowed as usual, and followed Qaramat out.

As soon as they were gone, Abhi called Anamika.

'What is it, Abhi? Do you want to go back to your bed now?'

'It is not going to be an easy evening tonight. I expect we will be up till late.'

'Why?'

'It will be Abdul Khan next at our doors.'

'Why?'

'He will learn soon that Qaramat Ali was here and he will be angry with us, that we have given money to his enemy.'

'He knows us. We are his friends.'

'He may not think that now. You may have to deal with him.'

'Why?'

'Only you can deal with Yamaraja.'

Anamika went up to where Abhi was sitting and hugged him. She had tears in her eyes. Abhi held her tightly and kissed her. 'Do not worry. We have each other,' he said.

'I am never worried as long as you are with me. Let Yamaraja come. I will deal with him.'

Anamika busied herself in the kitchen. She had to talk to Niloufer to find out more about Nadya and Qaramat. They sat in the kitchen, talking and making preparations. At first, when she had arrived, Niloufer had not been sure that she should enter the kitchen, but Anamika had put her mind at rest. She had become like their surrogate mother. Ganga did not mind either, since Anamika did not. She took extra baths every day to clean herself, but beyond that, she was willing to have this beautiful Muslim woman come into the kitchen and teach her new recipes.

Abhi was right. It did not take long after Qaramat and Nadya had left for the sound of yet another horse's hooves to appear outside their door, followed by a furious pounding on the door.

'Sethji, open the door.'

Niloufer knew who it was and got up to open the door. Anamika came along with her. Abdul Khan stood there, glowering.

'Where is Sethji?'

'At his galla as always, Khan sahib.'

'Lalla, how are you? Are you alright?'

Abdul did not wish to speak to his mother. He knew full well that she was on Qaramat and Hassan's side. Had she been party to Abhi and Anamika betraying him? He did not know. He had to see to his business with Abhi first.

Abhi greeted Abdul with his usual politeness. 'Khan Saheb, welcome to our home. What can I do for you?'

'Was Qaramat Ali here?'

'Yes, Khan sahib. He left just half an hour ago. He did not stay very long.'

'Did he come to borrow money from you for Hassan's army?'

'He did come to borrow, but he did not tell me what for. I did not ask.'

'How much did he borrow?'

'I cannot tell you how much someone has borrowed from me. I have to keep that secret.'

'Why did you give him money? I thought you were my friend.'

'We are your friends. But lending money is my business. It was my father's business. It has been my family's business for generations.'

'But you know Hassan is my enemy. You know I am fighting him. You know I have to defeat him. Why then do you help my enemy?'

'Huzoor, try and understand. We are your friends. We pray you will win in your battle against Hassan and become the shah of Ramgarh. But Qaramat Ali and Hassan are your enemies. They are not my enemies, nor are they my friends. They are my clients. I have to treat all my clients alike.'

'No, no, no. You have betrayed me. You have helped my enemy to destroy me. You have joined my enemy and become his friend. I should treat you as my enemy.'

Abhi kept calm, but he could see Abdul itching to do something violent. He was getting redder in the face. Abhi had been smiling when Abdul came, but he had realized that to smile anymore would only anger Abdul. He had answered all of Abdul's questions with a serious but friendly demeanour. The more he stayed calm, the angrier Abdul got.

Abdul took his gun from his shoulder and began to load it. Anamika heard the sound—one she was familiar with from her childhood. She rushed in.

'Lalla, what are you doing?'

Abdul Khan was taken back. He had not expected Anamika to come in and use the private name they had decided upon. 'Stay out of my way. Your husband has betrayed me. He is my enemy. I cannot have him help my enemy.'

Anamika swiftly moved past him to shield Abhi. 'You will have to kill me before you kill Abhi.'

'I have no quarrel with you. He has become my enemy's friend and so he is my enemy.'

'He is not your enemy. He is your friend. I am his wife and I am your friend as well, as you know.'

'If he gives my enemy money to fight me, then what else do I call him? Get out of my way.'

'You cannot kill him. You promised me. We promised each other that you will protect Abhi for my sake. Remember we sealed our pact in blood, your blood and mine.'

Abhi was the least surprised among the two of them at what Anamika had said. He had guessed as much. He did not yet know what the pact could be, but he knew there was an intimate secret between Anamika and Abdul. Abdul, meanwhile, was flabbergasted. He had made his secret pact with this beautiful woman in order to have her. At that time, the promise to save her husband seemed innocuous, since Abdul did not see who would want to kill this harmless disabled man. But now he was in a rage. At the very moment he could see himself dominating Hassan, suddenly Hassan had acquired new sources of power. Abdul was about to be thwarted again.

'You have tricked me. You are clever people. You are a diwan's daughter and Sethji is a clever bania. I am a simple soldier. I only understand the law of the gun. If I see an enemy, I kill him before he kills me. You are helping Hassan to defeat me. So, just as I was about to win and get my rightful prize, you have let Hassan thwart me.'

'Lalla, let me explain. It is not like that. We are on your side. We want you to win your battles. I want you to be the shah, as I have told you before. We will all be happy when you win. You will win because you are a brave soldier and you are a better fighter than Hassan. Ammijan has told me how you nearly killed him that night in his tent. You will win. You have the big guns that Raja Devi Singh has sent to you. Quli sahib can come anytime and take money if you need it. We are here for you. I am here for you.'

Abhi marvelled at his wife. He discovered a new side of her every now and then and he knew she had hidden depths. Here was his young wife, just twenty years of age—how had she acquired such depths?

Abdul Khan was in despair. His anger was not assuaged, but he was frustrated. He had been diverted from his idea of killing Abhi. He knew that what Anamika was saying made sense, but what he felt was not what his head was saying. He sunk down on one of the seats near the galla.

Abhi was quick to see what had to be done.

'Anamika, please take Abdul sahib with you and give him something. He has been riding hard and fast and he needs some refreshment. We must feed him before he returns to his tent.'

'Lalla, come with me. Abhi we will call you when it is time to eat together.'

Abdul Khan followed the woman he loved; the woman who had enchanted him like a lamb. His anger had not dissolved, but it had been deflected. He felt thwarted, but in a way he could not comprehend. Had this been combat, he would know what he had to do. He could fight his way out of a fierce battle. But this was a complicated melee of emotions—anger, frustration and now, desire.

Anamika took him upstairs as always. Niloufer had realized from all the shouting that she had better keep out of the way of her son. Anamika sat Abdul down on the bed. She took his gun and put it aside. Then she took his face and buried it in her bosom. Abdul Khan sobbed with rage. Anamika held him tight. She could feel Abdul's mixed feelings of anger and despair. He was seeing himself losing the war to Hassan. He had to be perked up.

'Lalla, I am yours as always.'

She took his face in her hands, lifted it up, and kissed him full in the mouth. Soon, she could see the tide turning as he hungrily kissed her. She let him do as he pleased. She let her pallu drop; her blouse was tied at the side with strings and she began to undo them. He was roaming all over her body, kissing her on her lips and wherever he found bare skin—by her neck, around her waist. He began to undo her sari. She just let him to do whatever he felt like doing. She knew he had to feel that he was in command.

'Lalla, treat me like one of your zenana houris. Take me as you like.'

By now he could explore her nakedness. Anamika let him be as frenzied as he felt. She helped him along as she loosened his belt and felt his trousers drop. He grasped her hands and let her feel his hard self. Anamika egged him on. 'Command me, my King. How can Saki please you?'

Abdul looked at the woman who was offering herself to him. She was a vision of beauty and sensuousness. She had lust in her eyes. He felt a wrench in his heart. His anger disappeared. He held her close for a long time. Now he was no longer kissing her nor clawing at her. Anamika could see that something had gone wrong. She became anxious.

'Lalla, what is the matter? Do I not please you any more?'

'I have to win. I have to become a king.'

'Of course. But you know I am here for you whether you are king or not. Saki is always here for her Lalla.'

'You belong to him. I know why you love him so much.'

'Are you still angry with him and me?'

'No, Saki. I am not angry any longer. I understand my position. I am powerless to do anything till I prove my strength with my gun. I have to win. I have to become king before I can possess anyone.'

'Why do you say that? You know you have me to do what you want with.'

'Yes, but I know that you will only love him. Ours was a pact, and you fulfilled it.'

'So did you, Lalla.'

'But I see that his power does not depend on his physical strength. He has power because he has ways of conjuring up money from nowhere.'

'But you can have as much money as you like. You know he will give it to you.'

'But then he has you. You are only mine because you love him.'

'Is that such a bad thing?'

'No. But I must know my strengths. I have to go and start preparing for the battle.'

'Hold me and tell me you are not angry with me.'

'No, Saki. I am not angry with you. I have to do what will give me the right to be angry. I have to win and become king before I am truly powerful.'

'Come back whenever you want. I am here whether you are king or not.'

'I know. I will never forget our first meeting here. It has given me the strength to keep going. But now I want to win. Then I will have something that I can truly call my own.'

Anamika held Abdul for what seemed like a long time. She understood that they were now breaking up. Abdul had come angry at Abhi, but ended up angry at himself for not being king. She knew she had calmed him down, but only as far as Abhi was concerned.

'Let me give you something to eat before you go.'

Anamika swiftly dressed herself, took Abdul by his hand and went down the stairs noisily.

'Abhi, I will bring the thali for you and Abdul sahib in a few minutes. You can talk business.'

Abdul went sheepishly into Abhi's galla. Abhi was as calm as he always was.

'Come, Khan sahib. Tell me about your battle plans.'

★ ★ ★

That night, as she snuggled up to him, Anamika was surprised by how passionate Abhi was. He had been calm while Abdul was pointing his gun at him. But the sense of danger lingered even when Abdul had calmed down and talked in a friendly way. Abdul had eaten with the family and then taken his leave in the most pleasant fashion. It was when they were finally in bed together that Abhi realized what he had been through. He began kissing Anamika passionately. She was thrilled at his ardour. Something new was happening in their lives. Abhi was eager for her body, sucking and even biting with unprecedented ferocity. Anamika rubbed her thighs against his and began exploring him with her arms. He held her close to him and wrapped his legs around her. This had also never happened before. Anamika adjusted herself so he could ride her. As she touched him all over, she suddenly realized what it was. For the first time ever in their married life, Abhi was hard. She sobbed and grasped him in her hands. She laughed and cried and said, 'Please Abhi, come closer, come to me.' She slipped herself under him and gently helped him enter her. It was a miracle. Niloufer's ointments had smoothed the passage of blood, but his anxiety at what Abdul was doing and indeed his anger had made his blood run faster in his veins.

He was not long, but it felt like they were inside each other for ever. Anamika was sobbing and laughing and kissing Abhi all over. He was also happy clawing, biting and kissing. She kept him inside her, holding him tight. He was spent, but still it felt good to have him inside her. He was happy beyond belief. He had suddenly been able to do what he had given up hope of ever doing.

They stayed intertwined for a long time, mouths over each other's sensitive parts, touching, stroking and gently hitting each other. Anamika was laughing and crying. Abhi was happy and held her tight, possessively. It was as if he had finally asserted his rights. She had never really questioned this dominion over her. Now she knew she was right to pray and hope and have faith in Niloufer.

Halfway into the night, Abhi woke up and asked Anamika, 'What happened to Yamaraja?'

'He won't come back. I have got my Satyavan back.'

'But you have to do one more thing, my queen.'

'What is that?'

'Prove the astrologers right.'

'A few more nights like this, my lord, and I will fulfil all your wishes.'

39. The Wazir's Gamble

Their way back was swift and silent. Qaramat Ali and Nadya knew that their first priority was to get out of Abdul's reach. The horses felt the burden of the long trip. But they were hardy creatures and sensed that they had to gallop.

It was sometime before Qaramat spoke.

'Maybe we are now safely out of Abdul Khan's reach.'

'How could he have found out that we were there?' asked Nadya.

'When we arrived, there were two soldiers guarding the house. When we left, there was only one. So I reckon one went to tell Abdul of our visit.'

Nadya was again astonished by Qaramat's sharp observation skills.

'What would have happened had we been caught in the house?'

'I had thought about that. I guessed that Sethji would protect us from anything violent. But I must confess, I had a plan if Abdul Khan had threatened something worse.'

'What was that?'

'I had brought you along just in case I had to give him some ransom to be able to get the money back to Huzoor.'

'Would you have given me away to him?'

'Only as a token of our sincerity. When the war was over, whoever won, you would be returned to Huzoor.'

'But he must remember what I did to him. Why would he not kill me in revenge?'

Nadya was trying to be as cool as she could. Underneath, she was angry that she had become a pawn in the royal battle.

'He would not kill you. He would want you in his zenana. He wants everything Huzoor has and that includes you.'

Nadya had been through a lot in her life. She had been handed from slave owner to slave owner. She had been in khanates and kingdoms and in moving caravans, beholden to whichever male was the top dog. She was used to being used. But this revelation shocked her. She had become fond of Qaramat and thought of him as her protector, just as he was for Niloufer. Nadya had also, for the first time in her life, developed an attachment. Hassan had been rough with her at first, but she had realized that he was the first person who saw her as more than a mere body. He had asked her to do things for her and had appointed her as his daytime guard. She had been sent to scout out Pierre and his guns. He had been impressed by what she had done and in a rare gesture that she had never before experienced, he had rewarded her by giving her that bath. And then had come the time of restoring his confidence using every trick she knew.

Yet in the intrigues of the State, she remained a pawn. She knew that Hassan was not as good a fighter as Abdul was. Perhaps Qaramat thought so as well. If Abdul were to become king, Qaramat would still be wazir. His loyalty was not to a person but to the kingdom. Nadya was then bound to become Abdul's plaything, one of many from Hassan's harem which would pass on to Abdul. Nadya wished she could escape that prospect if it were ever to come to pass. She wanted to be with Hassan even if he lost. But then, chances were that Hassan would be killed by Abdul. After all, that was what nearly happened on her first night with Hassan.

Qaramat knew that the impact of his words would be harsh for Nadya. But he had his own priorities. He had to preserve the kingdom against any conquest by Devi Singh. If Abdul won, Qaramat wanted him to secure Ahmad Shah's kingdom for himself and not become a vassal of Devi Singh. Everything else—and indeed, everyone else—was but an instrument of his policy. He was fond of Nadya, but he could not be sentimental. She was good for Hassan, but that was that. If Hassan was to be killed, Nadya had to be pushed on.

By the time they got back, it was quite late. Soldiers came out to take care of the tired horses. Qaramat asked them to unload the leather sacks and take them to his tent. He gestured to Nadya to come with him. They went into Qaramat's tent. Nadya was intrigued as to what the old wazir wanted with her. He opened a leather sack and took out one of the smaller bags, which he handed to her. He knew that she would go back to Hassan's tent.

'Tell Huzoor his mind can be at rest about the money. Show him this bag.'

Nadya made parting salaam to Qaramat. 'Wazir-e-Alam, it shall be done as you say.'

Nadya knew that Hassan would be worried about them. When she entered his tent, she was surprised to see that he was sitting up on his divan reading something by the faint light of candles. There was a bath and towels, but no water as yet. Nadya was intrigued. She salaamed him thrice. He bounded down and hugged her close.

'Huzoor, what are you doing?'

'I was waiting up till you came back. I wanted to be quite sure that Qaramat had not traded you for his safety.'

Nadya was again astonished. These men seemed to reside in a different world, a man's world, in which her fate was better known than what she knew herself. Hassan was concerned, and yet he seemed to have no control over what Qaramat may decide.

'Huzoor, Wazir-e-Alam has asked me to present this small bag to you so you know that the money is here.'

'The money can wait. It is only going out again to the firangi. Let me take care of my Nadeer.'

Saying that, Hassan clapped his hands. Servants rushed in. Hassan ordered them to get hot and cold water. Nadya was astounded. He had really been worried for her. Tired as she was, she felt elated. After all her doubts, she was still dear to Hassan. But even so, she could have been dead by now or in Abdul's harem. How was she to understand men? After all the men who had used her, she had still a lot to learn.

The bath was filled soon. Hassan said, 'Where is my Nacheez?'

Nadya took the hint. In fact, she was relieved to get rid of her soldier outfit. There she stood before Hassan as she had that first night, with just her cross flashing in the dim light. He picked her up yet again. She was exhausted and worried. But she played along. She was limp and willing in his arms.

Once again, he put her in the bath. Nadya squeaked at the touch of the hot water but soon sank in. This time, Hassan joined her. They had to squeeze in together tightly. He began to rub her back and neck. It felt good. She was not going to resist. This was delicious, whatever the intrigues in the big world of men. Nadya wanted to savour the moment, and leave tomorrow to take care of itself.

Soon, the rubbing and the touching became mutual. From a bath to refresh the tired bones, it became a silent dialogue of two young bodies. Nadya enjoyed the way Hassan pleasured her, and she began to reciprocate. The water kept sloshing out of the bath as they laughed and kissed and twined themselves around each other.

Eventually, Hassan got out. He helped Nadya out and wrapped her in a large thick towel. He began drying her vigorously and she squealed again. Then, he picked her up and placed her on the divan. He wrapped a towel around himself and stood in front of her.

'What does my princess Scheherzad wish? Her slave is ready.'

Nadya was surprised once again. This was a new game. She had been the slave to his desires. Now he was making her a princess. But of course, Nadya knew that Scheherzad was the princess who had to tell a thousand tales to save her life. She had to play along.

Nadya also realized that this was probably their last night together. She had to show Hassan what she could do. She threw off her towels and lay back. Spreading herself, she said, 'Where is my wine, slave?'

Hassan laughed. He bowed, and filled a silver cup with the wine from the Surahi, and offered it to Nadya.

'My princess, here is your wine. What more can your slave do for you?'

Nadya knew what to do. She threw the wine at Hassan. He laughed. She grabbed her breasts.

'Please us as we wish.'

Soon there was no stopping them. It was as if they both knew that such nights may not come again. Ahead lay the battle and an uncertain outcome. Tonight, they had each other's body to enjoy, and that they did. Hassan wanted Nadya to have a memorable night, and she knew that. She let him play as he liked with her, letting him dominate and make her do things she only pretended to resist. Then again, he let her ride astride him and command him as if he was her slave. They went through many of these games before they played them again and some more.

40. Muzaffarshan Jalalabadi

Fatima's retinue was small by her normal standards. She took Najma and Timur with her, and Salamat Ali to make quite sure she had someone young and energetic on her side. Salamat had never met the Pir before though he had heard a lot about him and was thrilled at the invitation. He knew that the Afghani begum would be difficult. He had also sensed that what he had told her had made her fearful for her son's life. She had also brought cook, her masseur and her servant-slaves along, just in case the stay stretched on longer than anticipated, but they were to stay behind while she met the Pir.

The horses, camels and palanquins finally made it to the part of the Sreni across from the temple, which Sangampur's main attraction. This was the confluence of the Sreni and the Yamuna, and the river ran very broad and deep here. But there were many boatmen who were eager to transport the royal party across. It was still early morning. Fatima intended to approach the Pir in her bare feet, without any horses or palanquins. She was carefully dressed in white and had her head covered as well as a veil across her mouth and nose. She was a simple supplicant before the Pir. That was the way she wanted to win his favour. So it was the small party of Fatima, Salamat Ali, Najma and Timur that crossed the river in the first boat, leaving the rest of the retinue to catch up with them as and when they managed to come across the river.

Fatima was getting very nervous as the boat approached the other bank. She held Salamat's hand very tightly in her own. Salamat was amused that he, at his young age was providing support to the dowager Queen. But being Qaramat Ali's grandson, he had been brought up to be discrete and observe everything with care. He could see that Sangampur was a confluence of faiths as much as of the rivers. There was the big Kali temple, of course. But there was also a mosque, away from the river bank, whose tall minarets could be seen from a distance. The town attracted believers of all sorts. The confluence of rivers made it holy and the Kali temple even more so. People came from vast distances by boat and bullock carts, and on foot, to fulfil their promises to Kali or perform namaaz at the mosque. Reaching the other bank, Salamat could see naked sadhus and others wearing nothing more than langotis, with ashes smeared over their bodies, long unkempt hair and garlands and necklaces of beads. There was a smell of charas in the air, as the holy men were all smoking it. He could see the begum perking up at the familiar aroma. But she had to be on her best behaviour today.

Timur seemed to be familiar with the layout of Sangampur. He had also found out the whereabouts of the Pir. They had to wind their way through narrow lanes and across puddles of water which seem to gather wherever people had established yet another small temple to worship at. Water seemed to be the universal solvent for all sins, as far as the Hindu pilgrims were concerned. Timur warned the party to be quiet as they neared the Pir's residence. But he need not have bothered. There was loud singing, with drums and cymbals being played. When they got there, an astonishing sight struck their eyes.

A crowd had gathered and formed a circle, in the middle of which was an old man with a grey and white beard and disheveled hair, dressed in a long thick robe, dancing away. He was oblivious to all around him as he whirled and swung his arms, chanting and singing. He had a beatific smile on his face, and, for all he cared, there was no one within miles of his presence. Muzaffarshah Jalalabadi was doing what he most liked. He was whirling around in a dance, communing with his God without a thought about the world.

The begum was in a hurry. She knew time was of the essence if she was to get the Pir to intervene in the battle about to commence between her son and Abdul. The battle ground was at least a day and a half away, if they rode their horses hard. But she also knew better than to disrupt the Pir's dance. She began to feel the enchantment all the others did as they watched him in his ecstasy. Many in the crowd felt they were as close to God as they would ever be just watching this holy man whirl around chanting poetry and singing songs.

After what seemed like ages, he stopped and fell on the ground in a heap. This was the end of his dance, as the many who came everyday to watch him knew. He danced when the spirit took him and once he began, the word would spread that the Pir was enjoying his ecstasy. They began to withdraw one by one to get on with the tasks of their daily lives and soon only the begum and her entourage were left. The Pir's acolytes made sure that the people left him in peace, and began to fan him so he would recover from his vigorous dance. This was not necessary, as he was perfectly fine, but they wanted to show their devotion. The begum's party had to wait patiently till he regained his consciousness and became his worldly self. That took its time, much to the begum's chagrin.

Once back in his wakefulness, the Pir noticed that he had visitors. He raised an enquiring eye. Fatima Begum fell down at his feet and made several salaams. The rest of her party followed suit. The Pir saw the gathering and knew what was coming.

'Huzoor auliya, please bless this unfortunate woman who has come to seek your help and guidance.' Fatima had rehearsed these sentences in her mind several times. Salamat Ali did his salaams, as did Timur and Najma. They did not say anything, as they knew that the Begum saheba wanted his exclusive attention.

'Fatima Begum, what brings you here? Are you worried about your son?'

'Huzoor, you know everything. Nothing is hidden from you. You can read a mother's mind like an open book. I have come to seek your help for my son. He has embarked on a battle. I am afraid for his life.'

'He is not a brave fighter like his father Ahmad Khan, is he?'

'No, Huzoor, you know all about him. Abdul, his half brother, will kill him unless you can stop this battle. You helped his father become the shah. You must help keep my son alive and let him enjoy the kingdom.'

'We do not decide anyone's fate. There are times when we can foresee a man's future, but not change it.'

'Huzoor, what do you see in my son's future? Will he be alright?'

'When I saw Ahmad Khan that day in the Diwan-e-Khas, I could see he would be a king some day. I did not see how his heirs would fare. I have not even seen this boy for many years now. Where is he?'

'Huzoor, he is in his war camp, a day and a half's ride from here. He is about to fight Abdul Khan and the king of Purana Zilla, Devi Singh. My son faces two armies and only you can go and stop them from fighting.'

'We do not see his future clearly now. We may not be able to prevent the battle. But let me see the boys face before I can tell what will happen to him. Bring him here.'

'Huzoor, that may be impossible. By the time we reach him, the battle may have already started.'

'What would you have me do then, Begum?'

'Huzoor, as a poor mother, I spread my arms before you and beseech you to come with us to where the battle will happen. You alone can stop the massacre that will surely follow if you don't come.'

'God decides who is just and who is unjust. He alone can decide who lives and who does not.'

'Huzoor, you are our god on this earth and you alone can help this poor mother, whose tears will wash your feet everyday of her life if you save her son.'

'I can come but I cannot say what God will do.'

'Huzoor, thousands of shukriyas and duas for taking pity on this poor mother.'

The astonished Salamat Ali realized that now he had to guide the royal party, along with the holy man, to where he alone knew Hassan was. He began to organize their expedition. Timur had to be instructed to arrange the horses, which would have crossed the river by now. Then Salamat had to arrange something for them to eat on the long journey. Salamat did not want to guess what the holy man might need. He simply asked the Pir's acolytes, and then instructed Timur on what to do. He also gave Timur a message to send to his grandfather by pigeon. Timur knew where to find such facilities. He was useful in that way.

By the early afternoon, the slim party of the Pir and the begum, along with Salamat Ali, left Sangampur for the battleground. Timur was relieved to be left behind to take Najma and the rest of them back to Muzaffarabad. At least tonight he would have time to provide solace to some distressed member of the zenana without the fear of a sudden summon from the begum.

41. Qaramat's Dilemma

Qaramat knew that it was not wise to visit the prince early in the morning. He took his time with his ablutions and his prayer. He spent more time than he had done lately reading the holy book. He knew it well, but each time he read it, he was surprised by its novelty.

Even so, he had to think of his present predicaments. He assessed that he had to neutralize Devi Singh directly or at least bribe Pierre away from the fighting. There was no way of knowing if Pierre would take the bait, but he had to try. The question was how to do it without getting caught in the act. He had to retain Abdul's trust and not lose Hassan's. There seemed to be no one to whom he could give the task of approaching Pierre.

Of course, Qaramat knew who he had to ask to do it. But he knew that Nadya had not been pleased to know that he had meant to use her as a possible ransom. There was a change in her attitude towards him. She had hardly said anything on the way back after that conversation.

But he knew that it was her idea that Hassan had taken up. Qaramat was beginning to revalue Nadya's abilities. As soon as this battle was over, whichever way it went, he would have to reward her specially. If Hassan was to survive the battle, it would be largely due to Nadya's discovery of Pierre moving his gun behind Abdul's lines. She had also been ready to be at his side when visiting the banker. It had to be her. But how would he persuade her?

It was late enough in the morning for Qaramat to go to Hassan.

42. The Battle 2

The first blows were struck by Devi Singh and his army. They had crossed the Sreni quickly and made straight for where they knew the artillery was located. As per the orders from Zail Singh, the camels and the elephants had begun their slow movements. The guns were heavy; even the smaller ones required strong animals to drag them across uneven ground. But the small army led by Selim Turki, the master gunner, had no clear orders except to report back to Hassan as soon as they could.

Devi Singh had his cavalry mounted with small guns, with the camels dragging some bigger guns. The camels would take their own time but the cavalry was fast. Before the enemy artillery could organize itself for an attack, the cavalry swooped down and began slashing the animals dead. There was a commotion in Hassan's small army. It was heavy with guns but short on soldiers. Faced with guns firing and swords flashing, the elephants ran amuck.

Selim Turki had been in confusing battles before. He had to quickly decide to retreat and reform his forces. He began giving orders for the guns to regroup away from the river and towards where he knew Hassan was located. Soldiers were sent out to tell Hassan of what had happened. Selim wanted to tie down Devi Singh's army at this end, even if he could not defeat it.

Once the guns began firing, the artillery regained its nerves. Having lost some guns and camels, this was the first retaliation they could make. Devi Singh realized that his intial advantage was now gone. He too had to fall back and regroup if he was to halt the enemy's march towards the bigger battle.

He moved his mounted camel soldiers with their swivel guns to confront the enemy's camels and elephants, bringing up the big guns. He had to save his cavalry now, because it would be massacred if it went full frontal in battle. He had to move the cavalry around and behind the enemy army. This was a territory he knew well, being part of his kingdom. He split his forces and let the crack cavalry get behind Selim Turki's formation. His guns could hold down the enemy guns and his cavalry could swing around to sow more confusion in their ranks.

43. The Battle 3

Qaramat Ali was in attendance at Hassan's tent as soon as he had finished his morning prayers. He expected Hassan to be in a good mood, with the money now safely in his hands. He had also expected Nadya to have added to Hassan's joy. She was good both for his pleasure and for keeping his fighting spirit up.

'Wazir-e- Alam, how much money did you get from the bankers?' Hassan asked.

'Huzoor, five lakhs as we had decided. We now have one lakh in coins to pay the soldiers as you wish. We have the rest in hundi notes to do as you wish.'

'What would that be?'

'Huzoor, I was thinking about our battle on two fronts. Our guns are still a day away and I am sure Devi Singh will attack them as soon as he can. He is nearer and has the advantage as he knows the terrain.'

'What will happen then?'

'I expect our artillery will be delayed in arriving here and perhaps, tied down at that end, unable to move.'

'Do you know or are you guessing?'

'Huzoor, I do know that Devi Singh was planning to cross the river in the very early hours of this morning. I do not yet know whether he did so and how our army reacted. I am expecting some messengers soon.'

'What do we do then?'

'We have two choices. One is to try and see if we can bribe the Frenchman to come to our side for the five lakhs we have. He is known to be greedy. We could send a message across that if he were to abandon Abdul now, we will look after him. The hundi for four lakhs is just a beginning. You could offer him a jagir as well.'

'What is the other choice?'

'We start moving our army rapidly and attack Abdul's army as soon as we can. We will need to split the army into two so that one section can get behind his army and take out the big gun with a surprise attack. The other section, which you would lead, can confront

Abdul in a battle.'

'Can we trust the firangi to do as he says? Will he not take the money and betray us to Abdul?'

'Huzoor, Abdul has nothing to give him as yet. The firangi is in Devi Singh's employ. We can tell him that we are not interested in fighting Devi Singh. We don't want to conquer Puarana Zilla. We just want to defeat Abdul.'

'But we need to tell Devi Singh that before we tell the firangi.'

'I can arrange that quickly if you give your command.'

'And who will we send to tell the firangi?'

'My answer to that question would be: the only soldier we can trust to do such a delicate task is Nadeer.'

Nadya had been listening to all this, standing behind Hassan as his guard in her manly garb with her sword and dagger at the ready. She had learnt not to say anything; indeed, she had mastered the art of impassive listening regardless of what she thought of the proceedings. She had begun to rethink her life since last night. It was clear to her that her future was no longer secure with Hassan and Qaramat.

'Nadeer, what do you say?'

'Huzoor, I am here to follow whatever command Huzoor gives me.'

'We know that. But what do you think of Wazir-e-Alam's advice? We trust you to tell us the honest truth as you have done before. You found out about the firangi and warned us about him. I have not forgotten that.'

'Huzoor is very kind. There is one problem which may cause some difficulty.'

'What is that?'

'Huzoor, Devi Singh's sister has gone along with the firangi to fight in this coming battle. As long as she is there, Devi Singh may not agree to let us fight Abdul alone. He will worry about his sister. The firangi has taken the responsibility of protecting her.'

Qaramat Ali was yet again surprised that Nadeer knew something he did not. This had not often happened to him before. But it was the second time Nadeer had done this.

'How do you know this?'

'Huzoor, last night when you were talking with Sethji, Niloufer

Begama told me about meeting Sonal, who is the raja's sister. Sonal had told her that she wanted to learn about artillery battles and the firangi had brought her along.'

'Wazir-e-Alam, what do you say now?'

Before Qaramat could answer, a breathless soldier was ushered in. He came in and bowed low thrice to Hassan, and saluted Qaramat as well. Qaramat asked, 'What news do you bring us?'

'Huzoor, the raja of Purana Zilla has attacked our forces. Khan Selim Turki sahib has sent me to give the news to you.'

'How bad is it?'

'Huzoor, I was sent away as soon as they attacked. We did not expect it and several camels were wounded and the elephants were running wild. The Khan sahib told me to report that he was engaged in battle, which may take some time.'

Hassan could see that his well-laid plans were coming unraveled.

'Wazir-e-Alam, what do we do now if the guns are stuck at the other end of the battlefield?'

'Huzoor, as I said a while ago, if we cannot turn the firangi away from Abdul we have to start quickly and mount an attack on Abdul's forces. One flank can go for the firangi and his guns and do to him what Devi Singh has done to us. You can mount a straight attack on Abdul and his troops. He has one-fifth of the numbers you have got.'

'But he has Devi Singh's cavalry, which will soon come and join him. We lose our advantage then, don't we?'

'Huzoor, as I said, we offer Devi Singh a truce. We tell him we will not cross into his territory and do not want to make him an enemy. We can then keep him from coming to join Abdul.'

'Who will do that?'

'If Huzoor wishes I can go myself and meet Devi Singh. That will give him confidence that it is your own wish.'

Hassan turned to Nadya.

'Nadeer, what do you say?'

'Huzoor, Wazir-e-Alam knows best what to do. But Huzoor has to start marching as soon as our soldiers can be organized by Zail Singh.'

'Wazir-e-Alam, do we give some money to our soldiers before marching out?'

'Huzoor, I would say you promise to reward them once the battle is over. There is no time now to organize a distribution. We need to get ready. The money is in my tent. I can have it brought to your tent's. It can be kept safe here. Nadeer can stay behind and guard the sacks.'

'What do you say, Nadeer?'

'Huzoor, I wanted to be at your side when you go out fighting. But I will do whatever Huzoor says.'

Nadya had imagined that she would be riding alongside Hassan during the battle on a horse, or at his back astride an elephant. She had thought yet again of coming between an assassin's sword and Hassan. But last night had changed her mind. She did not feel at ease among these men. She knew that Hassan was on a losing streak. He had been outsmarted by Devi Singh twice, once with Pierre coming with the big guns around the river and then Devi Singh's attack in the morning today. She did not know what would happen to her if Hassan was to lose the battle, and perhaps even his life. She had seen many masters, and one more would hardly matter. Yet, lately, she had seen that the masters were not that smart. She could think through these problems of strategy as well as they could. Maybe she was meant for better things. She had been impressed by the way Anamika had taken charge of giving the money to Qaramat, and the way she combined charm with ability. Nadya, for the first time in her life, thought she could do better.

'Wazir-e-Alam, go and tell Devi Singh we desire peace with him. We will not enter his territory. Tell Selim Turki that he is not to join the battle we are fighting. That will reassure Devi Singh. We shall start immediately for the battlefield. Nadeer will stay behind and look after our treasure. Call Zail Singh.'

This was Nadya's signal to step up and go in search of Zail Singh. Qaramat saluted Hassan and went back to his tent to organize the transfer of the leather sacks and the hundis, before he got on his horse and galloped off westwards to where he knew Devi Singh would be.

44. The Battle 4

This was the day Abdul had been waiting for. He had got the news that Devi Singh was to cross the river early in the morning. He had got up early to get his soldiers ready for the big gest battle of his life. Quli had been instructed already and was to be with Pierre's big gun, defending them against any sudden cavalry attacks. Abdul was to have the bulk of the soldiers with himself, confronting Hassan. He knew Hassan would come down for him with his large army. He had to make sure that Pierre's big gun was there to upset the horses on the enemy's side and give him an early advantage.

Quli was glad he had been assigned to look after Pierre and the big gun. That way, he could keep an eye on Sonal and ensure her safety. Now that the artillery barrage from Selim Turki was to be delayed, as far as they knew, he had confidence that Sonal would be unharmed. The new plan was to keep Padmini on the left flank of Abdul's army, which would be on the right side of Hassan's approaching army. Had the artillery from Selim Turki come, Pierre was to swing to the right flank. But now they knew it was unlikely.

Sonal was very excited that she was about to take part in her first battle. She had been learning about loading the big gun with shots and balls. She had even practiced lifting the heavy gunpowder balls just to show that if needed, she would fight like any other man. They had persuaded her to wear light armour at least, but her enthusiasm was worrying.

Pierre was very calm. He had already set up his position. He had instructed his marksmen and made sure that they had cleaned and polished all the guns. He was particularly careful of Padmini, his prized possession. There was to be no hitch in the operation. Artillery battles were fought at a different pace than cavalry wars. Each big shot took its time to load and then fire. Its impact could only be felt after some minutes, when the noise would let one know that it had landed, allowing them to gauge how much destruction it had caused. Then, it would take time to cool down the gun for the next shot. Pierre believed in setting things up and then sitting back, inspecting his soldiers as they did the work they were trained to do. Not for him any running around. He left that to the cavalry and the mounted camel gunnery.

His main task done, he sat down and pulled out his pipe, filled it with tobacco which he carried in a pouch and began smoking. This was his routine before a battle. He took out from his coat pocket a small book, *The Imitation of Christ* by Thomas à Kempis, and began to read it. He had read the book several times before, but even so, he liked reading it whenever he wanted to soothe his nerves. But he was not to have his peace. Sonal came and made a bow.

'I am here to fight, Pierre sahib. What should I do?'

'Rajkumari, make sure that you are well protected. We expect that Hassan will send his cavalry very soon to attack our position. As soon as we hear the hooves in the distance, we must load our first shots and be ready to fire. Do not wait till you see them coming. You have to judge the direction the noise is coming from and swivel the gun accordingly. Then fire. The gun will recoil so stay away after firing. It will also make a lot of noise. You will see many horses and soldiers killed or injured. You have to be strong-minded and not feel any pity. See how you like it. If you cannot face it, we can shift you behind the lines to a safer place.'

'I have come to see for myself what the men in my family go through. Why sometime they do not come back, and why we have so many widows among us. I need to be strong if I am going to be part of a family where the men fight battles as their principal task.'

'I wish you luck.'

Pierre resumed his reading, indicating that he wanted to be left in peace. But Sonal had other ideas.

'What are you reading?'

'It is a devotional book about Jesus Christ, whom we Christians worship.'

'Which language is it written in?'

'In Latin. The author, Thomas à Kempis, was a monk and he spent his life in a monastery copying the Bible, our holy book, and writing his contemplations.'

'Is it a very old book?'

'About four hundred years.'

'You must tell me more about him.'

'Another day. You better go and get ready for the battle.'

Pierre had anticipated the timing well. Minutes after Sonal left his side, he heard a shot being fired. The noise of the approaching cavalry was not too far behind. Pierre knew then that the initial attack by the enemy cavalry had been thwarted. He ordered the smaller guns to be shunted to the right so they could be ready for Hassan's larger army when it came. Padmini had to now be cooled and cleaned for the next shot.

Quli Murshid was waiting to attack the cavalry Hassan had sent to take out the artillery. As the first gun shot had halted the attack and caused its damage, Hassan's soldiers and horses were in a state of confusion. This was his chance to go on the offensive. He had only two hundred horses, but the element of surprise was crucial and he began to engage the enemy cavalry in close combat.

Abdul had to be patient. It was difficult for him to contain his excitement after all these days. He had to win and become king. That night in Ranipur with Abhi and Anamika was still burning in his head. He had been defeated by a cripple who had a power that he could not match. He had to have the kind of power he understood, the power of the sword and the gun. If he had the power, he could be king and then everything else would follow. Then he could lay claim on Anamika as more than just the protector of her husband. He would have in his possession that tall blonde woman who he had seen dancing naked for Hassan that night. She had hurt him, but he knew that one day he would be her master. Had he succeeded in killing Hassan then, he would have enjoyed her charms that very night. He had often thought about how that might have been. That was another vision also burning in his head. Abdul was primed for winning this battle. There were glittering prizes at the end of it.

But, as of now, he had to wait for Hassan to mount the attack. Hassan had many more soldiers than him, five times as many. So the tactic was to let him come the distance. Along the way, Hassan would face the smaller guns which were ready to attack first. That would sow confusion in his ranks. It was only when they were no more than fifty yards away that he would give the order to his troops to launch their offensive. He had prepared them well. They were well-fed and had been rewarded with the money he had got from Ranipur. Hassan may already have distributed the money Qaramat had got for him from Sethji. But even so, he knew that Hassan's soldiers had been starving for the last few days, as he had prevented them from looting the villages nearby.

He waited to hear the approach of Hassan's army.

45. The Battle 5

*H*is troops had been gathered by Zail Singh. Hassan had his elephant ready to mount. Nadya saw to it that he got on his elephant along with the standard, which told his soldiers that he was leading the troops. A big cheer went up when the elephant stood up and everyone could see their shah sitting atop. Hassan had arranged his troops to take account of his lack of artillery. In the front were the foot soldiers. They would rush first and face the small guns which Hassan knew would be deployed against them. But once the initial shock was over, then his cavalry would begin its attack. He had plenty of soldiers to spare, compared to Abdul. Sheer numbers should overwhelm the pretender and re-establish Hassan's legitimate rule in Muzaffarabad.

He signalled the soldiers to be silent. He turned his elephant around so he faced the infantry at the front and the cavalry further back.

'My faithful followers, today is the day we will crush that insect Abdul who has been flying around, stinging us. You are heroes and each of you will be rewarded one hundred rupiahs when the battle is over. This is your chance for glory and rewards. May Allah be with you.'

Nadya said a silent prayer in her head, clutching the cross as she always did when times were stressful. She wished Hassan well, but she knew that he had little chance. She could wait for him to come back in the evening, but most likely by tomorrow she would be serving in Abdul Khan's zenana. Whatever Hassan may have promised, she did not think those leather sacks were going to be opened for Hassan's soldiers.

The troops left noisily and Nadya returned to Hassan's tent. It was a huge tent and now she was alone in it. The leather sacks were there safely hidden under the divan where she sat down. Hassan had left the hundi notes with her to guard carefully.

There were still a few servants left behind who would be looking after the troops when they returned after the day's battle, but they knew to keep out of her way unless asked. Nadya had to think about what she would do with her life. She knew that by the end of the day, her fate would be sealed. If, by any chance, Hassan won, he would return to Muzaffarbad and she would be back in the large zenana competing with the Salmas and the Lailas, with daily intrigues and backbiting. She would no longer be Hassan's bodyguard and he would not be seeking her advice on crucial matters. She had been in an illusory heaven these past few days.

But Hassan was not likely to come back. Abdul was an unknown entity. Of course, she would adapt herself to a new master, but this one had been stabbed by her. He would not have forgotten that. Niloufer may intervene on her behalf, but she knew that Abdul did not have much patience with his mother. In any case, he was hardly likely to keep his mother as the woman who would choose his objects of pleasure night after night. Hassan could do that as to him Niloufer was just another woman, albeit an older but yet seductive woman. Abdul would want his own Niloufer, whoever she might be. So Nadya was to lose the one patron she could rely on as far as the power struggles in the zenana were concerned.

Nadya kept on thinking about what to do. She clutched her cross as she brooded on her choices. After a long life of servitude, she was ready for something else. She just did not know what. She was smart. She could ride a horse and wield a sword or a dagger. She had been taught how to handle a bandook. Long ago, she had learnt to read a few words in her church school and then picked up some more in each harem she had lived in.

She had not realized, but she had fallen asleep thinking these thoughts. The journey to Ranipur and back had been exhausting and while the following night had been full of pleasure, it had been a little short on sleep. She woke up as a servant from Qaramat Ali's tent came into Hassan's tent.

'What is it?'

'A pigeon has brought a message for Wazir-e-Alam. He is not here. So I brought it for you to read it.'

Nadya realized that she was now being treated as a confidant of the wazir and of Hassan. A servant would not otherwise have told such an important news to a pleasure girl.

'Let me see it.'

The servant handed a small roll of paper to Nadya. She did not like what she saw. Qaramat Ali was away sealing the truce with Devi

Singh. Hassan had departed for the battle. And here was a message that the Afghani begum was arriving later today. There was some cipher that she could not decode. But she had understood enough to know that there would be interruptions ahead. If the Queen Mother was coming, this meant a big entourage and some interference with what Hassan may or may not do. She remembered that the begum had ordered her arrest along with Niloufer. If that was what she was coming to enforce, it was time for Nadya to run away. Had Hassan been there, he could have defended her against his mother's orders. But, as it was, he was unlikely to return, and Qaramat could not be regarded as her friend any longer. He would sacrifice her to save his skin. That much she had learnt last night.

Nadya had to think fast. She needed to get away from the camp before the Afghani begum arrived. But where was she to go? Who would shelter her? Who could protect her from the winning army? She thought of Niloufer in that house. Perhaps, she should find a way back there. Anamika and Niloufer could be the answers to her prayers. But it would be difficult to get there. She could not go back by the route they had taken yesterday, as now there were armies across that route. She would have to go a long way around.

She remembered how she had found out about the Frenchman and his guns. She had to head for the river going north. Then if she was lucky, she could avoid the battle and swing around the back towards Ranipur. She had to get out as soon as possible. She called a servant. In came the man who had just brought her the message.

'Get a horse ready for me. The message is important. I have to go and help Huzoor.'

The man was quick to withdraw and Nadya was pleased that her commands were being obeyed. All she had to do now was to escape. Her horse was fast and strong enough to carry the leather sacks. She also had the hundi notes and so she knew that if the worst hit her, she could buy her way out of trouble. She had risked her life to get the money and rather than have it wasted by Abdul's winning army capturing it, she may as well use it for herself.

46. The Battle 6

Qaramat was carrying a white flag with himself. He had a sure instinct as to where Devi Singh would be. This was familiar terrain to him. He had been with Ahmad Shah in his long campaigns to conquer Purana Zilla. He had to head west and then swivel slightly southwards to get near the other bank of the Sreni. He was sure that Devi Singh's army would be there.

He could hear the guns being fired, which directed him to the battle. Qaramat was unafraid about riding into a battle. He had done this often. His horse and his demeanour would be noticed and people would see that he was no ordinary soldier. He kept on going westwards until he could see the colours of the Rajput army. There were tents struck some distance from where the guns were firing. He knew that that was where Gulabchand would be holding the consultations with Devi Singh. Gulabchand would not enter combat himself, just as Qaramat. Qaramat unfurled his white flag as he approached the tent.

He was seen from afar, and soon, Gulabchand had come out to meet him.

'Wazir-e-Alam, what a surprise. Welcome to our humble tent.'

'Diwan sahib, it is I who am humble in your presence.'

Qaramat got off his horse. A Rajput soldier took it away to give it water. Qaramat embraced Gulabchand. They had known each other for decades and had been keen enemies. Each knew the other's style of operation and yet, each could surprise the other. Gulabchand was ready for his surprise. He took Qaramat by his arm and entered the tent. There were some cushions and a simple carafe of water, placed where Gulabchand had been sitting. Gulabchand filled a silver cup of water and gave it to Qaramat. Qaramat was grateful for such solicitous care.

'Tell me, Wazir-e-Alam, how can I help?'

'Diwnaji, as you can guess, I have come to ask for a truce with Raja sahib.'

'What do you mean?'

'My Huzoor has sent me to tell you that he will not fight you. He does not covet Purana Zilla. He will withdraw from your territory the troops that have crossed over. He wishes to have a truce and seek your friendship.'

'Will he not fight at all? What about Abdul Khan?'

'My shah wants to settle the score with his half brother. He wants to defeat Abdul Khan. He does not want to fight Raja sahib.'

'I can ask Raja sahib, but I foresee a problem.'

'What problem?'

'We have made a treaty with Abdul Khan to help each other against your shah. He needs our help right now and we cannot abandon him.'

'But you are helping him with the big guns that the Frenchman has taken there. Is that not enough proof of your friendship?'

'Wazir-e-Alam, as you know, you don't measure friendship by spoonfuls. Once you have promised full help, you give it.'

'We can offer you full friendship and promise to remain friends for ever.'

'Perhaps, but it may be too late. We have to assist our friend Abdul Khan. If he loses to your shah then we can never sure be that Hassan Shah will abide by our friendship.'

'I can offer you five lakhs as compensation for your losses this morning and then more if you wish.'

Qaramat was aware that he was now losing the argument.

'No, Wazir-e-Alam, the Rajasahib's sister is in the battle on Abdul's side. We have to make sure that she is safe and that means we have to go to Abdul's assistance.'

'You are right. Perhaps I am too late. Perhaps the rajkumari has sealed the friendship you have with Abdul Khan. Maybe we can resume the talk when Hassan Shah has emerged triumphant.'

'Perhaps. We shall see.'

Qaramat was quite downcast. He was not used to being on the losing side. He usually won his arguments by arriving at a possibility of compromise early. But this time he had been too late. Too many things had escaped his grasp. Nadya had not said as much, but twice she had got to important information before he did. Maybe it was time for him to give up. *Maybe I should go to Mecca and retire there for my last years*, he thought.

47. Ranipur

Abhi had realized that his suggestion that Abdul have his camp near Ranipur had its disadvantages. Now that the battle was on, he began to worry about the villagers. The battle itself was some distance away from Ranipur, towards the south. The armies were gathering in a large plain just this side of the border between Ramgarh and Purana Zilla. But Abbhi was sure that as the day went on, the wounded and the dead will be coming back to Ranipur. He had begun instructing Shivnarayan to make arrangements for the vaid and the blacksmith to be ready to help. The men of the village were told to be vigilant, but not get anywhere near the battlefield. The women were frightened, but Abhi was sure that the village was safe as long as Abdul Khan was alive. Even if Hassan Shah was to win, he knew—though the villagers did not—that he had a hold over Qaramat Ali, thanks to the loan.

Even so, he was in a high state of excitement. Anamika could see this and was especially careful when she bathed him. She made sure that he had plenty to eat in the morning since the day was going to be busy. Messengers were coming in and out bringing news about the battle as well as all the usual trade matters to deal with.

'Mika, are you alright?'

'Of course, Abhi. What is worrying you?'

'Abdul Khan may lose and then Hassan Shah will not spare him.'

'I have thought about that. But Abdul Khan knows that as well as we do. He knows the language of the sword and the gun. That is his language. But I think he is a better soldier than Hassan is. I told you about that time when he nearly killed Hassan Shah.'

'Yes, but that tells me that he was not fully prepared for every possibility. He thinks of one thing at a time. He is simple-minded that way.'

'Maybe you have to be like that to be a soldier who can win battles. Too much thinking and he could lose his focus on the main goal.'

'Perhaps. I still hope Hassan Shah does not win.'

'Why are you afraid he will attack Ranipur?'

'Difficult to say. While he needed the money, he sent his wazir, but if he wins, he may get arrogant.'

'Can he defeat Abdul Khan and Raja Saheb?'

'Maybe not. But I am worried about you.'

Anamika went to where Abhi was sitting and took his face in her hands. She then kissed him. They had never done this in the galla in all these days. But Anamika knew that Abhi was very worried.

'Nothing will happen to me. I am here as long as you are here. Whatever happens, whoever wins, I shall remain with you and if we have to go, we go together.'

'How many Yamarajas can you deal with?'

'I only have one raja in my life and that is the one who is right here.'

Anamika kissed him again and held him close. She could feel Abhi's heart beating faster normal. She held him closer and buried his face in her bosom. It was minutes before she let him go. He calmed down and got back to his ledgers. She kissed him once more and left him at his work.

48. Battle 7

*H*assan had thought out the battle well. As his foot soldiers began advancing in their large numbers, Abdul ordered the small guns to start firing. One could see the foot soldiers stumbling and falling, but still they kept coming. Abdul had to tell his army to wait till they came much nearer. He was sure that sooner, rather than later, the army would come from Vishalnagar to bolster his forces. He had to conserve his meagre forces till they arrived.

The small guns were firing and still they kept coming. Hassan was behind them, high on his elephant where all the soldiers could see him and his standard. His cavalry was impatient to rush at Abdul's men but he held them back. He also had to conserve his forces against the big gun and the small guns. He was not sure whether his gamble of truce with Devi Singh would work. Delaying was the right tactic.

Abdul could see that the small guns were not stopping the onrushing troops. He sent a man around to Pierre asking the big gun to pivot in the direction of the big army approaching. The battle on that flank was still going on with Quli Murshid in close combat with the cavalry which had come as a surprise attack on the big gun. Pierre was considering if he needed another big blast at that cavalry, but the danger was that he may kill Quli's people as well. Getting Abdul's order, he shouted at his men to begin moving the big gun rightwards. This was not easy. Camels had to be harnessed to move the big gun three furlongs to the right. Sonal went along enthusing, as she was about to see more of the battle.

The foot soldiers were in sight now and Abdul was getting impatient. He was straining at the leash as much as his horsemen were. But even so, he knew it was too soon. Then he heard an almighty noise as the big gun sent off a shot. This did the trick. There were loud cries and Abdul could see many foot soldiers were now lying on the ground fatally injured, if not already dead. The ground was now clearer and he ordered his army to advance upon them. All together, with a mighty shout, the horsemen in Abdul's army advanced upon the remnants of the foot soldiers of Hassan'a army. They had to climb over bodies and the ground was already getting muddy with blood and gore. But they were used to this. This was their life. They exulted in this surrounding.

The big gun had to be silent now till the situation clarified. Pierre wanted to avoid killing his side inadvertently. The big gun had done its initial work, both for the attacking cavalry and now for the infantry. Now he had to wait till a strategic situation developed where he could employ Padmini again.

Hassan saw that Abdul was walking into the trap he had set. He let Abdul's men have a go at the infantry. That was his line of defence. He could sacrifice the foot soldiers. But once Abdul's men had come forward and were engaged with the foot soldiers, he gave command for his cavalry to begin the attack. His superior numbers would make the difference as the day wore on.

49. Jalalabadi

Their progress was not as swift as the begum would have wished. Each village they passed had somehow come to learn of the Pir passing by. Villagers came out in their scores. Some with offerings, others with requests. Small children had to be blessed, young women wanted blessings for a husband or a child. Older people just wanted to have a look at the holy man. They were offered food and gifts and had to receive the hospitality of each village along the way.

Fatima was impatient but there was little she could do to hurry the holy man along. He seemed to know precisely what he was doing. If he was not hurrying, there must be a reason for that, she thought. He will save my son, she kept on thinking. Indeed, her mind was focused throughout the journey on prayers directed at the Pir and Allah and every passing temple they saw. She was desperate for her son's survival; it did not matter which God would save him.

For Salamat Ali, this was a fantastic experience. He just watched the Pir and made quite sure that whatever the holy man wanted he was ready to find for him. Not that the holy man wanted much and the villagers along the way were willing to provide so much that he need not have loaded their horses with the provisions that Timur had rustled up for them in Sangampur.

They had been proceeding for a while in the direction which Salamat Ali knew would take them to the war camp when Muzaffarshah halted.

'The battle has begun. We will not go to the camp. Let us go to where the battle will end. Follow me. I will take you there.'

'But Huzoor, if the battle is finished, how will we save my son?'

'I did not say the battle is finished. They are fighting the battle now. I know where we have to be. Just follow me.'

Salamat Ali was duly impressed. Was it some divine knowledge or had the holy man worked out that what with the delay along the way in coming, the battle must have begun and so he had to find a better vantage point to make his intervention. He had a lot to learn at his young age. He just had to observe and work out for himself how much was divine knowledge and how much good guesswork. After all, some day, he was going to be a wazir.

All this time they had been going westwards from the river and Salamat Ali knew that the camp would be just a few more miles away. That much he had been told in messages by his grandfather. But now, the holy man turned right and then began to proceed northwards. Salamat was intrigued, but Fatima grew more and more anxious as to where all this was taking her.

50. Nadya

Nadya headed straight out of the camp towards the river. Sangampur was further eastwards from where the camp was. So the Afghani begum would be coming from the east before she pivots south towards the camp. Nadya had to keep out of her way and move northward and out eastwards to where Devgarh was. Her best bet was to hug the river past Devgarh and get to Ranipur via a longer but safer route.

She could hear the noise far away but it got indistinct as she moved away from the battlefield. Then, suddenly, she heard a big blast. Ah, the big gun, she thought. Proudly she remembered how she had spotted the firangi coming at Devgarh when the wazir and everyone else had been misled by the diwan of Purana Zilla. She savoured the moment and indeed the joy of the night after her discovery.

She was quite lost in her thoughts as she galloped towards the river. It was quite hot. She unloosed just one button of her tunic and touched the cross just for luck. She was startled when she heard someone shouting. She looked and there were three people on horses riding towards her. She was surprised as she did not expect anyone riding around unarmed at such a time. She could not now escape them so she decided to go to them.

As she got close, she realized who it was. The old man with a white beard had to be the Pir of whom she had heard so much from Niloufer, Qaramat and Hassan. Muzaffarshah Jalalabadi had been a looming presence in all their lives. But then there was a woman who had to be the Afghani begum and a fine looking young man whom she had seen during their march, riding along with Qaramat when they had first struck camp on the banks of the Sreni all those days ago.

Nadya hoped that her soldier's outfit would fool them and no one would inquire into the sacks on her horse. She went up to them.

'Salaam Huzoor. Salaam Begum Saheba. How can I help you?'

It was the holy man who spoke.

'Take us to Ranipur. You seem to know your way around here.'

'Huzoor, there is a battle taking place. Are you sure you wish to go to Ranipur?'

'Do as we ask you. We can see you are going there.'

'Huzoor, you know everything. How did you guess?'

'We see you are carrying sacks of coins. It must be to deposit it with the Seth in Ranipur.'

Nadya was humbled. She had no defences left. Did he also know she had stolen the money?

'Huzoor knows everything. I was going around away from where the battle is raging. I am hoping to get to Ranipur avoiding the guns. If you are with me, I will feel very safe.'

The party of three now became four and with Nadya in the lead began to make their way northwards towards the river. Afghani begum was not sure who this soldier was. Was he a soldier in her son's army or in Abdul's army? She dare not ask such questions since the Holy man was there and that restrained her. Salamat had seen that the soldier was a woman. He had noticed the green eyes and the nape of Nadya's neck where tiny blonde hair were visible. He realized that this was most probably the woman who had been with his grandfather in their escape from the camp that night which left him to take the zenana back. But he was a discrete young man. He would not betray any of his knowledge or even his feelings. After all, here was the one person who was closer to him in age than his travelling companions.

Salamat decided that this was also not the time to tell the begum that here indeed was the woman who had saved her son whatever the rumours she had heard. But again, at this juncture, the begum had no other thoughts than her son's survival. This diversion of the party towards Ranipur had baffled her and she was clinging close to Salamat as she rode along.

The Pir and Nadya went ahead. Nadya realized that the Pir was leading her forward for a purpose.

'Beti, you are beautiful. That much I can see. Will you tell me why you have decided to ride out on your own? Was Hassan Shah cruel to you?'

Nadya was flabbergasted. How did this man know everything. Her disguise had worked on many people, but he had seen through it. Did he just conclude that she must be from Hassan's camp because she was coming from that direction or did he really have divine knowledge.

Nadya wanted to get down from her horse and fall at his feet. But it was best to ride along and distance themselves from the other two.

'Huzoor, nothing is secret from you. Hassan Shah, my master, has gone to battle with Abdul Khan as you know. The sacks contain one lakh which he wanted to give to his soldiers after the battle. I fear he is going to lose the battle as he is no match for Abdul. There are also two armies he faces since Raja Devi Singh has made a treaty with Abdul. I thought the money will only fall in Abdul's hands so I took it to hide it away. I had not quite thought about Ranipur. But you divine everything.'

'You keep the money for yourself. You have earned it.'

'Huzoor, many shukriyas. How did you know?'

'I see you are an honest woman. You are a believer in Isa. I see your cross. Believers in Isa are good people. They are people of the book like Muslims are. We share many prophets. Ibrahim is our common ancestor.'

Nadya had no idea what Muzaffarshah was talking about. In her church all those years ago, no one had read the Bible to her. She had heard various chants and the old men with beard and black robes had been forbidding. But as to the contents of her religion, she knew the cross stood for what had happened to Christ. That much her mother had told her. But Ibrahim was news.

'Huzoor is very kind.'

'You are right about Hassan and Abdul. But your life will change now. I see you becoming a ruler some day. You will meet someone and marry him. You will rule a kingdom together.'

Nadya was overwhelmed. Here was her fortune being told and she had not even sought such knowledge. She had heard how the Pir had foretold Ahmad Shah's fortune. That much was folklore among the zenana women and Niloufer had mentioned it to her several times. Nadya clutched the cross with one hand while firmly holding the reins and said a small prayer.

51. The Battle 8

The day was getting hotter as the sun moved up the sky. They had now been fighting for some hours. The soldiers were getting tired and thirsty. The battle had reached a stalemate. Abdul's men were trying to advance towards where Hassan was. Their small guns kept on firing. But even so, Hassan's infantry had not been eliminated. His cavalry had joined the battle and there was a standing combat between rival horsemen.

Abdul wanted to have a go at Hassan who stayed on the top of his elephant. But there were too many soldiers in the way. He had to cut his way through patiently. This was going to be a much longer and harder battle than when he had attacked that night and surprised Hassan. He looked around for where Quli was. He had not yet come back from his defence of the artillery flank. Abdul asked a horseman next to him to go and fetch Quli for him.

Sonal was getting very excited by all that was happening around her. So far she had taken part in two big shots from Padmini. But she was also looking at the battle to figure out what was happening. From her stance at the back she could not see much, but realized that things were moving very slowly. Quli came riding by on his way to see Abdul.

'Are you alright, Rajkumari?'

'Yes, I am. Do not worry about me. Do you think we should use the big gun to throw Hassan off his elephant?'

Quli was in too much of a hurry to think about this. He said what he thought was the easy thing.

'Ask the firangi. He will know when to use the big gun.'

Encouraged by that answer, Sonal went behind the lines to find Pierre where he was sitting calmly, still reading his book. Sonal was impressed that he could be so relaxed in the midst of a battle.

'Are you a yogi?' she asked Pierre.

'Why do you say that?'

'You are so calm when everyone else is fighting and wounding and dying. You sit there reading your holy book.'

'It is not my holy book. It is a book written by a man who could be called a holy man, I suppose. But I know that my being agitated will not add anything to Abdul Khan's fighting power. My task is a simple one and that is to deploy the big gun when I think it is needed. I can rest in between and read my book.'

'That is what I have come to ask you. Should we fire Padmini once more at Hassan Shah to knock him off his elephant?'

Pierre was surprised by the audacity of this young woman. She had just witnessed her first battle and she was already thinking strategically.

'We could. Does Abdul Khan wish it?'

'I could go and ask.'

'No. Please not you yourself. Let me send out one of our gunners.'

Sonal was quite disappointed. But she knew her safety was important. She did not want to cause a problem by getting injured.

'Can I go with him?'

'No. But since you had the idea, if Abdul Khan agrees we can fire Padmini, you can arrange the shot yourself. Ask the soldiers to help you set it up as you wish.'

Sonal was now bubbling with excitement. It was not long before the permission came. She made her way to where Padmini had been placed at its last shot. She asked the soldiers around her to move it a bit further out. This took its time but was done. Then she asked the men to fill the gun with the powder and the shot. She wanted to do it herself, but even as she went to lift up a big ball, the men stopped her from doing that. Gun placed, gunpowder ball stuffed, the shot was placed and Sonal lit the firewood to light the shot.

Two things happened one after another within minutes. The almighty bang of the gun was heard as it travelled towards Hassan's army. Sonal was not wrong in her aim. The howdah was blown off and the elephant began running wild with Hassan's mahout goading it to bring it under control. A big cheer went up from Abdul's army. But Sonal had forgotten about the recoil in her enthusiasm of firing the shot. She was thrown back. Her head hit a box full of gunpowder balls and she lost consciousness.

Pierre was alarmed when he heard the gunners shouting. He abandoned his book and rushed to Sonal's side. She had to be moved out of the way first before anything could be done. He did not want to let Abdul or Quli know as they would be diverted from their fighting.

She was his responsibility. The young woman had been allowed to go only because Devi Singh was confident that Pierre would look after her.

It was not likely that Padmini would be harnessed again any time soon. Pierre told his gunners he was withdrawing back to the camp and they should call him if required. Saying that he picked up Sonal on his shoulder and started walking briskly back to their camp. He was a big six foot man and the burden felt light. But he was worried as to what damage the young woman had done to herself.

He stopped when they were some distance away from the battle and looked at Sonal's wound. She had hit her head and there was blood. She had lost consciousness due to the shock. Pierre took a handkerchief from his top pocket and began cleaning up the wound. It needed to be washed but there was no water nearby. He took out his trusted bottle of brandy from his inside pocket and wet his handkerchief with it. He began cleaning up Sonal's wound. The brandy had its effect. It stung and Sonal opened her eyes.

'What happened?'

'Don't worry. You fell and hit your head when the gun recoiled. You will be alright soon. You must rest.'

'I will be fine. I cannot just lie here and trouble you. Let us get back to the battle.'

'Not before I have bandaged up your wound. I need to take you back to the camp to get some bandages.'

'Just use any rag. You have this red handkerchief. Just tie my wound up for now. We will worry about bandages later. I don't want Quli sahib to worry about me. The battle is most important now.'

Pierre had heard a lot about brave Rajput women throwing themselves on the funeral pyre of their husbands. But this young woman was showing a simple kind of courage which impressed him. She had come to watch the battle and she was not going to be other than a soldier.

'The bandage smells of something. What is this pungent smell?'

Pierre had to be discrete.

'It is a soldier's quick medicine for healing wounds. It will do you no harm.'

On the battlefield, Abdul's army was joyous. They had hit Hassan.

But he had not been killed. Hassan knew the elephant would be a liability now. He left his mahout to take care of the beast and jumped off and got on the horse which had been going along, specially for him. His standard could still be seen from a far. A cheer went up in his army that their shah was safe. The big gun had done a lot of damage beside knocking down the elephant's howdah. Hassan had lost a score of his horsemen and more foot soldiers. The field was now choked with bodies and muddy with blood. But this was the way it was supposed to be. Hassan tried to recall the battles he had read about. He knew that he had to rethink his tactics.

He rode in front of his cavalry and sought out Zail Singh. Riding along, he asked Zail Singh, 'How long do you think Abdul's men can hold out? Can we defeat them soon?'

'Huzoor, it is the big gun which has made the difference. I was not expecting the last big shot. It killed some of their people as well but it has made our task difficult.'

'You charge forward. I will take a part of our troops around the left and come at them from their right. Their guns are on the other side.'

'Huzoor, that is a good plan. That is also where Raja Devi Singh will come from if we do not have a treaty.'

Hassan saw that Zail Singh had given up any hope of Qaramat being successful. Why his wazir had not come back and reported to him was a question Hassan had asked himself. No doubt, he has some other trick up his sleeve to get some help for. In the meantime, he had to finish off Abdul.

Hassan swung around and rode to the left periphery of his army. He called out to his horsemen at the periphery to follow him. They saw his plan immediately and enthusiastically began to form behind him. Hassan had seen that Abdul's right flank was exposed as there was no artillery there. He would only just edge over the boundary between Ramgarh and Puarna Zilla but not by much. He had promised Devi Singh via Qaramat that he would stay away from the Purana Zilla territory. But maybe the truce was holding, and he could just do a quick and short detour through the edge of Purana Zilla.

Quli noticed that Hassan had left his elephant. He could see his standard moving around. He pointed out Hassan's movement to Abdul.

'Sardar, I see Hassan is coming around our right side. I better go there and stop him.'

'No, you stay here and take the main battle. I will go around and confront him. He is my quarry.'

Quli was pleased that Abdul's fervour for defeating Hassan had not been abated. He was happy in whichever position he had to fight. He had had an exhilarating time first thing in the morning, taking on the cavalry charge Hassan had sent to attack the artillery. That had got his blood racing. Now, he could calmly manage the main battle, which had slowed to a sedate pace.

52. Nadya

Nadya's plan to take a long detour hugging the river was not going to work. The holy man had his own ideas. He had sensed where the battle was and moved them along in a westward direction. Nadya saw that they were headed in the direction of Ranipur, where Abdul's army was camped. She did not have any courage now to argue with the Pir about where she wanted to go or not go. He was in total command and the begum and Salamat were silent followers in their train.

'Huzoor, where are you taking us?'

'Beti, don't worry. I know where we are headed. We have to see if we can save Begum saheba's son from being killed.'

'Can we get there in time?'

'Trust me. I know a quick way. Let us speed up our horses.'

Saying this, he broke his horse into gallop and Nadya took a while to catch up with him. The two followers also woke up and sped their horses. The begum was now quite sure that the holy man was on his way to save her son. As they rode, they could hear the noise of bandooks firing and shouting. Suddenly they heard a big bang. Nadya realized that Pierre was in action again. She was not sure where her loyalty lay any longer. She would have prayed for Hassan's survival, but she was quite resigned to his defeat and death. It was as if she had worked Hassan out of her system. She felt quite empty.

She was also thinking of the words of Muzaffarshah. She was intrigued to know that she could be married and be a ruler. Who would marry her? Surely not Hassan, even if he survived. Certainly not Abdul, who would spare her life only if she was lucky. She did not know any other man around here except for Qaramat and Zail Singh. The Pir had said she would meet someone and marry him. That means I have not met him yet. Who could it be and what would he be like? Her mind had not been trained to daydream much but still, it was pleasant to fancy her future as she followed the holy man.

Soon enough, they were approaching the battle. The Pir had selected a path which took them to the back of Abdul's army. This was not very far from Ranipur in any case, so her instinct was not wrong. But she had no idea what would happen to her if Abdul saw her behind his lines. But the Pir was single minded and rode on. The two laggards were trying to keep up, but he had decided that this was his own mission.

As they rode nearer, Muzaffarshah stopped by a big tall man who was calmly reading a book and smoking a pipe. Pierre got up and said, 'What brings you here my friend? I thought you were gone to Mecca.'

'Gun masterji, how is the battle going'?

'Badly for both sides. Neither can win and so far it looks like we shall go on for a few more days.'

'Get me a camel. I want to go in the middle of the battlefield. I must stop this madness.'

'Are you sure you want to brave the bullets?'

'If I am on a camel, they will see me and not shoot.'

'I would say you are safer riding on the end of the big gun—our Padmini. Everyone will take note and the big gun will silence the soldiers on both sides.'

'That is a better way perhaps. Where is the gun?'

Nadya was flabbergasted by the speed with which the Pir was moving. She was also intrigued by Pierre. So this was the firangi who had brought the big gun from Vishalnagar. How could he just sit there and read a book when all around him were fighting and killing? But now, she had to worry about what Muzaffarshah was up to. What if he is killed? Will she be blamed for misleading him here?

The holy man was single minded. Sonal was standing by the big gun. Her accident had not curbed her enthusiasm. She saw the old man approaching her along with Pierre.

'Rajkumari, Saheb Muzaffarshah Jalalabadi wants to ride Padmini. Let us get him on to it.'

Sonal had not heard about Muzaffarshah but he was clearly a holy man. She fell down at his feet. He blessed her and moved on. Padmini was brought nearer to where they were standing. The soldiers manning the gun lowered the front end and Muzaffarshah was helped up by Pierre using his full six feet height, and his strong shoulders. It was a strange sight, the tall white Frenchman helping the old grey and white bearded Sufi saint in his flowing white robes on to the shining metal front of Padmini.

The Pir was quite agile and was riding the gun in no time. The question now was of dragging it in front of the fighting armies. As soon as the camels were harnessed to pull the gun forward, everyone in the two armies could sense that something important was about to happen. The cavalry began to clear a path for the gun to advance inwards to the middle of the battlefield. Quli saw the Pir and ordered his soldiers to stop fighting as did Zail Singh.

Farther away, Abdul was heading to the edge of his right flank to confront Hassan. He was struck by the sudden silence of the guns behind him. He turned around and saw the big gun being wheeled out, with Muzaffarshah Jalalabadi on top. He had not seen the Pir for a year now. He had gone to him to seek his guidance when Hassan had dispossessed him. The Pir had urged patience and told him his fortunes were going to improve. Now what was he doing here?

Fatima Begum was happy to see the Pir rushing in to the middle of the battlefield. She had almost despaired of them reaching in time to save her son. She could not chide the holy man, nor could she divine what was on his mind. Now she understood why he took the turn on the road that he did. Salamat was having the lesson of his life. Here was a man who could be spiritual one moment and then leap up a big gun like a young man the next. What now?

Abdul signaled to Hassan that the Pir had come. Hassan stopped his horse and moved around. He saw the big gun approaching behind four camels and with a distinct figure in a white robe seating. How had Muzaffarshah got here? Who had brought him? What will now happen to the battle?

Hassan began to move back to where he was before, in the middle of the battle lines. Abdul was doing the same on his side. It was clear to both that now the Pir was here, the battle would take a very different turn. He hoped that Hassan would not escape his sword once again with the help of the Pir. But then, he was devoted to the holy man and would do whatever he asked. It was best to see what will happen now.

The camels had brought Padmini in the middle of the two armies. Soldiers had been disengaging from the fight and retreating to their sides. A small area was clear right between the middle of the two armies. Muzaffarshah shouted at the camels to halt and they obeyed instantly. A soldier got off his horse and unhitched the camels from the gun. The front end was lowered and Muzaffarshah jumped down. Everyone was now silent, waiting for the Pir to speak. But instead of speaking, he bent down on his knees and started praying, facing west towards Mecca. The armies on both sides felt ashamed that the old man had remembered what they had routinely forgotten—to do their namaaz daily five times if possible—no one moved, however or joined him.

Jalalabadi got up from his prayers and began to address the armies.

'In the name of the Compassionate, stop this bloodshed. Lay down your guns and bandooks and sheath your swords.'

Hassan came to the front and got off his horse. Abdul saw that and he got off his horse as well and came to the place where the Pir was standing. He bowed down and did salaams thrice. Hassan saw this and quickly followed. Abdul was the first to speak.

'Huzoor, what brings you here? Let us finish our battle and then you can anoint the winner as the shah of Ramgarh.'

Hassan had to have his say.

'Huzoor, stop this rebel who is challenging my right to the throne of Ramgarh as the only legitimate son of Ahmad Shah. He will obey what you tell him to do.'

'Huzoor, he has no more right than I do. I am the first son of Ahmad Shah and his older brother. The throne should be mine. Give me time and I will defeat him in battle.'

'Huzoor, I was about to crush him with my superior army five times his numbers. Let us finish what we have started.'

The Pir listened to them patiently. But, almost as if by design, they could hear the sounds of hooves of horses hastening towards them. The soldiers looked to where the noise was coming from. It was from where Abdul and Hassan were just moments ago. Devi Singh had arrived with his cavalry. For the next few minutes, the noise of the arriving army was deafening. They were shouting and firing their guns in the air and looking forward to the fight.

But even they noticed, as they came nearer, that fighting had stopped. Devi Singh, who was at the head of his troops, came forward and saw that in the middle of the two armies stood Hassan and Abdul with Muzaffarshah Jalalabadi. Devi Singh got off his horse and made salaams to Muzaffarshah.

'Huzoor, how fortunate that we have your presence here. How can we serve you?'

Muzaffarshah saw what had happened. Abdul went to Devi Singh and proffered his hand in friendship which Devi Singh clasped firmly. Gulabchand was also getting off his horse as was Qaramat Ali who had decided to stick with Devi Singh's army for his way back. Qaramat went to Hassan and whispered something in his ears. Hassan nodded. Hassan realized that his boast of how much larger his army was seemed hollow now. Here was Devi Singh to help Abdul, and his own artillery was far behind by the banks of Sreni on this side of Vishalnagar. The battle had been stopped just in time. He would have lost it in the next hour. The Pir may have saved him.

'Raja sahib, Wazir-e-Alam, Diwanji, I have come to put some sense in these boys. They should stop fighting and killing. They have a quarrel, I know. Let us find ways of settling this quarrel. But let not hundreds of soldiers die for the sake of this quarrel between two brothers.'

Gulabchand could see that the battle was over. The Pir was about to solve this issue in his own unique way.

'Huzoor, what do you suggest?'

'We want to think about this. I had seen Abdul over the years. But I have not seen Hassan for the last fifteen years. I can only make up my mind when I see the faces of people. I want to sit somewhere and look at them carefully. Then alone can I suggest what should be done.'

Qaramat Ali spoke up.

'Huzoor, nearby is the village of Ranipur where our Sethji Rathore has a haveli. He is married to the daughter of diwanji. We can meet there and you can decide what is to be done.'

Muzaffarshah looked at Hassan and Abdul.

'Is that agreeable to you both?'

Together they nodded their assent.

Now the armies had to disband and the soldiers could get some rest. They could get back to their respective camps and catch up on their food and water and tend to their wounds. Hassan, Abdul and the others got back on their horses. The camels were harnessed again and the Pir got on his gun and rode back to where Nadya and Pierre were standing along with Fatima and Salamat. Fatima fell at the Pir's feet as soon as he got off his big gun.

'Huzoor, thousands of shukriyas and duas for your health and happiness. You have made a poor mother's heart stop crying. You have performed a miracle.'

'Begum saheba, nothing has happened yet. I have not yet done anything. Let us see what the rest of the day brings to us. Right now, let us get on our horses and get to Ranipur.'

The soldiers were resting and only the leaders made their way to Ranipur. Quli noticed that Sonal was bandaged. He asked her what had gone wrong. Sonal made light of her wound. But Quli would not hear of it. He asked her to get on her horse and sped off ahead of the rest to Ranipur. He did not want Devi Singh to see his sister injured and uncared for. Behind them came the Pir, Abdul, Hassan, Devi Singh, the diwan and the wazir with Fatima and Salamat following. Nadya had decided to fall back and wait till Pierre got ready to come. She had to guard her horse with the sacks. She felt safe in the company of this tall man who reminded her of the grown up men she had seen as a child.

Pierre was the first to speak.

'I see you are a Christian like me. Are you a Catholic or a follower of Luther?'

Nadya had no idea what he was talking about.

'I cannot say what I am. I was taken from my village many years ago and the church was a dark and gloomy place with old men in black cassocks and long beards. They never told us what they were.'

'Where is your village?'

'I am told I am from somewhere beyond Marmara. They call it Abkhazia.'

'You belong to the other Church. Not the Roman one but the Constantinople one.'

'I have not heard about either Rome or Constantinople. What are they?'

'It is a long story which I may have time to tell you some day. We all believe in Christ and we wear the cross but otherwise, we quarrel with each other.'

'People quarrel anyway about religion or money.'

'Or women or territory. I am happy if they go on doing so as my task is to help them with my big gun.'

53. Ranipur

Anamika was aware that there was a battle going on not far from where they were. Abhi had prepared the village for what might happen at the end of the day. No one had come yet all morning and now it was past noon. She went along with her house work of cooking the meal for Abhi and Niloufer. Ganga was there to help her. She thought that keeping busy will help her calm down as well. The day was going to be a long one and who knew what it would bring.

They had finished their lunch. Niloufer and Anamika were resting in Niloufer's room, worrying about the battle. Niloufer was worrying about Abdul as much as about Hassan. She would lose either way which of them won. Abhi was as usual, busy with his ledger books with Shivnarayan's help. Ganga had to wash up and clean the vessels which had been used in the lunch. There was a calm about the house which they knew could not last for long.

Soon enough there were sounds of horses rushing to their door. Anamika got up and opened the front door. There stood Quli Murshid and Sonal on their horses just as they had arrived those many days ago. Anamika immediately noticed that Sonal had a bandage on her forehead.

'Rajkumari, what happened? How did you get hurt?'

Sonal jumped off her horse as if nothing was wrong and embraced Anamika.

'It s nothing. I just fell down and bumped my head.'

'Come and let me look at the wound. Quli sahib, welcome. I am glad you brought my little sister home sooner. How is the battle going?'

Sonal was still reluctatnt to admit she had any problem.

'Didi, there is nothing to worry about. Pierre has tied a bandage but just to make sure it does not get any worse. It is just a small wound.'

'Behenji, the battle has now stopped. Pir Muzaffarshah Jalalabadi arrived and stopped the battle. He is coming here along with Sardar, Hassan Shah, Rajasaheb and others. The Pir has said he will decide what to do about the quarrel between them after he has looked at the two combatants.'

Anamika realized that there will be many people coming to their door. She called Niloufer and Ganga. Niloufer came out to the door.

'Ammijan, can you look at this foolish sister of mine and see what she has done to herself? I knew she was taking a risk going to fight out there.'

Niloufer embraced Sonal and took her to her room to examine the bandage. Quli was stuck in the room with Anamika, not knowing what to do with himself. Anamika saw his predicament. It was best to send him to talk to Abhi.

'Quli sahib, you better tell Sethji what has happened. He will have to get ready for the many people coming to our village. I better get ready to receive the guests. Ganga, get some milk warmed up and take the barfis out on a thali. Also get some flour out of the storeroom and begin preparing for the evening meal.'

Anamika had to get ready for the guests. She disappeared back to her room so she could dress a bit better for the guests and make sure that Abhi was ready to receive them. There was now a bustle in the air. Soon, she could hear the steady march of many horses coming towards the village.

Quli called Jibril to come in to the galla. Abhi had decided that he had to come out to greet the guests, especially since Pir Muzaffarshah was among them. He could walk now by himself, but still needed some help to get over high thresholds which separated the rooms from each other. Also, walking out of the house was going to pose problems for him even after his recovery. Abhi told Shivnarayan to alert the villagers about the important people coming to the village.

Anamika heard Quli calling Jibril and she went into the galla.

'What is it Abhi?'

'I have to go out and greet the guests. If the Pir is coming, I cannot sit here and greet him. I hear your father is also coming with Raja Saheb along with Abdul Khan and Hassan Shah and Qaramat Ali. So we will have our hands full.'

Anamika could feel the pride in Abhi's voice that he was determined now to walk out and greet his guests. She also felt her heart glow and offered a silent prayer to Kali, thanking her for their good luck.

'Let me help you walk out.'

Quli would not hear of it.

'No, Behenji, you stay here. I will go along with Jibril and make sure Sethji is alright. This is my work.'

Quli handed his gun to Anamika as he would not need it now. Anamika slung it across her shoulder as she had seen Abdul do it. She knew about guns so it was not likely it would go off without her knowledge.

Jibril and Quli escorted Abhi out of the galla and into the living room and then very carefully, out the main doors. Abhi had not been outdoors since the day they went to the Kali temple. He could feel the difference in his own strength. He was looking forward to meeting the guests as he would have always liked. He could now be a Seth, just like his father and his grandfather.

The first horses were arriving. Pir Muzaffarshah Jalalabadi was at the head of the procession along with Gulabchand and Qaramat Ali, who had been conferring with him. Abdul was with Devi Singh and Hassan was with them. As soon as the horses reached the village square, Wahid and Jibril began to help the riders down and took the horses to the well to water them. Abhi advanced towards the guests. Of course, the priority went to the Pir.

'Huzoor, many many salaams to you. We are fortunate that you have come to our village.'

Abhi walked along with Quli and bent low before the Pir. Then he greeted his father-in-law and Qaramat.

'Welcome, Pitaji. Welcome, Wazir-e-Alam.'

Abhi tried to touch Gulabchand's feet but he stopped him from doing that and embraced Abhi. Qaramat made his salaams to Abhi, astonished that the Seth whom he thought crippled, was walking out to meet them. Abdul and Hassan were not far behind, with Devi Singh, carefully keeping them apart. As he got off his horse, Abdul was also amazed that the Sethji whom he nearly killed only the other day was now in the village square greeting the guests. Hassan had of course never before seen Abhi, so he failed to notice what a big change this was. Villagers had heard about the big people coming and had begun to gather at the farther edge of the square. Thus far, only men had dared to come out.

Abhi continued his welcome.

'Please, come in and make yourself comfortable.'

The Pir looked at the house and the square. He saw that there was a short plinth around the well. On one side was the trough from which horses drank but there was room enough for some people to sit down.

'We will sit here as it is in the open. Please take the others in. We need the sunlight to look at the two princes and see what we can do.'

Anamika and Niloufer had been looking out at the square from within the house. When she saw the Pir, the wazir and then Hassan Shah, Niloufer could not stay within. She came out and made her salaams to the Pir who blessed her. He was now sitting down on the plinth by the well. No one else had joined him so far. They were standing around waiting for his next pronouncement. Niloufer then salaamed the wazir and Hassan Shah. She acknowledged her son. But then, she saw the Afghani begum following on her horse. Niloufer was not sure what she should do. But the begum got off her horse and embraced Niloufer.

'Many many shukriyas for saving my son's life. I was misled by some false gossip about what had happened. But Salamat Ali who has been helping me all these days, told me the truth. I had to come to Ranipur to thank you for what you did.'

There was a melee all around. Anamika had now come out, deciding that it was alright given the many people present. She bowed down before the Pir who blessed her. She then touched her father's feet, who lifted her up and embraced her. He had tears in his eyes.

'Your mother will be so happy when I tell her how well our son-in-law and you are looking.'

'It is Mata Kali's blessings. Why don't you come in and rest? You must be tired.'

'Beti, you know I cannot come in to my married daughter's house. I will sit here outside with the Pir.'

Abhi heard this and he intervened.

'Pitaji, let us forget the old conventions. The times we are living through are so different from what happened before that we need to change our ways. Look at us. We have learnt to welcome sardars and begums in our house as our friends. Please, come and rest in our house.'

It was Muzaffarshah who came to everyone's rescue.

'Diwanji, I need you and Wazir-e-Alam by my side while I make up my mind about this dispute. When I have said what I need to, you can go and enjoy your rest in your daughter's house.'

That was an order for everyone to get ready for the Pir's decision. Devi Singh saw that the Pir kept him out of the decision making. As a rival king, he was not the right person to be involved. Qaramat and Gulabchand sat down on either side of the Pir. Niloufer took the Afghani begum and Salamat Ali with her to the house. They all sat down on the front porch of the house where Jibril and Wahid used to spend all their time. Abdul and Hassan were too tense to sit down or relax. They stood slightly apart from each other, facing the Pir but wary of each other. Quli stood by Abhi to make quite sure he could help Abhi to move when he wanted to. Jibril and Wahid were also in attendance. On the far side from all stood Nadya and Pierre. They were there almost like strangers. Hassan had been too preoccupied to notice Nadya. Qaramat had concluded that Nadya wanted to be left alone and he was happy to let her.

Anamika was keen to bring some refreshments for her guests but was not quite sure how to do it. She could sense the tension rising as everyone fell silent. The Pir spoke up.

'Come near me, the two of you, so I can judge for myself who shall be the shah.'

Abdul and Hassan stepped close to where the Pir was sitting. For Abdul, this was where the latest chapter in his life had begun. This was the well where he had spotted Anamika and their lives had been intertwined since then. That memory alone could get his blood rushing faster in his veins. She was right there but he knew he could only claim his prize if he was the shah. If not, he was less than the Sethji, who could conjure up money from nowhere. This woman and all other women will be for ever a trophy too far for him.

Hassan was sanguine. He knew he was the legitimate son of Ahmad Khan and after all, the Pir had anointed his father as the legitimate shah. The Pir only had to look at him and recognize who his father was. He was also not sure what might follow if the Pir had other ideas.

Muzaffarshah Jalalabadi looked at the two princes for sometime with great concentration. He then took a ring off his finger and turned it between his cupped hands. He closed his hands and asked Gulabchand to choose one hand where the ring maybe. Gulabchand indicated the hand he thought contained the ring. The Pir then cupped his hands together again and asked Qaramat to choose the hand which had the ring. Qaramat chose one hand. The Pir looked at them both and laughed out loud. Everyone was baffled by this open hearted laughter. It did little to break the tension. What was the Pir up to?

'The answer is clear. Neither of you is the true heir to the throne. We therefore ask you to fight it out. Just the two of you in front of us. Whoever wins the duel will be the king.'

The Afghani begum cried out.

'Huzoor do not say so. My poor boy would be slaughtered by Abdul Khan. 'Please save him.'

'Begum saheba, you brought us here to intervene in the battle. We told you then that we do not decide anyone's future. We can only foretell it. As of now, we cannot see who the next shah of Ramgarh is. He may be here but we cannot divine who he is. So the best way is for the two boys to fight it out.'

Niloufer knew what the Afghani begum was thinking. She also felt Hassan had no chance but she did not say anything. Her heart was torn between her loyalty for Hassan and her concern for Abdul. Abdul had never liked her much. Hassan would treat her better if he survived. But as a mother, she wanted Abdul to win. Anamika found herself strangely subdued. Abdul was once her passion. She had done a deal with him to protect Abhi. Hassan was nothing to her. But whether Abdul would win or not was not her concern. She was more concerned that Abhi should not get too tired standing outside or collapse. But Quli was there so she was reassured. Quli was solid. She suddenly remembered that she had left Sonal alone in the house. She ran inside her house in search of Sonal.

A hush descended on the square. The Afghani begum had gone back to her place on the edge of the house sitting alongside Salamat and Niloufer. She was terrified. Salamat was trying to be calm, sitting with his gun across his knees. Fatima leaned closer to him as if for assurance. Salamat wondered what solace he could offer to this imperious woman. But he had to be on his best behaviour.

The Pir spoke again. 'Each has a sword and a dagger. No guns and no other weapons. Each is on his own. Let the battle commence.'

Abdul was quick. He dropped his gun on the ground. He had unsheathed his sword in anticipation. Hassan looked around and saw Abhi. He gave his gun to him and unsheathed his sword. Abhi put the gun down by his side. Hassan took his time. He was going to be calm in the face of Abdul's excitement. Each had his dagger in the belt.

Abdul lunged at Hassan with his sword. Hassan was ready, unlike the last time they had met when he was in his cups being entertained by his women. Now he was alert. He parried the thrust and threw Abdul off. They were both good swordsmen. There was a balance between Abdul's ferocity and impatience to get this duel over with and Hassan's presumption that he had the legitimacy and the time to win. Abdul had expected a quick win. Hassan had anticipated a long struggle.

All around, the people were stunned to see this fight. It could end in one of them dying. Who would it be? Each had his favourite. Gulabchand and Devi Singh wanted Abdul to win. Qaramat had mixed loyalties. He wanted a strong king for Ramgarh. Either would do but he knew Abdul was the better fighter. Abhi was fascinated to be part of the group watching the fight. He had no feelings either way. Abdul had been their friend, but he could turn murderous, as he well knew. His wife had made some deal with Abdul, but now it seemed that the deal had been annulled. Whoever won, the two of them—Abhi and Anamika—would have to deal with a new reality. Nadya was surprised how disengaged she had become in the fortunes of Hassan, whom only the previous night she had taken close to herself. Pierre knew, as a soldier would, that Hassan had no chance.

When she went back inside the house, Anamika found Sonal wandering around, talking to Ganga. Sonal had now a fresh white bandage which Niloufer had tied on her. She was very cheerful but feeling slightly faint. Anamika told her what had happened. She took Sonal upstairs so they could watch the duel out of the zarokha. Anamika was still carrying the gun Quli had entrusted to her.

The battle was ferocious. The two duelists were moving around the middle of the square, watched by the villagers. The Pir was calmly watching with a smile on his face as if he knew what was going to happen. Qaramat and Gulabchand were watching, but also turning over in their minds how they would react when they knew the outcome. Devi Singh was calm, as he was sure Abdul would win. He had by now remembered that his sister should be somewhere nearby. He knew Pierre would look after her so he was not overly worried. He had seen Pierre in the distance and he seemed to be his usual relaxed self.

Abdul knew Hassan's weakness. As he had done the other night, he relied on Hassan's lack of concentration. Before anyone could see, he stabbed Hassan. Fatima shrieked. Hassan staggered and fell. Abdul was triumphant. But he did not wait to savour his victory. He turned towards Abhi, who was standing there.

'Sethji, I am the king now. I want you out of my way so I can have your wife as my own queen.'

There were gasps all around. Abdul rushed at Abhi, who was unarmed. Quli was standing next to him and immediately unsheathed his sword.

'Sethji is under my charge and his wife is my sister. You will have to kill me before he gets hurt.'

Quli moved in front of Abhi to confront Abdul, but he was too slow. Abdul had his blood rushing in his veins and he was combat ready. Quli parried one thrust but soon was on the defensive. Abdul struck at Quli's shoulder. He did not mean to kill, just wound. As Quli stumbled, Abdul turned to Abhi. But before he could get to Abhi, Quli intervened again. He had recovered quickly from his stumble and had another go at Abdul. But he was unwilling to kill Abdul. He just wanted him out of the way till he could whisk Abhi away. Abdul had other ideas. He wanted to kill Abhi. He slashed Quli's arm and the sword fell.

Abhi stood his ground fearlessly. Gulabchand was rising up in alarm and Devi Singh had unsheathed his sword. But before Abdul could strike, there was a loud noise. Abdul fell. They looked up. Above the haveli, in the zarokha, stood Anamika with a gun in her hand.

There was silence all around. Everyone was stunned by what they had seen. The two princes lay dead. The Pir suddenly got up and began his dance. He whirled around and around, chanting and singing. No one understood what he was chanting but he was in in his ecstasy. He whirled around the village square. Women of the village who had stayed away now appeared in the village square suddenly, as if they knew the danger was past. All watched the Pir as he danced. Fatima was sobbing loudly and uncontrollably. She could not get up and see her dead son as she too was intrigued by the Pir's dance. She had seen once before how he had to have his ecstasy. Niloufer was crying silently. She had lost two of her favourite men, but somehow she was resigned to what had happened. She knew the story of Anamika and her son by now, from the many hints Anamika had dropped. She had now acquired a new family in Abhi and Anamika. Her new family was still there.

When the dancing stopped, Muzaffarshah fell silent. He returned to his seat by the well. No one had moved and no one had tended the two dead bodies. Anamika had now come down and run to Abhi. She hugged him and stood by his side.

The Pir had spoken quietly to Gulabchand and Qaramat Ali. Now was his time to speak.

'Allah has spoken. We tried to divine his meaning before the duel but there was no clear sign. The two oracles I consulted gave me two answers as to who should be the shah. Now we know neither could be.'

Devi Singh was the first to speak.

'Huzoor, Ramgarh needs a shah. Who will you choose?'

'We don't choose. We only recognize who ever Allah has chosen. There is one such among us.'

Everyone was surprised that the Pir had chosen the next shah. Qaramat Ali had to know who his king was to be.

'Huzoor, who have you seen as the next king of Ramgarh?'

Muzaffarshah summoned Quli Murshid. Quli was nursing his wound. Blood had begun to thicken around the sleeve covering his right arm, which had been slashed. Thus far, no one had noticed his plight. As Quli staggered to make his salaams to the Pir, he almost stumbled. The Pir stood up and held him.

'This is the next shah of Ramgarh.'

Anamika rushed to Quli's side. She held him and wrapped one end of her sari around Quli's bleeding arm. Qaramat Ali stood up and salaamed Quli.

'Huzoor, I am your humble servant Qaramat Ali. I was the wazir for Hassan Shah. If it will please you, I can be your wazir as well.'

Quli was elated and confused and groggy. Anamika was holding him up. Wahid and Jibril rushed to her side and took over the task of taking Quli to the house. Sonal went down as well, concerned about Quli.

The Pir turned to Gulabchand and said, 'Diwanji, you can now go to your daughter's house.'

Gulabchand was still unsure.

'Huzoor, I will follow you.'

'No, we will sit here. We do not go into houses or palaces. We stay out, but tell your daughter to give us food and water.'

Qaramat and Gulabchand led Devi Singh into the house. Anamika was now ready to receive them. Quli had been taken to rest in Niloufer's room, where she tended to his wound. Sonal was there to help her. Abhi was still standing outside, stunned by what had happened, but Pierre and Nadya brought him gently back in. Fatima was outside, crying over her son's dead body.

The Pir asked Jibril and Wahid to bring sheets to cover the two bodies with. Soon, there were white sheets from Anamika's house covering the two men. Then they were asked to get some people to dig graves outside the village boundaries. Jibril knew people in the village and had no difficulty summoning up some men who could help him. Wahid stayed behind to look after the two bodies, making sure that no one came near them.

Anamika was out again very soon, with a brass bowl of hot milk and a plate of sweets. She put it before the Pir and bowed again. He looked at her.

'How many children do you wish for, Beti?'

'Huzoor, whatever you grant us, we are grateful.'

'I see you as the mother of a son and two daughters. They will all be famous throughout the land just as you and your husband will be.'

'Huzoor, many shukriyas for your blessings.'

'You must help the new shah. He needs your advice.'

'As Huzoor commands. Can I bring anything else for your comfort?'

'No. Just tell the Begum saheba and Niloufer begama that I wish to speak to them when they can come out.'

Anamika salaamed again and went back inside the house. Village women were now coming up one after another to seek the blessings of the Pir. Many had brought their children to seek help with their fortune. The Pir was patiently talking to each and every one of them.

Inside the house, there was a lot of activity. Abhi was trying to cope with the many-sided conversation in his galla since the men had all drifted in there with him. Devi Singh had seen that his sister was well except for a small injury. He did not worry too much about that as he knew Sonal was made of stern stuff. His worry was more about Quli Murshid. He confided in Qaramat Ali.

'Wazir-e-Alam, our new shah will need all the help you can give him. We are happy of course that now there will be friendship between Ramgarh and Purana Zilla. We are also ready to help in any way we can to build up his rule in Ramgarh.'

'He will need help as he has no experience in statecraft. He is a good soldier and has a head for money and accounts. But he has never led an army, being always a good deputy to Abdul Khan.'

'So, what do you suggest for him?'

'Rajasaheb, I am now getting old. This is my last battle. As soon as I can, I want to find a new wazir for my shah and take it easy for the rest of my life.'

Gulabchand was talking with his son-in-law.

'What made this change in your health, Abhijitji?'

'It was Abdul Khan who first suggested that I sit at my galla. He got his soldiers to lift me up and put me here. After that, everyday I was able to sit here, touch the ground with my feet. Then Niloufer begum came and she had some helpful ointments for me. Hot baths everyday and daily walking inside the house, even from one room to another, and here I am. I can walk with some support and soon, I hope, on my own.'

'Let us pray to Kali that you can walk on your own.'

'Can I make one suggestion, Pitaji?'

'Yes please. What is it?'

'I have seen the Rajkumari only for a few days. But I would suggest that if you want to strengthen relations between Vishalnagar and Ramgarh, it would be a good idea if Sonal could be offered in marriage to Quli Murshid Shah.'

'What does Anamika say about this? Is this one of her ideas?'

'Both of us thought about it. Rajasaheb may not agree but you should try and make it happen. He may prefer a Rajput king for his sister.'

'Vishalnagar rajas have a tradition of marrying in Mughal nobility over the years. Rajasaheb may agree. We shall see.'

The Pir had sent word that he now wanted to see the begum and Niloufer. Qaramat decided that he would also go with them, and take Salamat with him. The women were still crying. The only consolation they had was that the Pir had supervised and blessed the burial of their sons.

'Fatima Begum, your sorrow will not go away soon. It is sad when a mother outlives her son and indeed, the only son, as you have done. But God is great and will heal your wounds. You should think very soon of going to Mecca.'

'Huzoor, you always have told us the right thing for us to do. Your advice will be our command.'

'Wazir-e-Alam, what do you think?'

Qaramat Ali had been contemplating his own future since he had failed to make a truce with Devi Singh. He had sensed that his powers were failing. He had been outsmarted by Gulabchand and even Nadya had found out one or two things which he had not seen coming.

'Huzoor, I will take Begum saheba myself to Mecca. With your blessings, we will be able to make our Hajj and return to Ramgarh to be with you.'

'Niloufer Begama, will you go with them or will you stay in Ranipur?'

'Huzoor, I hear your command. But this is my new family. I will stay here.'

'There is no time to lose. Let us begin our journey back. Wazir-e-Alam, get us the horses and the camels so we can begin our journey.'

'As Huzoor wishes. We can get to our camp tonight, and tomorrow, set out for Ramgarh. From there we will arrange all the provisions for our Hajj.'

It was leave-taking time for everyone. Anamika was glad to see that Niloufer was staying with them and not going away with Qaramat, who had sent her to Ranipur those many days ago. She had become like a second mother for Abhi and herself. Gulabchand was sad to be saying goodbye to his daughter, but he too had to make his way back to Vishalnagar with his king.

Quli Murshid was better now. His arm was bandaged but he felt fine. He came out and bowed again to the Pir.

'Huzoor, I need your blessings to be a worthy successor to Ahmad Shah. Please give me your guidance.'

'Make sure you honour the memory of the two princes who died today. Build a maqbara for their graves just outside Ranipur.'

'Huzoor, it shall be done.'

'Wazir-e-Alam has decided to go to Mecca with Fatima begum. You need a new wazir.'

'Huzoor, how can I choose a new wazir now?'

'Whose advice do you trust?'

'Sethji and my behenji, the Sethani, have given me good advice so far.'

'That is your answer.'

Abhi had come out again to say farewell to the Pir. He spoke up, 'But Huzoor, how can I be a wazir? I have difficulty riding a horse. Muzaffarabad is far away.'

'Ranipur can be the new seat of Shah Quli Murshid. We shall come when he is ready to sit on the gadi of Ramgarh, with its new capital at Ranipur."

Quli Murshid immediately saw the advantage of this arrangement. He was a stranger to Muzaffarabad and its courtiers. He would have to get to know their ways and their intrigues. This way, he could start with a clean slate and build up his kingdom. Vishalnagar was nearer and his familiarity with the terrain would come in useful. Quli once again bowed down at Muzaffarshah's feet.

'Huzoor, I need all your blessings to succeed in my new life.'

'You are the shah of Ramgarh. Now rule like one.'

Soon they had left the village behind. Qaramat, Fatima, Salamat Ali and the Pir went across to Hassan's camp. Devi Singh, Sonal and Gulabchand went westwards to Vishalnagar. Quli Murshid found himself still in Ranipur with Niloufer, Abhi and Anamika. Pierre and Nadya had also stayed behind.

'Gun masterji, you have not gone back to Vishalnagar. Why is that?'

'My job is to find places where there are battles and they can use my big gun. Now, there will be peace between Purana Zilla and Ramgarh. I have to move on.'

'Where will you go?'

'I am not sure. There is so much anarchy in Hindustan I am bound to find some king somewhere who will have me.'

'Will you stay with me for a while? I need to be quite sure I can bring the whole territory of Ramgarh under my control. I have no knowledge of Muzaffarabad. There will be sardars there who may challenge me. If I can rely on you to help me with the other side of the river, then I can build my new capital here.'

Abhi and Anamika could see that Quli was already beginning to think like a king. He had a fine strategic mind and he was making his plans.

'I don't know about Muzaffarabad but this fine lady whom I have just met knows the place. Maybe she can be my guide.'

'I was just a lowly zenana woman. I know the names of some sardars and I am sure Salamat Ali, the wazir's grandson, will help us. Niloufer Begama knows a lot more about Muzaffarbad. She can help us.'

'Then I give you a jagir of one hundred villages on the other bank of the Sreni from where you can keep an eye on Muzaffarabad. Pierre Saheb, you will be the khan khanan of Ramgarh.'

Pierre and Nadya were as astonished as Abhi and Anamika. Niloufer had also never seen Quli be so commanding. Here he was, a king for just an hour, if that, and he was already giving firm orders. Maybe he would be a good king, like Ahmad Shah.

Pierre and Nadya had to leave. Nadya embraced Niloufer and promised to see her again. Pierre shook Abhi's hands and made a namaste sign to Anamika and Niloufer. Abhi was curious.

'Where are you headed now?'

'My tent is with Abdul Khan's army. I will go there now and get back tomorrow morning to take my orders from my new master Shah Quli Murshid Khan.'

Nadya said nothing but everyone understood that now she was with Pierre. They had said nothing to each other but it seemed natural that they would be better together. Nadya had knowledge of Ramgarh and

Niloufer's support. Pierre had the gun and military knowledge. They shared a religion, though it was not clear what each believed in that the other could agree with.

Niloufer came out with them. In the stillness of the night, she wanted to go and see where Abdul Khan and Hassan Shah had been buried. She wanted to say her own silent farewell to the two boys who had meant so much to her. Nadya and Pierre went with her till the outskirts of the village where the two bodies had been buried. They left Niloufer with her private grief and moved on.

That night, as they lay intertwined, Anamika could sense that Abhi was still excited. His heart was beating faster than normal. She kissed him deeply and let him roam all over her body. The near danger of Abdul attacking him had once again got his blood racing faster in his veins and arteries. The evening had just added to that excitement, what with Quli making him Diwan of Ramgarh. Abhi was active and assertive. Soon, Anamika could sense that this was going to be another one of those nights for them. She let him do what he wanted to. He wrapped his legs around her and she got the message. She slid under him and let him get above her. The ardour of their first night of lovemaking was again reignited. This time, Abhi manged to stay inside her for longer. She was laughing and crying and kissing and biting him. He was keen to stay inside her as long as he could. She kept him in by holding onto him tightly. He went on for a while and then there was a sweet moment when they both knew that the magic had happened. They lay happily together.

After a while Abhi asked, 'What did the Pir tell you?'

'He promised me a son and two daughters.'

'What will you call him if it is a son?'

'Lalla, of course.'

'And if it is a girl?'

'Saki.'

Acknowledgments

I thank Kishwar Desai, Namita Gokhale and Prof Anjana Sharma for reading the manuscript and offering advice. I claim ownership of all the shortcomings remaining despite their best efforts.